A Secret Infatuation

The Earl's Sisters

JENNIE GOUTET

Copyright © 2025 by Jennie Goutet

All rights reserved.

No part of this book may be reproduced in any form or by any electronic or mechanical means, including information storage and retrieval systems, without written permission from the author, except for the use of brief quotations in a book review.

This is a work of fiction. Names, characters, places, and incidents are either the product of the author's imagination or used fictitiously. Any resemblance to actual persons, living or dead, events, or locales is entirely coincidental.

NO AI TRAINING: Without in any way limiting the author's [and publisher's] exclusive rights under copyright, any use of this publication to "train" generative artificial intelligence (AI) technologies to generate text is expressly prohibited. The author reserves all rights to license uses of this work for generative AI training and development of machine learning language models.

Human Authored™, Reg #: 4917415

Line edit by Theresa Schultz @ Marginalia Editing

Proof edit by Joanne Lui @ JL Editing Services

Cover Design by Shaela Odd at Blue Water Books

For my friend, Géraldine Heuzé Darouti, who is amazing—and a little shy.

The Earl of Poole and his Sisters

PROLOGUE

June, 1802
Leatherwood, Surrey

At fifteen years of age, Lady Sophia Rowlandson, second daughter to the fourth Earl of Poole, was the least interesting person in her family. She'd been told she had inherited her mother's beauty, but as far as she was concerned, neither beauty nor rank were worthy compliments. Such things were left to the chance of birth, and what honor could there be in that? She was not particularly bright and not at all ambitious. One had only to look at her elder sister Dorothea to see how Sophia lacked. While Dorry was already planning her come-out, when she might marry respectably and take her place in Society, Sophia dreaded her own come-out and wished to put it off as long as possible.

She was not funny like Camilla, or a talented equestrian like Joanna. Matilda—whom everyone called Tilly—might still be a girl, but she knew her own mind. Sophia could not say the same of herself, for whenever someone stronger came along, she would bend herself to that person's will.

And, of course, there was Everard, a year older than Tilly and the only son and heir to the earldom. Evo was full of pluck—or grig, as he might say—and would easily fulfill his role when the time came. Every Rowlandson had varying degrees of courage except Sophia. Oh, people called her sweet, but it never felt like a compliment. Rather, it seemed like a bandage they threw over a personality that was found wanting. It was this quiet belief about herself that caused her to seek refuge—to hide—in her neighbor's drawing room in the midst of a party.

The view from Chawleigh's drawing room was famous for its pleasing prospect. A large expanse of grass stretched out in either direction with imposing trees to give shade at regular intervals. At a distance, the land dipped slightly. Not enough to miss the shiny ripples of a pond that was at present dotted with small boats maneuvering their way back to the boathouse. Merry shrieks could be heard through the multipaned glass where Sophia stood. She would have liked to have gone boating with a gallant gentleman, if only she'd had the courage to risk the necessity of conversation.

She reached out to touch the sheer linen of the curtains framing the window, running her fingers over the seam and laced edge. Sophia was a bit like the decorative lace. Pretty and serviceable, but designed to blend into the woodwork. Her mother was not in sight and was likely engaged in harmless gossip with some of the neighbors under the shady trellis in the flower garden. Her father, though, sat within view with Lord Chawleigh and other gentlemen on chairs set out on the terrace. He reached for a drink from the tray of a passing servant, letting loose a bout of hearty laughter at the baron's cryptic jest.

Sophia brooded over what she'd heard that morning when she had neared the breakfast room at Chesmere Park. Her approach was silent enough that her parents had spoken freely, unaware they'd had an audience, the clink of cups on saucers punctuating their conversation. They'd not meant for her to overhear, but she had, and the words caused a painful twist in her heart, then and now.

"Dorry does not want for sense," her father had said, "but I am not of a mind for her to have her come-out next year. It is inconvenient for me to arrange it so soon. She had best wait until she is eighteen." After a muffled reply from her mother, the earl went on. "Sophy's head is empty, but that does not matter now, does it? She has a pretty face, which will serve her well enough. You had best teach her some conversation, however, or the *ton* will take her for a lackwit. I'm not entirely sure she is not one myself, for the girl is struck dumb whenever she is in my presence."

Sophia's feet had stilled before she'd reached the door, and her breath left her lungs entirely. Her father had always intimidated her, but she had thought he at least possessed some fondness for her. Apparently, he did not, or he would not speak of her in that way. He truly thought her head empty? She had *many* thoughts. *Many.* She just found it difficult to express them. Not even her dearest friend, Marie Mowbray, knew everything. She could tell Dorothea certain things, but she sometimes suspected her sister regarded her along the same lines as their father. Dorry loved her, she knew, but her elder sister was so capable she must certainly find her a trial at times.

Gentlemen's voices brought her back to her surroundings when they rang in the corridor outside the drawing room where she stood. They bantered like friends, jesting and teasing each other, and Sophia froze as her predicament dawned on her. She was not supposed to be in here. She could say she had come in search of the retiring room, but she knew Chawleigh Manor well enough to know it was not to be found through the drawing room. No one would believe she was merely lost. Heart pounding, she swung her head wildly, wondering if she could dive behind the sofa. But no—one glance underneath it and they would catch a glimpse of her crouched down. Oh, pray, let them continue on their path and not discover her hiding here.

The door to the drawing room opened, and the voices flooded in to where she was. Sounds of a scuffle echoed in the corridor, and it seemed as though they had stopped to engage in a friendly fight. Someone entered, and Sophia turned, bracing herself. Robert Cunningworth, Lord Chawleigh's son, stopped short when he saw her.

"Lady Sophia, what a surprise to find you here." He wore a peculiar smile, insincere. His smiles always seemed forced, meant to achieve a purpose rather than express delight.

As Chawleigh Manor stood within five miles of Chesmere Park, their families were close. They had known each other since childhood, but Sophia endeavored to escape his notice whenever she could. She clasped her hands in front of her and stared at a spot on the floor somewhere in the middle of the room. Nearly soundless footsteps brought him into the periphery of her vision.

He laughed, a harsh sound. "Now, Sophia, you aren't going to pretend you don't know me, are you? Not when we've grown up as neighbors." When she said nothing, he continued his approach until he stood before her. Still she said nothing, hoping her trembling would not show.

"I might court you in a few years if you talked more. That would save you from having to speak to someone you don't know. We are well-suited, you and I, aren't we?" After a short silence, he went on. "We come from the same sphere, and our fathers would approve the match."

Sophia remained mute. The thought of marrying Robert, who had teased her cruelly throughout childhood until he began to harass her with his attention, was too dreadful to contemplate.

"But then, I suppose I don't need a wife who talks. Might be more comfortable to have one who doesn't." Another ill-fitting laugh. Behind him, the door banged against the wall, and noises spilled into the room.

"Who's this?"

Sophia had no idea how many gentlemen followed Robert into the room, and she didn't dare to look.

"This is one of Lord Poole's daughters," Robert said. She felt his eyes on her. Though she didn't dare meet his gaze, his tone told her what she would find there—cold and unrelenting speculation. "Allow me to present Lady Sophia. I would have you make your bows, but I daresay she won't lift her eyes to see them." This sally prompted humiliating laughter.

"Come, Robert. Leave the lady to her solitude. Let's get the jack we came for."

Sophia did not glance up to see who had spoken, but his authoritative tone provided a sense of protection, like a tall fence around her. If only they would heed the suggestion, she might remain here alone until she had regained her composure. Then she could slip outdoors to join her mother. Or, if she could find one of her sisters, that would serve.

"Lady Sophia should greet us properly," Robert shot back. "I will not have my friends think I have any connection with a lady who has only hair for brains."

The cruelty of these words brought her head up in shock. How it pierced to hear words so similar to her father's on her tormentor's tongue. She could feel the color rise in her cheeks as she glanced up at the four strangers standing next to Robert, each wearing looks of amusement or resignation. Their forms shimmered in her rising tears. His insult had produced a few more chuckles, although these were more half-hearted. Perhaps they'd begun to lose interest in teasing her.

"Leave her be. You've made her uncomfortable." This had come from the same gentleman who'd mentioned the jack, and his voice was now tinged with steel. She risked a glance in his direction but could not see his features through her blurred vision. He stood beside Robert, his hand lifted slightly. Robert pushed his arm away.

"No, I've had enough of this. I shall be greeted properly in my own home by Lady Sophia. Trust me. Our fathers are long-time friends, so I am within my rights to demand it." He folded his arms, waiting.

"Ah, Cunningworth, what shall we do with you?" The man clapped a hand on his shoulder. His voice had turned cheerful, cutting the tension. "Lady Sophia is beseeching us with her eyes to be spared the courtesy of your attention. She does not lack brains; she lacks patience for forced conversation with Philistines." This was accompanied by a few snickers. Just when Sophia thought surely Robert must take offense, the man continued. "As do I, for you have been promising to beat me soundly at bowls, so let us have the jack you were searching for and be off."

"True enough! We are wasting precious time," another gentleman said. She recognized Tom Perkins, the squire's son and a friend of Robert's who was content to follow his lead.

Robert hesitated still, but the first gentleman—her rescuer—went over to the desk in the corner of the room. "Here it is, and the paint's dry. Let us go."

To Sophia's surprise, he put his arm around Robert and steered him out of the room, the others following. She heard Robert's laughter above the rest, which meant the friend had been able to take the sting out of his words—although, it was not out of the realm of possibility that Robert did not know what a Philistine was. Regardless, she couldn't believe anyone was capable of managing him that way. She had never known one able to do so, not even his own father.

Her vision cleared, and she had a sudden desire to see the face of the man who had come to her aid. All she had perceived was his olive coat and buckskin breeches—hair that fell in golden-blond waves like an angel. Heart racing, she hurried to the doorway and peered out. There was no one in sight.

Once outdoors, she rejoined a group of girls that included her sister Camilla, walking in the direction of the game being set up on the lawn. No one took notice of Sophia, which was precisely what she had hoped for. The players were in high spirits as they chose teams for a game of fours. There would be many more spectators than players, but no one seemed to mind it.

Sophia's first glimpse of the gentleman she was seeking was a rewarding one. The man had a handsome face with pale blue eyes underneath unruly brows; his nose was perfectly proportioned, and his lips remained on the edge of a smile. The faint lines on either side of it hinted at good humor. She could not draw her eyes away, but watched as he naturally took charge of the players, reminding them of the rules with an ease that showed him a born leader. She wished she could ask someone what his name was, but doing so would reveal her interest. If, however, she paid attention someone might address him, and she would have her information.

"Harwood, stop. If you put me with Perkins, we shall be soundly beaten. Give me one of the ladies instead." This was from one of Robert's university friends.

Laughter came from all sides at the friendly slight, but Sophia focused on the words. He had called the gentleman Mr. *Harwood*. She had not expected victory to come so quickly! She scarcely took in his response because Robert joined in with the teasing.

"Felix always offers to organize the games. It's so he can hoard the best players on his team and cover his own deficiencies."

Robert's crack was met with more amusement, and Sophia found herself smiling along with everyone. Mr. *Felix* Harwood. She knew his Christian name now, too. As if Mr. Harwood felt the pull of her interest, he turned and approached the group of girls where Sophia stood. She went still behind Bernice Milton, fearful he would speak to her—wishing he might speak to her.

"Can I persuade any of you ladies to join us?"

"I will," Camilla offered, stepping forward, and he turned to Sophia's sister with a look of pleasure. That her younger sister could so easily win such a smile from him dimmed Sophia's feelings of victory at having learned his name, but she could not do what Camilla did. She could not join the game, for as with many things, she was not good enough.

"No one else?" Mr. Harwood asked the group at large. It felt like his voice was directed toward her, but she kept her face lowered. His offer was met only with the shake of heads and hands covering their giggles. Bernice stepped to the side, leaving Sophia exposed.

His boots moved into Sophia's vision. When she dared to look up, she found his eyes on her, but he did not press her to play. Instead, he smiled and gave her a wink, which stopped her heart from beating for a full pause. He then turned to where the game was being set up, and she could breathe again.

"Grantly, go and see if some of those returning from the boathouse wish to play, and we shall have our eight."

Mr. Grantly lifted his hand and went off to Mr. Smithson, who was walking beside Dorry, but Sophia could only think of Mr. Harwood's smile and the wink he had sent her way. He had not only protected her, he had *seen* her. She could scarcely say that about her own family. She stared at his retreating form as he went and picked up one of the balls. He tossed it up and caught the ball easily, then laughed when another of their friends pretended to throw a punch. And suddenly...suddenly it was as though the world had color.

Mr. Felix Harwood. She had not thought that such a kind and handsome and *honorable* gentleman could exist.

CHAPTER 1

March, 1806
Grosvenor Square, London

There was no satisfaction to be found in returning to London for another season, especially one that featured Sophia's come-out. Last year, she could hide behind Dorothea, who was on a mission to find the most eligible bachelor London had to offer. No one had expected Sophia to court suitors and be at her most charming, since her elder sister had drawn the attention. Dorry had ended up marrying Miles Shaw, who was not London's most eligible bachelor. But that mattered little, for she was made to see what great worth there was in becoming Mrs. Shaw, even if it had taken nearly losing him to realize it.

Sophia sat on a cushioned Chippendale chair, which matched the mahogany desk and bed frame. She liked her yellow and gold baroque-papered room with its view that overlooked Brook Street and the houses opposite. The quiet hours spent here gave her solace, helping in a small way to equip her for the activities that must be spent without.

That night they were to go to Lord Chawleigh's London house to begin their season. It had been two years since they had seen their Surrey neighbors. First, Sophia's father had died. Then, last year, Lady Chawleigh had taken ill, and her sickness progressed over the course of the spring. Robert remained with her on the estate, while Lord Chawleigh traveled back and forth from London, first tending to his wife, then returning for the most urgent parliamentary sessions. Lady Chawleigh died early in the summer, prolonging the absence of social calls that had begun with the earl's death. Sophia had not regretted it, for Robert still made her uncomfortable. He was not unkind as he had been in his youth, but he paid her more attention than she wished for. With any great hope, he would have turned his attention elsewhere since they had last met.

Restless, her attention fell on her reticule that lay on the desk. She pulled open its strings, and from the bottom of the cloth bag removed a tiny key, tied to a blue ribbon. Listening for any hint that one of her siblings was about to invade her sanctuary, she inserted the key into the narrow desk drawer and pulled it open. Inside was a supple book with a pastel-blue cloth cover whose pages were bound together by ribbon-covered wire. She allowed her fingers to explore the soothing, familiar texture, then set it on the desk and opened it carefully. She had not looked at it in recent months, but something about having to begin her London season caused her to reach for its comfort.

The first page contained a date: June 7, 1802. Underneath was a drawing of the stretch of lawn in front of Chawleigh Manor. A few of the lawn balls could be made out, but there were no people. Sophia did not draw figures well enough to have attempted it. She turned to the second page, which held the words, "Mr. Felix Harwood." Those she had written in the prettiest hand she possessed. And although she had been tempted at the age of fifteen to write it again and again, and to add "Mrs. Felix Harwood" underneath it, she had resisted the childish impulse. Next to his name were three pressed yellow trefoils, which had been trampled under his feet from where he stood at the start of the game. A scant memento from the day, but they were all she had. That, and the words her father let fall over dinner about how Lord Chawleigh held the advowson for Mr. Harwood's father. The vicar had boarded and tutored Robert before he went off to Eton.

"Apparently," her father had said, "Lord Chawleigh saw potential in young Harwood and paid for his schooling with a charge to keep his son in line." Sophia had seen for herself how gifted Mr. Harwood was in this. It appeared, then, that both Mr. Harwood and his father had a patron in Lord Chawleigh.

"His benevolence paid off, for he worked as a quarter-sessions clerk and helped enforce game laws, which benefited both Chawleigh and myself." Her father had given one other precious bit of information—Mr. Harwood was to transfer to a more prestigious post in Customs in Brighton, where he planned to join the yeomanry to guard the coast from the French. Therefore, she knew not to expect to see him again when she visited Chawleigh Manor.

She turned another thick, worn page of her memento book, and on this was a newspaper clipping from the *Surrey Gazette*, dated February, 1804.

"*Mr. Felix Harwood, only son of the Vic. Thomas Harwood of Farnham, has accepted a commission as Lieut. in the East Surrey Yeomanry.*"

Sophia remembered the day she had stumbled on the article. It had been during a dull season when their father had once again left for London without them and invitations at home were few. With nothing to do, she read the newspaper from front to back and gasped audibly when she stumbled upon his name. Fortunately, no one had been there to question her reaction. What a shock to read of Mr. Harwood in the paper when she had almost given up hope of hearing of him again! Once she was sure that the newspaper had been read by everyone, she slit the page with the article before Mrs. Pratt could take it. That had been mere weeks before her father's untimely death—before their lives had tumbled into the chaos of grief.

Nothing else occurred to feed her secret hopes regarding Mr. Harwood since the article, but she kept them alive by remembering how deftly he had managed Robert. How he had defended her, and the smile and wink he had sent her afterward on the lawn. She sometimes wondered if he thought of her, too, after that day. Perhaps he was also shy and dared not pursue her?

But then she laughed at herself for entertaining such a ridiculous notion. Mr. Harwood was not a feeble creature like her; he was not shy. And even a ninny would know that without a proper introduction, he could hardly approach her—even less begin a correspondence when they were near strangers. Besides, who was to say he had ever viewed her in any way but a poor, diffident creature?

Mere facts did nothing to dampen her thoughts in his direction, however, and hope persisted.

Desperate for more to fill her memento book dedicated to Mr. Harwood, she had at last attempted to draw a portrait from memory, but it was badly done, and she took a knife to the page and removed it. The three pages were all she had, but it was sufficient; she was now wise enough to know that nothing would come of this *tendre* she had developed from a chance encounter four years ago. Still, it soothed her to look over the pages whenever she had a social event she did not look forward to attending.

"Sophia!" Her sister was coming down the corridor toward her bedroom.

She hurried to put her book in the drawer and managed to close it before Camilla opened the door and strode in. Heart beating fast, Sophia tucked the key under a stack of papers in what she hoped was a discreet gesture.

"Are you ready to go? I've just learned it is not to be only our family and Lord Chawleigh's this evening, so we *do* have hope of a pleasant dinner." Camilla gave her a droll look, and Sophia smiled. Having noticed Robert's budding interest two years ago, Camilla had won her heart by declaring that he was the very last man whom Sophia should marry. "*For he would crush you,*" she had said. It was comforting to have an ally in her sister.

"Who else is to be there?" Sophia intertwined her fingers, steeling herself for a larger crowd than she had prepared for. No social situation was easy, but at least when it was just Lord Chawleigh and his son, she had learned that by merely offering a few banal remarks, she could pass practically unnoticed.

"Mr. Perkins, whom we know, and a Mr. Harwood, whom we don't." Camilla went over to Sophia's wardrobe and examined the gowns that hung there. "I wish I could wear this gold-colored one. It would suit me nicely, if only it fit."

Sophia's mind had remained stuck on the name. *Mr. Harwood.* After so many years of thinking of him but never breathing the name aloud, she was suddenly adrift. Her next comment flew out unguarded. "But we do know him."

Camilla turned, her eyebrows lifted in inquiry, and Sophia was forced to go on. "I...I think we met him once at Chawleigh Manor some years ago. You played lawn bowls with him."

"Ah, true. I had forgotten him," Camilla replied, fingering another gown with coquelicot trim.

Really! Sophia was astonished that anyone could forget Mr. Harwood. He was the gentlemanly ideal in every way. And now she would see him again for the first time in four years. Would he remember her? Surely, he must! If only he would not recall her as a spiritless creature. She would have to make an effort to be as lively as was in her power. She licked her dry lips and reached up to pinch her cheeks before stopping herself. Her sister must not know that she was anticipating this meeting.

"I will tell Mama that you are ready." Camilla swept past Sophia on her way to the door.

"No!" Sophia stood suddenly, and her sister turned back in surprise. "It...it's only that I have worn this gown so recently. I am of a mind to change. Perhaps the one with the leaf embroidery?" The gown she had thought good enough for Robert Cunningworth was not nearly elegant enough for Mr. Harwood. She attempted a smile, hoping her sister would not think her behavior overly strange.

Camilla considered this, then went over to the wardrobe to pull it out. "Yes, it becomes you very well. You should wear it more often." She shook out the dress. "Here, I will help you into it."

"Thank you." Sophia shivered as Camilla unbuttoned her plain silk gown, and she hoped her sister would think it was from the cold. The evening had gone from dull to significant all at once. She stepped into the emerald gown with the embroidered leaves on the net overskirt, attempting to suppress her emotions. She had thought herself over this childish infatuation with Mr. Harwood, but her racing pulse told her otherwise. Was she fanciful for holding on to the idea of him for four years? A man she had met only once and with whom she had not even exchanged a word?

The answer was yes. Fanciful and foolish. And yet, she was helpless to feel anything differently. After all, he was the only one who had ever defended her without knowing her or requiring she give a response. He was the only gentleman who appeared to *see* her. The effect of that smile and wink had not faded, no matter how many years had marched by. Of all the gentlemen she had met since, he still stood out as singular and ideal. At least tonight, Mr. Harwood would see her at her best. She had grown more loquacious than she was at fifteen and now dressed stylishly. He would find before him a woman grown.

"Your cheeks are pink. It's becoming," Camilla noted as she stepped around Sophia to observe the effect of the new gown. "Here, let me slip this diamond leaf comb into your hair."

When this was done, Sophia reached out impulsively and hugged her sister. Camilla looked at her in surprise. "Thank you for buttoning my gown. I daresay the servants are busy."

"Mama is certainly keeping Margery busy with Joanna's hair. It seems a comb has not gone through it in ages." And in an odd reversal of roles, she added, "Don't dally. I shall wait for you downstairs."

Sophia nodded and went over to sit at her dressing table. She stared into the mirror and turned her face first to the left to see her unsmiling mouth from that angle, then to the right. She tried to smile as she hoped to do for Mr. Harwood but could only swallow convulsively. Pulling on her gloves, she leaned her forehead onto her fingertips.

Let me be interesting tonight.

THE BARON'S London house was located at 20 Grosvenor Square on the opposite end from the Earl of Poole's, and Sophia and her family went there on foot. Only Tilly was left at home with the governess. Evo was away at school, and Dorothea and her husband had been invited but were unable to attend. As soon as they knocked on the front entrance, a footman ushered them into the brightly lit interior. After taking their cloaks, the butler led them to the drawing room.

Lord Chawleigh came out to greet them, stopping first in front of Lady Poole. "Welcome to our home, my lady. Welcome, Ladies Sophia, Camilla, and Joanna. It is good to see our dear neighbors once again, although we have both suffered a life-altering loss in the interim."

"It is sadly true." Lady Poole left her hand in his, adding, "It must be particularly hard for you, my lord, since it has been only one year."

Sophia's mother had improved since her initial wave of grief had passed—and after gaining a son-in-law upon whom she might rely. Lord Chawleigh inquired after her health, then took her elbow and led her into the drawing room as Robert bowed before Sophia. His features had filled out, and his expression was almost considerate.

"Good evening, Lady Sophia." He greeted both of her sisters as well, offering his arm to her and Joanna, who was closest. "I apologize, Lady Camilla, that I do not have a third arm to offer you."

"You would look very strange if you did," Camilla replied. "Please do not trouble yourself. I am perfectly capable of walking without tripping over my feet."

This elicited a smile, and Sophia began to hope that the years had indeed improved him. So far, he had not yet overwhelmed her with excessive attention, and he had found humor in her sister's playful retort.

Once they entered the drawing room, all other thought fled Sophia's mind. Two gentlemen stood near the mantelpiece, and her eyes traveled from Mr. Perkins to Mr. Harwood. When the latter gentleman turned and met her gaze, she managed to keep her own steady. She would show him that she was not the same tongue-tied maiden she had been at the age of fifteen. At least, that was her intention, but her courage lasted all of two seconds before she averted her eyes.

Mr. Harwood had changed very little, except for a certain bulk to his shoulders and arms, which was visible through his coat. He watched their approach, and she was able to assess that although his face had matured in the ensuing years, his eyes were still kind; his lips hinted at that same smile.

Breathless, she halted in the center of the room as the gentlemen left their position and approached. She returned Mr. Perkins's greeting mechanically and turned to face Mr. Harwood.

"This is Lady Sophia," Robert reminded him. "And these are her sisters, Lady Camilla and Lady Joanna."

"Your servant." Mr. Harwood bowed before them, and before Sophia had time to ponder whether he had remembered her, he turned to her sister. "I recall meeting you, Lady Camilla. You were my partner in the game of fours, and you had the steadiest of hands."

Camilla looked pleased. "I should write you off as a flatterer, except that I do enjoy playing bowls and think I am not terribly ill at the game. However, you must play against my sister Joanna if you wish to be truly challenged. She is accomplished at any sport she sets her mind to."

"Hardly worth boasting about," Robert murmured, and Mr. Perkins snickered, but Mr. Harwood looked intrigued and brought his eyes to Joanna.

"I shall look forward to the opportunity, then, my lady. Would it be unkind to confess to my hope that you will not outplay me?" This was accompanied by a charming smile.

"Not at all. I will not go easy on you, however," Joanna replied without an ounce of bashfulness. "You must decide if you wish to risk it."

He laughed and bowed again before rejoining the other

gentlemen, who had each taken a glass of claret. Lord Chawleigh indicated for the servants to bring ratafia for the young ladies and sherry for Lady Poole before encouraging everyone to take their seat.

Sophia did so numbly, trying to wade through the shock of being of so little consequence in Mr. Harwood's eyes. He had remembered Camilla but not her. She must have imagined that his defense that day had been for her sake and not so that they might proceed with the game of bowls. She had imagined that his knowing smile had been given specifically for her. She was clearly trivial in his regard, for he could scarcely treat her with less significance. Meanwhile, she had held on to the unwavering hope that he might have retained some small thought for her throughout the years. What a simple creature she was.

The conversation swirled around her, but she did not participate, not even to give the usual commonplaces that would show her to be a woman of interest. When the butler announced the dinner, Robert leapt to her side and bowed before her.

"Lady Sophia, I would be honored if I might escort you into dinner."

Wordlessly, she took his arm, now sentenced to eating beside Robert and struggling to follow his conversation. He never left much time for silence. Behind her, she heard Mr. Harwood solicit Camilla, and Mr. Perkins offer his arm to Joanna.

As the footman helped her into her seat, Robert turned to her and smiled. "I haven't forgotten about you in these two years' absence, Lady Sophia. I hope we may see much of each other this season."

He had never revealed any compelling reason for his interest in her, other than a desire for her family's connection—that and he thought her biddable. Neither were traits she wished might inspire a man to pursue her. It had not been Robert Cunningworth she hoped would pursue her.

Sophia managed to arrange her lips in something that looked like a smile, but her heart grieved. She had always known the fantasy she'd created out of Mr. Harwood would not hold, but she was unable to help it. Her heart followed its own desires. As for Robert, it mattered little that he seemed determined to please this evening; she did not have any feelings for him at all.

The dinner passed more tolerably than she might have imagined, given the fact that she was heartsore and hard-pressed to perform socially. Mr. Harwood was seated across from her, and she allowed herself to listen to his conversation whenever the pauses in her own permitted it. She conversed with both Robert and Tom Perkins on her other side, whom she did not feel particularly close to, considering how easily he had joined Robert's harassment in years past. Once, Mr. Harwood met her regard across the table, and the surprise of it caused her to turn away with a frown. He could not know that he had been anything special to her. She must let him think she had forgotten him, too.

Once the dinner was concluded, the men stayed behind in the dining room for port, while the women went into the drawing room. As soon as they were alone, Lady Poole called the attention of Sophia and her sisters.

"Lord Chawleigh has laid claim to our long friendship by inviting us to dine with him although there is no hostess to serve at his side. He requested that one of you might pour the tea when the gentlemen join us after their port. Sophia, dear, I think it had best be you."

Camilla sent her a look of concern at the same time that Joanna protested, "But, Mama, Sophia is tongue-tied around gentlemen. Had you not better do it?"

Instead of answering, Lady Poole held Sophia's gaze. "She must overcome her bashfulness if she is to have a successful season. It is best if she begins now."

Sophia tried to give voice to the protest that rose up in her, but nothing came out. Was this not akin to announcing some sort of understanding with Robert? Her reluctance warred with her inclination to be an obedient daughter. She swallowed and nodded her head.

They were not made to wait long before the sounds of the gentlemen's voices approached the drawing room. A footman entered through a servant's door with a tea tray, followed by a maid carrying the hot water. They set these down on the table on one end of the room, and Sophia glanced at her mother, who leaned in.

"The Chawleighs have always been good neighbors—almost like family," her mother whispered. "There is no need to make any ado about such a simple request."

Sophia smoothed the skirt of her gown and stood. The porcelain jar of tea sat on the tray, and she pinched the leaves and put them in the steaming teapot, hoping she was preparing it to Lord Chawleigh's satisfaction. Around her, the discussion settled on Vice-Admiral Nelson's state funeral, which the baron had attended. No one seemed to remark on her position beside the tea tray, which was a comfort. When the tea had steeped long enough, she moved to pick up the pot, then hesitated. She would have to ask each gentleman how he took his.

It was easiest to begin with Lord Chawleigh, who reached over and patted her arm. "Thank you for performing the service, my dear. I will have sugar. Two spoons."

She nodded mutely and went to Robert and Mr. Perkins, mumbling the same request. Then she stood before Mr. Harwood, who lifted his eyes. His seemed uncommonly bright, giving the same impression he could see through her. But that was an illusion; he did not even *remember* her. Her throat worked, but nothing came out.

"If you would be so good as to bring mine with milk, I would be much obliged to you." Mr. Harwood smiled warmly.

Unable to hold his regard, Sophia turned, and it was not until afterward that she realized she had not returned an answer. He would see her in the same light as he had four years ago. It had been naive to think she had overcome her timidity, even a little bit. She brought everyone their tea and avoided looking at Mr. Harwood when she brought his. What a ninny he must think her. There was only one thing to do now, and that was to put aside this secret infatuation she had maintained all these years. To forget about Mr. Harwood completely.

The only problem was, she was not sure she could.

CHAPTER 2

Felix Harwood entered his rented lodgings at No. 123 on the Strand. The rooms were located on the second floor of a narrow, red brick terraced house. He had taken them before being promoted to junior commissioner at the Sick and Hurt Board, but he had been disinclined to move into something larger because of the unobstructed view it gave him of the Thames.

He responded to a knock that came minutes later, allowing a servant to bring in his laundered items and hang them in the placard placed against one wall. Felix thanked him and handed him a coin. When he was alone again, he went over to the window, folded his arms, and leaned against the frame as he stared out. Below him was a stretch of garden enclosed by a wrought-iron fence that allowed a glimpse of the service lane beyond it and stone steps on the bank leading down to the water.

It was difficult to credit how far he had come in the past three years. The son of a vicar with a modest living, he had secured a distinguished post in the Admiralty and, most recently, a seat in the House of Commons. Lord Chawleigh had given him some early advantages by paying for his schooling and calling in favors for his first position as a quarter-sessions junior clerk. But Felix had obtained his transfer to Brighton as a customs clerk by his own industry. There, a fortuitous meeting prompted the Admiral Mowbray to recommend him to a position in the Admiralty, after they had discovered a sympathy in their ideas for reform. The admiral then pulled strings so that Felix might win the pocket borough of Gatton and serve his constituency in Parliament. When he learned of this, Lord Chawleigh had expressed some discontent at the shift in Felix's political views, but he had been distressed by the loss of his wife and mostly left Felix to make his own way.

Last night was the first time Felix had seen the baron in many months. Lord Chawleigh had recovered some of his equanimity after Lady Chawleigh's death, but at first glance seemed far from the imposing man he had once been. It was astonishing to think that he could have been in love with his wife, for in every other way he seemed beyond such human emotions. However, as they waited for the lady guests to arrive, Felix was soon made aware that the baron had not forgotten what he owed him and would be expecting his vote on certain bills that had to be carried through both Houses. Felix nodded and tried to appease without giving promises, but he was relieved when they heard the arrival of more guests. For all the ways both Robert and his father might try his patience, he cared for them. They had given him opportunities he otherwise would not have had, and he knew that deep down there was goodness in both.

His mind drifted to Robert's neighbors from Surrey—the Earl of Poole's daughters, whom he had not seen for several years. He did not remember having met Lady Joanna, but he did remember Lady Camilla—and her elder sister—quite distinctly. Lady Sophia had been a couple of years his junior then and now was fully grown. She appeared still to be excessively shy, and he wondered why that was. She was titled, wealthy, and a beauty besides. It bothered him to think that some event or ill treatment might have caused such timidity. As though she had been crushed by someone in her life—some *one* or many—although perhaps that was his imagination. Her father had seemed perfectly congenial when he was alive, and her mother and sisters were all that was agreeable.

Ah, well. It didn't do to dwell on the issue of Lady Sophia's bashfulness, for even if she was of an age to consider as a woman of interest, she was far above his touch. He had no ambition to embark on a courtship with the daughter of a peer. Felix would not have given her a second thought, except that she had seemed upset with him last night in the way she turned away with a frown. Not just cold and indifferent, but upset, and he did not know why.

Enough of that. He pushed away from the window frame, willing himself into action. He had just returned from riding, so would wash up before heading out to Brooks's, where the admiral had promised to make him a member. He owned to having some nerves at the idea of applying for membership to such an illustrious club, but he must remember that he was an MP now, and this was where he belonged.

When he arrived at Brooks's, Admiral Mowbray led him into the dining area that was open to guests. He leaned in to avoid being overheard.

"Your membership is a sure thing," he promised. "Brooks's is friendly toward Whigs, and they will be glad to have your vote."

Felix knew this, but responded politely. "That is good to hear. Thank you for your sponsorship, Admiral. I will do my best to achieve our aims."

"Excellent."

The admiral had a good-natured visage, a jovial demeanor,

and a love for balls and parties. Someone who had never seen him command might be fooled into thinking him an ill fit for his post. Felix had seen him in action, however, and when Admiral Mowbray pressed forward, nothing deterred him. They settled down to discuss the most pressing parliamentary business, with the admiral recommending the committees Felix should be part of.

The year prior, a commission had been created to ensure that all new naval appointments would be merit-based rather than handed out by favor. Felix was barred from investigating appointments in the Sick and Hurt Board where he worked, but he would join the commission to investigate irregularities in other areas of the Admiralty. He would use his position to call for pensions to sustain the widows of seamen who had lost their lives in service to the crown. He had seen firsthand how the loss of a family's breadwinner plummeted all its members into poverty, and at present only the officers' families received some form of compensation.

Although serving with the yeomanry on the coast had given Felix a sense of purpose, it paled compared to all he hoped to accomplish in Parliament. The prospects were rich and exciting, especially with Grenville and Fox at the helm.

Upon leaving the club, his mind filled with committees and reform, he nearly ran straight into Robert, who was walking with Perkins and Grantly on Bond Street.

"You need to look where you're going, Harwood."

"My apologies." Felix grinned at his friends. "I've just been to Brooks's to meet with Admiral Mowbray."

Robert shook his head. "Did you hear nothing of what my father said last night? I cannot believe you are still bent on Parliament—and as a Whig? Why spend hard-earned money only to tire yourself on a lost political cause?"

Felix clasped him on the arm, laughing. "Not you, too? Why not let me just continue in my pigheaded way?"

Tom Perkins smirked. "You cannot argue with him, Cunningworth, since he has owned to being pigheaded."

Grantly waited until their laughter had died down. "Join us, Harwood?"

It took Felix no time to decide that he was far too restless to return to his rooms and would like nothing better. "Where are you headed?"

"To the stables, and then Hyde Park for a turn on Rotten Row," Robert said. "Come along if you've nothing better to do."

"Why not? I will meet you there, as my horse is stabled in the opposite direction to yours."

That was another thing he would have to look into. He kept his horse and phaeton in a stable and carriage house on Drury Lane, not far from his rooms. It had been convenient and affordable when he had first arrived in London, but it was not the nicest of areas. It was time to change stables, even if it meant three pounds more a month.

Robert waved, and they parted ways.

Felix had continued to call Cunningworth by his first name, partly because they had met as lads, and partly because his surname was a mouthful to say. For some inexplicable reason, Robert seemed truly to like Felix despite the disparity in their stations. He was not an easy person to get along with, especially when he considered himself slighted. But he had boarded with Felix's family while the vicar tutored him and prepared him for Eton, and they had shared enough moments in boyhood to develop a close bond. Robert was an only child, and Felix had only younger sisters.

When he finally reached Hyde Park, the promenade at the fashionable hour was well underway. As of yet, he had not made many influential connections in London, but he suspected that was about to change, now that he was an MP. He scanned all those gathered, some on horseback, some in carriages, and still others on foot. He didn't spot his friends, but his eyes came to rest on an open barouche carrying four figures in fur-lined cloaks and bonnets, for it was still early in the spring. One of them turned, and he recognized Lady Sophia with her sisters and mother. Another still in girlhood bore a resemblance to Lady Sophia and Lady Poole, and he assumed she must be the youngest daughter. He hesitated for a moment as he stared at the crested carriage. Should he ride over and greet them?

Perhaps Lady Sophia had sensed his regard, for she looked at him and seemed to grow still when recognition dawned. Her eyes latched on to his for a brief moment, before she turned away, chin up and mouth tightened. It reinforced his impression from the night before that she did not like him, but he could not guess what her reasons might be. It irked him, for he was generally considered to be an affable fellow. It was not as though he were pursuing her as a fortune hunter might. All he had done was to spare her Robert's harassment all those years ago in the drawing room. Even at last night's dinner, he had been careful to treat her exactly as he did her sisters, without giving any hint of what had happened in the past.

Lady Camilla turned and saw him in contemplation and lifted her hand in a wave, which he could not ignore. Regardless of Lady Sophia's disapproval, he had been tempted to go over to them. After all, he was not so far beneath her as to warrant a snub. They had met twice in a perfectly respectable social setting, for heaven's sake. He directed his horse over to the barouche and reached it at a timely moment, for the row of equipages had come to a stop as people chatted across carriages or to those on horseback.

"Good afternoon, Lady Poole." Felix smiled and bowed to

the countess, then repeated the greeting for each of the sisters, taking care to greet them with equal consideration. When he came to the last one, he paused for an introduction.

"This is my youngest daughter, Lady Matilda," Lady Poole said.

He bowed from where he sat on horseback, thinking that he had never heard Lady Sophia speak, other than a murmured response to what someone else had asked her, or her request for how they took their tea—a request she made to everyone but him. Not even on the day when he had turned Robert away from taunting her had she spoken. He supposed he could not blame her for that. His own sister was shy, and Lady Sophia had looked as frozen as Meg sometimes did when Society pressed its obligations on her. Still, it would be nice to hear Lady Sophia's thoughts.

"Are you here with someone, Mr. Harwood?" Lady Camilla asked.

"I am to meet Robert Cunningworth, Tom Perkins, and Grantly. We split ways since my horse is not stabled near theirs, and I have not seen them since I arrived in the park." At this, Lady Sophia surprised him with her direct regard. He was even more surprised when she opened her mouth to speak.

"Where is your horse stabled?"

The question was not an unusual one except that it had come from Lady Sophia, and it had the strange effect on him of slowing time. She *did* speak, and it was a sweet voice. Not only had she spoken to him, but the words had come from her lips voluntarily. This appeared to be an anomaly, for the occurrence produced an effect on her sisters as well. They all turned to stare at Sophia until she turned pink.

In his haste to pull the attention from her and release the strange tension, he answered, "My horse is stabled on Drury Lane."

"I see."

She nodded, then turned to stare at some point ahead until the moment grew awkward again. Felix had thought of Lady Sophia a handful of times since they had met in Chawleigh Manor all those years ago, and he could not sort out why every moment now seemed significant. He smiled through the discomfort that had settled on the party, then lifted his hat.

"It seems the carriages are about to move again. I shall not keep you, but will wish you all a pleasant afternoon." He rode onward, trying to make sense of the odd feeling that had filled him at the sound of her voice.

Robert was still nowhere in sight, so he went in search of him. The park was packed with people, but he recognized no one and was granted a few minutes' privacy with his thoughts. *Why* did every small moment with Lady Sophia stand out in his mind? He had mostly thought of her as an excessively shy young lady after the first meeting at Chawleigh Manor. During their dinner last night, however, he could not help but be more aware of her presence. He had to own to himself that he must like her at least a little bit, or his senses would not be heightened in such an unaccountable way whenever they met. He could not pursue her, of course, but he supposed it natural to be a bit infatuated with such a beauty. Especially since she gave so little of herself and remained something of an enigma. Was it not normal for a man to wish to unravel a mystery? That must be it.

"Felix!" Robert waved him over to their party from the stretch ahead.

He urged his horse into a canter, feeling suddenly and inexplicably hopeful. He brought his gelding alongside theirs and readily approved their idea to ride along the edge of the path and circumvent the carriages. They had no chance to talk as they performed the maneuver, and it gave Felix additional time to reflect. In doing so, his thoughts turned in a more sober direction.

When Lady Sophia spoke audibly and of her own volition for the first time, it was to ask him where he stabled his horse. Was it not so she might judge how wealthy a man he was? For she would assume at once when he said Drury Lane that he could not afford anything closer to the fashionable area. Was she using that as a way of measuring whether he was worth her attention? Given her extreme reserve with him, it seemed likely she was.

"What is it, Harwood?" Perkins had ridden beside him and was looking at him curiously. Only then did Felix realize he was frowning.

"*Hm*? Oh—nothing, I assure you. Just some dust in my eye that is irritating me."

"With this mud? Astonishing."

Perkins was not the brightest of fellows, Felix decided. He wouldn't let a man make up an excuse so he might keep his own counsel. He was saved from further scrutiny by Robert, who reined in and turned his horse.

"There doesn't appear to be anyone of interest here. I am hoping I might see Lady Sophia while we are out. Let us go to Gunter's instead. We might have better luck there." He turned his horse to follow a path that led directly to the teahouse and away from Lady Sophia. Grantly and Perkins turned to follow.

Last night, Felix had wondered if Robert was openly pursuing Lady Sophia, and now his suspicion was confirmed. He knew he should tell his friend that Lady Sophia was in the park and could likely be found if they retraced their path. It was only right to do so. But instead he kept silent and followed in Robert's wake.

CHAPTER 3

A week had passed since their dinner at the Chawleighs' London house—and six days since Sophia had seen Mr. Harwood in the park, where she had managed to *speak* to him. She had opened her lips to ask a completely unprompted question. He'd answered most naturally, but it surprised even her mother and sisters so much they exclaimed about it afterward. Sophia managed to satisfy their curiosity with the claim that she was attempting to speak up more—practicing so she might be ready for all of the season's events. Despite the fact that her resolve to put Mr. Harwood entirely out of her mind had been cast aside in that moment, she could not regret her impulse in having addressed him, for she had shown herself—and him—that she was capable of it.

Sophia held on to that small triumph now, as she was about to undergo the most terrifying experience of her lifetime. She was required to make her presentation to the queen, and the anticipation, the expectation, left her bound by fear like a prisoner awaiting conviction. Her tight corset, ridiculous puffed skirt that went all the way up to her bodice—completely removing any trace of a figure, by the way—and the feathers pinned to her hair in a Prince-of-Wales plume certainly did not help her to feel any more like herself.

"Dorry, I am not sure I can go through with this," she murmured breathlessly from inside their carriage as they inched forward in their approach to St. James's Palace. They were almost to where the road met Pall Mall.

Her sister, Lady Dorothea Shaw, had been married for just under a year and was already expecting her first child. She sat beside her husband Miles in the forward-facing seat, across from Sophia. It was the only way both sisters would fit with their wide skirts, a necessary part of their elaborate court dress, and Dorothea was too ill in the early stages to take the rear-facing seat.

"You can and must fulfill this obligation," Dorothea replied firmly. "How we ever managed to secure vouchers to Almack's last year without my having been presented is a mystery to me still. I can only suppose it was because our father had departed this Earth before he could properly introduce us to the *ton*, and we were accorded a measure of grace."

Sophia didn't respond, and after a moment, a mischievous chuckle escaped Dorothea. "That, or the patronesses consider their reign superior to that of the queen and did not care whether or not we'd been presented. But you may be sure no such reprieve will be extended to us again this year. We are not so distinguished as to forego this courtesy to the queen."

Sophia knit her brows, unwilling to contradict her sister but unable to stay silent at words she considered unjust. "I am sure the patronesses do not think themselves above the queen. Only think of how kind Lady Sefton is. And Lady Jersey, how droll! They were merely being gracious regarding our circumstances."

Dorothea smiled and shook her head. "You are determined to think well of everyone, but not *everyone* is deserving of it.

Regardless of what transpired last year, we must certainly present ourselves in the queen's drawing room this year."

It was unnecessary for Sophia to remind herself how much each social setting challenged her peace of mind, but to be required to make her curtsy before the queen without a single error was nothing short of terrifying. She glanced at Miles, who returned a sympathetic look. He seemed to understand better than his wife just how great the trial was for her. Dorothea was adept at most things and had trouble sympathizing with the challenges of others, although she was changing. A devoted and loving—but firm—husband, Miles softened those traits in her that might be described as managing. Goodness knew there was much to manage; now that their eldest sister had left their house on Grosvenor Square and moved into her marital home, it became clear how much responsibility she had always taken on. Sophia could only respect her for having carried it all for as long as she did.

After the ladies in the carriage ahead of them had been helped out, the earl's carriage inched forward. The line moving toward the palace had turned into a two-hour wait, and now it would finally be Sophia's turn to step into the court. She smoothed her hands over her white silk net gown with chenille embellishments. With the panniers placed close to the high waistline, she scarcely knew what to do with her arms. But it was useless to argue against the requirements of court dress. Her only stand was to insist upon wearing feathers from the humbler pheasant for the required three fanned out in her headdress. Dorothea would have had her wear the more elaborate ostrich feathers, but Sophia remained firm.

"Besides," her sister continued, "this year, we are in a better position to make our presentation. We do not need our mama to give us countenance, as I am married and can fulfill that role. Such a thing would have been too much for her."

Their mother, always sentimental and frail, had fully succumbed to her bereavement in the two years following the death of their father, which had caused Dorothea to sometimes grow impatient with her. Sophia could understand her mother's difficulty in moving on without the bulwark of their family to steady her, but could also sympathize with her sister's impatience over the prolonged expression of grief. Their father had not been an easy man to live with.

The door to their carriage opened, and the liveried footman standing outside of it bowed and held out his hand. Dorothea alighted first, followed by Sophia, and finally Miles. The gates to the palace were open, and ahead of them a line of people entered the courtyard. The swirl of white gowns indicated those who were as yet unbetrothed, and the more colorful gowns those who were married.

Sophia attempted to draw a deep breath but without much success. They crossed the courtyard and filed past the Chapel Royal before entering and following the procession to the grand staircase. The wall was papered in a blue flowered pattern, and the accents on the staircase were gold. On the upper level, they were led into the anteroom, where noble guests, seemingly from another era, advanced unhurriedly toward the Presence Chamber. A cluster of ladies, speaking in hushed voices and rapidly waving their fans, stood waiting to be announced. Contrary to the agitation around her, Sophia went perfectly still and reached for any thread of tranquility she might still have within. It was too much. She did not know if she could go through with it.

Dorothea leaned in. "Don't forget to breathe, my dear. You must not faint."

Sophia nodded and, just as the edges of her vision started to close in, she inhaled deeply. It helped, and her vision cleared. She was stronger than she realized and could get through this ordeal. *You managed to speak to Felix Harwood without having a question put to you directly*, she reminded herself. *You can meet the queen.*

"I can do this," she said. "It is unlikely she will speak to me."

"And if she does, you need only respond with the veriest commonplace, and *that* you can do."

The doors opened, and the chamberlain stepped out. He lifted the list in his hand and began reading off names. The designated ladies entered, and the door closed behind them. They were back to waiting, and Sophia decided to be resolute. This lasted until the door opened again, and the chamberlain announced more names. She had to force in another shaky breath when she heard, "Lady Dorothea Shaw. Lady Sophia Rowlandson." At least she would be presented at the same time as her sister.

"Lady Sefton should already be inside, since she is presenting us," Dorothea informed her in a thready whisper. Behind her, Sophia heard the excited whispers of smiling young ladies, eager to have their turn. It seemed that no one was nervous but her.

The Presence Room was richly decorated with dark red velvet curtains tied back to reveal the tall windows on the right side; a large Persian rug in similar tones covered the floor. A fire roared in the marble-encased chimney, and above that, ancient arms were displayed on the wall. Sophia scarcely took in these details as her feet carried her midway into the room. She focused only on the three plumes waving from her sister's head in front of her and the vague glimpse she had of Her Royal Highness seated on a red upholstered chair at the end of the room.

You are capable. She breathed. *You can make your curtsy to the queen, and you shall officially be launched for the London season. You have enough confidence. After all, you spoke to...*

"Lady Dorothea Shaw, eldest sister to the fifth Earl of Poole, married to Mr. Miles Shaw."

All thought fled as her sister glided forward and made a deep curtsy before Queen Charlotte. Lady Sefton spoke for her, and Sophia had a glimpse of the startling height of the queen's wig. She wondered if she always wore it like that, or if it was merely for court. Numb from fear, she heard her sister replying, "You are all kindness, Your Majesty." Then Dorothea backed up toward the door that would lead into the gallery, where freedom was to be found.

"Lady Sophia Rowlandson, second sister to the fifth Earl of Poole."

Now it was Sophia's turn. She clutched her train in her left hand, but an attendant rushed forward to take it from her. Legs trembling, she walked to where the queen now stood, talking to one of her ladies-in-waiting. As Lady Sefton presented her, Sophia dropped into a deep court curtsy. She had not needed to be reminded to practice this over and over until the gesture was flawless. She held herself perfectly still until the queen leaned down and kissed her forehead. Only then did she allow herself to rise.

To her inexpressible relief, the queen smiled graciously but did not speak to Sophia. It was then her turn to follow Dorothea, and she lifted her skirt just enough that she would not trip, inching back toward the door and taking care not to turn her back on the queen. Another lady had been announced and was now curtsying deeply.

She had done it! She had successfully made her presentation at court. Breathless with relief, Sophia was nearly at the door, where hands would reach out to guide her until she could turn forward again.

A mild outcry sounded from the gallery. The gentleman usher attempted to pull her out of the Presence Room from behind, but Sophia's heels bumped into something solid and she arched backward, her hands flailing to restore her balance. Ushers on either side grabbed her elbows before she fell, and she remained frozen in this posture, her stricken gaze on the queen, who had turned toward the commotion.

Sophia had the presence of mind to drop into another curtsy as soon as she was brought upright, and that was when she saw the fabric of her sister's gown and a slipper peeking out from underneath it. She pivoted her head quickly in shock before remembering she must not turn her back on the queen. In what seemed like an interminable amount of time, others hurried from behind to lift Dorothea and transport her inanimate form far enough so they could shut the door.

Once out of sight of the queen, Sophia whirled around and dropped to her knees beside Dorothea. She tapped her face and tried to revive her, but she would not wake. A commotion split the room as Miles, who had promised to meet them in the gallery after the presentation, hastened toward his wife, also dropping beside her, his face revealing his utter panic.

"She needs air," he announced to the room at large, and wasted no time in lifting her into his arms and carrying her in the direction of the exit.

Sophia hurried after him. There were hushed murmurs and an occasional giggle, but she was sure the ladies did so more to give vent to their nerves than from malice. All she could think about was that *her sister* had fainted. She had not thought such a thing possible. Nothing ever overset Dorothea.

FELIX STOOD in the Friary Court of St. James's Palace, waiting for the admiral to meet him there. A levee had been organized at the same time as the queen's reception, and Felix was to be presented as a newly elected member of Parliament. He was to stand before the king—or bow, rather. As a lad, he had not been particularly ambitious. He had known he would have an education, for his father, a scholar himself, considered such a thing indispensable. But Felix assumed he would live in a plain house in Surrey and follow in his father's footsteps as a vicar. That, or take on some other gentlemanly occupation, such as solicitor or steward. He had not aimed to reside in England's most prominent city and make history through policy change. Yet here he was, in London, a member of the Commons and now apparently about to rub elbows with the peers of the realm as they stood before His Royal Highness.

There was a commotion as people exited a palace door, and he turned to watch it. It appeared a lady had fainted at her presentation. He could hardly blame her, for such an ordeal must be extremely trying. In fact, he felt fairly nervous himself. Vaguely, he noted that her gown was plum colored, and even he knew anything but white indicated a matron rather than a maiden. This unusual detail caught his interest, for a matron would be more experienced in the world and not normally subject to a nervous crisis.

A gentleman with a pinched face carried her down the stairwell, and behind him was another anxious face that made Felix take an involuntary step forward. The small feathers in Lady Sophia's hair bobbed up and down in the breeze as she came to the gentleman's side and looked around. She appeared to be searching for their carriage, although there were not many of those in the court at present. Her eyes landed on Felix and, to his surprise, she hurried to meet him, hindered some by the large skirt of her gown. He strode quickly to her.

"Mr. Harwood, would you be so kind as to procure a carriage for us? My sister has fainted, and we must get her home." Her voice was breathless, but there was no weakness in her tone.

Her entreating eyes and plea touched a chord in him, and he bowed. "Immediately, my lady."

It was a shame he had already sent off his hired carriage with instructions for the groom to return at a set hour. He wasted no time in exiting Friary Court and hurrying along Marlborough Road until he reached Pall Mall Street. That was the likeliest place he would be able to find a hackney. It took a frustrating amount of time to achieve his purpose, but he eventually flagged one down and called up to the driver. "To Friary Court."

The driver furrowed his brows and tested Felix's patience by taking his time to respond. "I expect they won't let me in."

Felix waved his hand impatiently. "I have official permission to be there, and I will ensure that they do. We must hurry. A lady is unwell."

When they arrived at the gate to Friary Court, guards blocked the driver's way. Felix had anticipated this and stepped out of the coach.

"Forgive me for this unusual mode of transportation. I have hired a carriage to attend to a lady who fainted following her presentation."

The guards looked at his court dress and sword and moved to the side. Felix called to the driver to pull into the court and wait, then took a couple of steps forward before coming to a halt.

Near the palace wall, a crested carriage waited, and the same gentleman was settling the invalid inside of it. Lady Sophia, more animated than he had ever seen her, reached in to say something to her sister before withdrawing and coming around the coach to give directions to the groom and footman. The gentleman climbed into the carriage, and she hurried in behind him. The door was pulled shut, and the coach clattered over the cobblestones and exited.

Felix swiveled around to the hackney driver, who gave him a knowing look and spit out a stream of tobacco.

"Not needed, then, I'm to take it?"

"I am afraid you are not," Felix said with a rueful smile. "Here's a coin for your trouble."

He stepped aside as the driver turned his carriage and exited the court. Felix's thoughts were on Lady Sophia's expression, so full of concern and animation—so far from her usual look of shy reserve or cold indifference. There was clearly much more to her than what she showed to the world, and he wouldn't mind seeing some of it.

"Harwood, there you are. It wouldn't do to be late to the king's levee."

Felix smiled at Admiral Mowbray, explaining the cause for his delay. They turned and began discussing the likelihood of Grenville's affecting true change as they walked toward the state apartments. For once when discussing politics, however, Felix's mind was only partially engaged. In all of Lady Sophia's worry, he could not help but notice that she had called out to him for assistance without any reserve. Would she have asked just anyone? Or was it that she trusted him?

"Mr. Harwood?"

"Pardon?" Felix asked, realizing his mind had wandered. The admiral repeated his question of whether he knew how he must act inside the palace.

"Indeed I do. I have educated myself on what the proper protocol is. You need have no fear on that head."

"Excellent. Let us go up, then." Admiral Mowbray moved toward the same door Lady Sophia had exited a quarter of an hour ago.

He briefly wondered if he should pay a call on Lady Sophia

to find out how her sister fared, but it took no time to dismiss the idea. Merely asking a person for help was not the same thing as inviting such intimacy as an unplanned call. Perhaps, if luck were on his side, he might meet Lady Sophia at a social gathering in the near future where he could ask after her sister—and not be forced to wait until the season was half over before seeing her again.

CHAPTER 4

As soon as she heard the sounds of her visitor, Sophia hurried out of the drawing room to greet her. "Oh, you have no idea how thankful I am to have you in London."

Marie Mowbray, a friend of many years, removed a stylish blue velvet-lined bonnet from her light brown curls and turned humorous eyes to her. "You sound desperate. Has your season been very difficult thus far?"

Sophia handed Marie's poke bonnet to Turton and slipped her arm through her friend's, leading her into the drawing room, where the tea tray had already been set out. "You've no idea how much so."

Although the queen's presentation was the most pressing news she had to share with Marie, memories of her interactions with Mr. Harwood were what leapt to mind. There had been the dinner at the baron's house where she had met him for the first time in years, the chance meeting in the park where she had managed to ask him a question. And of course, there had been her urgent plea at St. James's Palace, which she had been unable to retract, for Mr. Harwood had arrived after Lord

Bartoff offered his services. But to speak of those things meant revealing something so deeply private, and she was not ready for that.

Camilla entered through the door leading to the dining room and glanced from the tea tray to their guest. "Welcome to London, Marie. I suspect you both will wish to be private, so I will take my tea to my room." She lifted the lid to the teapot, saw that the brew was ready, and poured herself a cup.

"Good day, Camilla." Marie placed her reticule on the sofa, adding, "I assure you, your company will not disturb me in the least."

A teacup balanced in one hand and a plate full of delicacies in the other, Camilla paused in her steps. "I may not disturb *you*; however, Sophia will not speak as freely if I am here, so I shall take myself off. I am sure you are more in possession of her secrets than any of her sisters are."

Marie sent Sophia a considering glance, along with a hint of her teasing smile. "Are you quite certain? She does not give up her confidences easily, even if she *is* my closest friend."

"Enough of speaking about me as though I were not here," Sophia said with a mock glower. "I tell you everything that's on my mind." She corrected herself. "Well, not everything. But then what female does that?"

Camilla laughed and exited through the door that led to the stairwell, and Sophia gestured for Marie to sit. It was odd timing for these chance remarks, for although she generally did share much with Marie, one thing she had never spoken of was her affection for Mr. Harwood. If Marie had been at Chawleigh Manor that day four years ago, the story of Mr. Harwood's heroism would surely have spilled out of Sophia. It was not that she minded telling her friend, it was just that as weeks had gone by before she saw her again, it seemed too irrelevant a thing to bring up. And then the moment had passed completely. It had become a story that went into her memento book, not something to share in whispered confidences.

Only now, Mr. Harwood was here in London, and that changed things. She wondered what he had thought about returning to Friary Court with a carriage, only to find out she had left. Was he irritated? Disappointed?

"Going back to your rather alarming greeting," Marie began as she settled herself, "I am eager to know what has happened since you've arrived. It has only been two weeks, so I suspect not much could have."

"How little you know," Sophia said, smiling with fabricated self-importance. As her mind spun through where she should begin—considering again the notion of bringing up Mr. Harwood as a person of significance and rejecting it—she poured tea for her friend and passed the sugar bowl to her. After pouring a cup for herself, she was ready.

"Dorry fainted in the queen's drawing room." The effect this piece of news had on Marie was pronounced, for her friend thought the world of Dorothea and her ability to manage all circumstances. She returned an open-mouthed stare.

"Lady Dorothea? I find that astonishing." She absorbed the news in silence for a moment, then glanced back at Sophia, a smile making an appearance. "I have sometimes felt she could lead an army against Napoleon."

Sophia laughed. "She did indeed—faint, that is—and *I* still cannot believe that it was not me who did so."

"Do you know why she did?" Marie sat back and sipped her tea. It already felt natural to have her in their London drawing room. Sophia had not realized just how much she missed having a close confidant, especially since Dorothea would not be taking on that role this season.

"I wrote to you that she is increasing," she began, and when Marie nodded, went on. "We all think that must be the reason for it. In any case, the doctor said there is no cause for alarm. It does not appear the baby was injured in the fall."

"And yet, women with less strength than Dorothea do not generally faint…" Her voice trailed away, and Marie sent her a guilty look. "But I do not mean to be alarmist, for the doctor has said all is well."

"Dorry said she cannot account for it either, except that perhaps she did not eat enough for breakfast. She admitted to being a little nervous to meet the queen, which surprised me, but assures me she is perfectly well now. Miles will not give any weight to her assurances and has insisted she remain at home for at least a fortnight. He would have her remain in bed if he could, but I do not think she will submit to that."

"Nor do I." Marie laughed. She set down her cup and clasped her hands, leaning forward. "And what of other news? How are your sisters doing? How are they filling their time while you attend all of the season's activities?"

"The start to the season has been slow, thankfully." Sophia sighed. "I would have loved for Camilla to have had her come-out this year, but she is only attending select events of a more private nature. Mama thought it best that the focus be on me this year."

"And I know how much you enjoy that."

This pulled a smile from Sophia. No one made her laugh as much as Marie. Her sisters tended to protect her, her mother to lean on her, and her brother to provoke her. Marie simply accepted her—and listened, teased, or recounted the most ordinary things.

"Camilla makes frequent trips to Hookham's for whatever latest novel is all the rage. Joanna, as you'd expect, is out riding every morning with our groom. She comes with us in the barouche when we go to Hyde Park, but I suspect that is just to see who is riding what horse."

"And Matilda? Everard?" Marie was a longtime family friend, and although she sometimes called the siblings by their honorifics when addressing them, she called Sophia by her first name and generally did the same when speaking of the others.

"Evo will not be home until Easter vacation, and I must say that although I miss him, my mind rests easy knowing he is under his housemaster's rule."

"And does not require you to keep him in line," Marie added.

Sophia nodded. "Tilly still follows Joanna around whenever permitted. And when Joanna pushes her off, she is content to sit with me and work on her embroidery or sketches. She prefers my company to the governess, although Miss Cross has been nothing but kind to us all. Dorothea plans to hire her for her own schoolroom when the time comes."

"That is good. Miss Cross is accustomed to your ways and you to hers." Their conversation had settled into its usual easy rhythm. "Was Dorothea's indisposition the only pressing news, then?"

Sophia thought again about bringing up the dinner and the other events relating to Mr. Harwood but decided they were too insignificant to talk about and nodded.

"Well, for my part, I am still astonished that my father has finally decided to bring us to London." Marie's pretty brown eyes were now positively glowing. "For two years, my mother urged him to rent a larger house and allow me to take my place in Society, and he has finally done so."

"What caused his change of heart?" Sophia handed Marie a piece of lemon cake when she noticed her guest had not served herself.

"Now that Papa is attempting to bring about reform through Parliament, he will spend the entire season in London." She bit into the cake. "*Mm.* My compliments to your cook. He hopes to end some of the corrupt practices, such as positions in the Admiralty being given based on favor rather than merit. I cannot help but confess my selfish pleasure that his goal coincides with my own—of spending the season in London, I mean to say."

"It is not selfish to wish to come to London. Or, if it is, then I am selfish for wishing you here." Sophia smiled and reached for the separate jug to add more hot water to the teapot. "I had not realized your father was to join Parliament."

"Oh, he is not. He does not have the stamina for the long debates. But he has seated someone he trusts in Gatton, and Papa will act through his proxy. He is from Sussex, not terribly far from us—a gentleman by the name of Mr. Harwood."

Sophia was in the act of stirring in more tea leaves, and she dropped the spoon into the pot with a small clatter. The loud noise jarred her as much as the news. Catching herself, she continued stirring without looking at her friend, her mind reeling at the surprise of hearing his name. Here, she had been trying to decide if she would speak of him to Marie, but her friend had done so first. Was that not significant? As her mind raced to find an appropriate response, Sophia settled on admitting to knowing him, for they would eventually all meet, and Marie would wonder at it if she said nothing about their acquaintance.

"I have met Mr. Harwood briefly. Once, years ago at Chawleigh Manor, and then again recently at their house in London." When she felt it safe to look up, she added, "In fact, he happened to be at St. James's Palace when we were coming out with Dorothea, and I asked him to fetch a rental carriage. I fear I sent him on a fool's errand, though, for we left in Lord

Bartoff's carriage before he returned. I hope he was not vexed with me."

Marie shook her head. "I cannot see how he would be. I have not met him, but my father promised to have him come to dine." She sent Sophia a mischievous smile. "He is purported to be handsome—is he?"

"I...I cannot say." In that moment, she wished she were anywhere but here.

"I think my father hopes to evade the London season altogether by having a match made right in his living room." Marie laughed.

Sophia wished she had the resolve to offer a smile to what was meant to be humorous, but the likelihood of such a design having success stole her will. Marie was charming. She had soft brown eyes to match her curls, and what was more, she was perfectly at ease with everyone. A man like Mr. Harwood must surely prefer a woman such as Marie over one who was too shy to string two words together.

When she had sufficient command of her voice, she said, "That sounds like a pleasurable evening. When is the dinner to be had?"

"We have only just arrived yesterday, so the date has not been set." Her friend turned considering eyes to Sophia and the corner of her lips tipped upward. "Shall I see if we might conjure up another gentleman and send you an invitation, as well?"

"Yes, why not?" Marie had probably spoken in jest, being confident that Sophia would reject the idea, but she could not resist an opportunity to spend more time with Mr. Harwood.

"Oh!" She looked at her more fully. "I hardly expected such easy capitulation."

Sophia smiled, but when Marie's questioning look held, she

felt like she should explain. "I don't mind a dinner when I am with friends. A small dinner," she added.

"Well then, I will be sure to arrange a very small one." Marie leaned in. "I do hope to see you enjoy your season, and I think it's a fine thing you are willingly accepting invitations. It is a good beginning."

"Yes," Sophia replied, somewhat weakly, already filled with guilt for her duplicity. "I hope we will both enjoy our seasons."

CHAPTER 5

Felix had successfully navigated his first weeks of sitting in Parliament, listening to proposed legislation and hearing a debate that had been carried over from the last season. He joined the investigative committee the admiral had pushed for—the Commission for Naval Inquiry—and another that interested them both particularly, the one to discuss providing pensions to soldiers and their families. Both he and the admiral felt strongly that it was unfair to serve the crown in good faith, only to end up begging on the streets because one had become infirm as a result of that service. This, and the lack of pensions provided to the widows of ordinary soldiers and seamen who fell in the line of duty, were matters that must be rectified with some urgency. His maiden speech on the plight of these could not be described as brilliant, but it had garnered applause and the echoes of "hear, hear!" from certain quarters.

He fully enjoyed his morning work in the Admiralty, and the afternoons and evenings he spent in Parliament, and felt he had come into a life that suited him. The only thing he had not figured out how to manage was the politely worded request he had received from Lord Chawleigh on behalf of his son. Aware of Felix's connection to the admiral, the baron had decided that as Robert lacked direction to seek out a career, a post must be found for him. In a recent interview, he intimated to Felix that the post that would most suit was that of assistant to the prize agent. Not only might he advance in the role and move from assistant to agent, he would be assured of a land-based, comfortable job that was likely to prove lucrative. After all, for every enemy ship captured, Robert would receive a percentage of the prize money.

"It is a trifling thing I ask of you. As you know, Robert is eager to be of service to the crown," Lord Chawleigh had said. "And now that you have connections in the Admiralty and are on intimate terms with Admiral Mowbray..."

Felix found it tricky to refuse without sounding ungrateful. Lord Chawleigh must come to understand that Felix could hardly present such a request to his patron, when the admiral was directing him to raise his voice to exert influence against such favoritism. For the moment he had not given a definitive refusal, but he would have to do so.

He was now on his way to dine at the admiral's house in Cavendish Square after two weeks of finding plausible reasons why he could not accept an invitation for dinner. He knew little about the other Mowbrays except that the admiral's first wife had died in childbirth, along with his son. His second wife was a good deal younger than her husband, and she had produced a daughter whom the admiral greatly cherished. There was no reason for Felix to be reticent about joining the dinner except that he suspected the admiral had ulterior motives for inviting him, and that those motives involved his daughter, the admiral's pride and joy. After all, he had said more than once with a particular smile that he was sure that Felix would find his daughter to be a charming, sensible girl.

The admiral was a worthy man, but one could not claim

him to be a handsome one. Of course, there was every possibility that his daughter had taken after her mother, the admiral's much younger second wife, who might well be a beauty. But this was pure conjecture. He supposed his hesitation came down to not being ready for his heart to be engaged; he therefore put up obstacles against the possibilities. That the image of Lady Sophia popped into his head at that exact moment must be pure coincidence, for he was certainly not interested in her. And even if he owned himself to be, he would not embark upon such a courtship. No, his future wife was likely to be practical and from a humbler station in life. With any luck, she would be good-humored and fair, as well.

On second thought, perhaps his reluctance to meet the admiral's daughter was unjust. Perhaps she was all of these things.

His rap on the knocker brought a footman to the door, who bid him enter. Felix found the interior warm and welcoming, with wooden floors and a staircase running along the right side of the main hall. The corridor walls were uncluttered, painted white, and boasted simple frames. On his left was a stone pedestal holding a potted fern. He handed his hat and cane to the servant and followed him into the drawing room, where the admiral stood to greet him.

Felix came and shook his hand, then bowed before the admiral's wife, who was indeed pretty, and who greeted him graciously. Perhaps he would be in luck and could hope for a pleasant evening if Mrs. Mowbray's daughter was anything like her.

"And this is my fair Marie. I am sure you will see why she is my pride and joy."

He turned to greet the admiral's daughter, but his attention faltered—came crashing to a halt—when he saw Lady Sophia standing at her side. Social correctness required him to greet Miss Mowbray first, since her father had presented her to him, but his lips seemed to stutter, along with his heart, for he greeted her with, "Lady Marie...Miss Mowbray...a pl-pleasure."

Felix was not a man easily overset, and this display of awkwardness hugely embarrassed him. He attempted to hide it in his bow.

Miss Mowbray studied him curiously with a small smile on her face, but he didn't *think* she was laughing at him. She would have every right to do so. Lady Sophia's brows were knit, and he could see she was concerned by his reaction. She probably thought he had gone mad.

"It is a pleasure to meet you, Mr. Harwood. My father has told me much about you." Miss Mowbray sank into a curtsy, then turned to the earl's daughter standing next to her. "And I am to understand you are already acquainted with Lady Sophia?"

"Yes. A little. Lady Sophia, your pleasure—your servant," he corrected himself hastily. Would it be too soon to ask for a visit to the retiring room so he could pull himself together? Where had his diplomacy gone? It was just that her presence was so wholly unexpected, he had forgotten how to perform the most basic civilities.

"Good evening, Mr. Harwood," she said quietly.

His attention slid back to her face, but he could not read anything there. Then again, he was not sure he would like to know what she was thinking. It was all so humiliating.

"Let us sit and have a drink while we wait for our dinner." The admiral had not seemed to notice anything amiss with Felix, or at least pretended not to. He resumed his seat next to his wife.

Lady Sophia and Miss Mowbray sat on the sofa, and Felix took the chair across from them. The knocker sounded again, and the admiral beamed with satisfaction. "What a pleasant evening we shall have. That must be Edwards."

Mr. Bartholomew Edwards was the admiral's personal secretary, and he and Felix had begun to develop something like a friendship in their common cause. When he was ushered into the room, the admiral waved him over. "You are not as late as you feared."

"No, sir. I was fortunate to escape as early as I did. But when I mentioned to the First Naval Lord's assistant that I had been invited to dine with you and Mr. Harwood—"

"Now, you must not speak too much of our connection with Harwood. Nothing is done in secret, mind you, but the less revealed, the better." This was accompanied by a laugh, but Felix knew he meant it. Although there was no secret about the admiral's having pulled strings to give him his MP position and that they shared a likeminded ambition for reform, they would make more progress if this fact was not constantly put in the limelight.

A new thought made him frown. Why was Lady Sophia here? He knew that Bartholomew Edwards was an untitled gentleman, but he came from an influential family in Worcester. If Felix were to be paired with Miss Mowbray this evening, was Edwards destined for Lady Sophia?

Felix closed his eyes briefly. He had become addled, for it was only his imagination that decided this dinner was for the purposes of courtship—or that he was destined for Miss Mowbray. That said, the admiral was now presenting Mr. Edwards to Lady Sophia, and he was bowing over her hand. If Felix was any judge, the secretary appeared to view her with an interested light. But then, that was hardly astonishing, considering her lovely frame, beauty, and gentle demeanor. Miss Mowbray seemed to know Mr. Edwards well, for they greeted each other amicably.

A servant brought out glasses of madeira, and the conversation was largely carried by the Mowbrays and Mr. Edwards, which allowed Felix to grow more at ease. He could only wonder at his having been so taken aback by Lady Sophia's presence as to overset his composure to such a degree. He sent her furtive glances, wondering what her thoughts on the evening might be, but she was listening to Mr. Edwards and did not return them. He could scarcely hear her murmured replies. Miss Mowbray was teasing her father, causing her mother to scold, and it made Felix realize he had been neglecting his hosts.

"Miss Mowbray, did you not come to Brighton while your father was living there?" he asked when a lull presented itself.

A smile still lingered on her face as she faced him. "Not generally, for he was always anxious to return to our home in Surrey. We did go twice, however, each time for a stay of two weeks."

"I am just wondering at not having made your acquaintance before, but I suppose that is understandable."

"And yet, you know our daughter's closest friend," Mrs. Mowbray said. "How did you and Lady Sophia become acquainted?"

He was about to reply vaguely about mutual friends, but at the sound of her name, Lady Sophia looked up. "He came to my rescue when I was a girl and diverted the attention of a gentleman who was harassing me."

Felix blinked. After her show of reserve at Lord Chawleigh's dinner, he wondered if she had remembered their encounter. He turned to their hosts.

"Young men are not always the most sensitive, and my friend is no exception. It was a trifling service I offered her, and I am astonished she remembers it." He smiled at her as warmly as he dared, then turned back to Mrs. Mowbray. "We met again in London this month, when Lord Chawleigh invited us both to dine. His son boarded for a time with my family so that my father might prepare him for Eton. And Lady Sophia"—he gestured to her—"is Lord Chawleigh's neighbor."

"Why, that is astonishing, for we are also within ten miles of Chawleigh Manor, and even less to Chesmere Park, although it is through Marie's friendship with Lady Sophia that we know the two families at all. Lady Sophia and Marie met at the reverend's house as girls to sew clothing for the poor, and they became inseparable." Mrs. Mowbray smiled at the two ladies. "Mr. Harwood, I had no idea you had such connections in our neighborhood."

"I am also surprised at your knowing Mr. Cunningworth," Miss Mowbray said before turning to Lady Sophia. "I suppose that is my own fault, for I did not ask you how it came to be that Mr. Harwood was at Chawleigh Manor when you first met him."

Lady Sophia did not offer up anything more of herself, but she had already surprised Felix by giving such a personal explanation for their initial meeting. Dinner was announced, and they moved into the dining room, where they sat informally around the table. Lady Sophia was once again seated across from Felix, depriving him of a chance to know her better. It began to frustrate him that this seemed always to be the case, although reason reminded him that it was only their second dinner together. He had never been so bent on seeking conversation with a woman before—even one he had no intention of pursuing.

SOPHIA HAD KNOWN in advance that Mr. Harwood would come to dine at Marie's house, but it had still been difficult to breathe when he walked in. She was quickly discovering that when it came to social discourse, her usual nerves and anxious heart flutterings were nothing compared to how she felt when in Mr. Harwood's presence. Somehow, it was more comfortable having him remain in the pages of her memento book, where she could allow him the space to be perfect while keeping her own heart safe from risk. It was more difficult to meet him in the flesh and expose herself to the constant threat of appearing ridiculous in his eyes.

Not that he seemed to view her that way. On the contrary, he was the one who appeared nervous this evening. Although she supposed that was normal after making her friend's acquaintance. Marie was everything a man like Mr. Harwood could hope to meet. She mixed freely in all types of company, and her conversation was peppered with humorous quips and easy discourse. It must be Marie who had set him off-kilter, for it was when he met her that he appeared to be the most overset, fumbling with his greeting. Following that, he had fallen silent until he finally gathered the courage to speak to Marie—although she must not imagine he needed such courage. She was merely projecting her own weaknesses on him. In the limited time she had spent with Mr. Harwood, he had shown himself remarkably able to handle all circumstances and all nature of people. Tonight's greeting was the exception.

He had asked whether Marie had been to Brighton to visit her father, and she assumed he regretted not having made her acquaintance earlier. With her ears tuned to everything that concerned Mr. Harwood, she had also heard Mrs. Mowbray's question of how she and Mr. Harwood were acquainted and spoke up to answer it for herself. It was a desperate attempt to let Mr. Harwood know that she had seen him in the light of rescuer that day in Chawleigh Manor.

Now she was seated at dinner beside Mr. Edwards, who

made himself agreeable and required little more from her than a simple murmur of encouragement as he spoke. She thought she was acquitting herself well in the conversation, but she could not be perfectly at ease in his presence, for his conversation was so lively, he scarcely waited for her tiny contribution before moving on to something else. He was able to eat at steady intervals while he spoke, but she was forced to leave her dinner almost completely untouched. What if he should require her assent while her mouth was full?

The conversation between the Mowbrays and Mr. Harwood appeared to be more interesting than her own, and Marie's laughter was so infectious that he had grown at ease and was responding naturally.

"How came you to sponsor Mr. Harwood?" Marie asked her father. "I am now learning he was not in the navy, but in the army, so I cannot fathom how your paths crossed."

Mr. Harwood raised his eyes to the admiral's, smiling but giving no answer. Admiral Mowbray returned the look, took a sip of his wine, and set down his glass. "I discovered Mr. Harwood's extraordinary diplomatic skills through a chance encounter while my officers were on shore leave. Is that not so, Edwards?"

Mr. Edwards returned a wry smile. "Indeed it is, and I can only thank the heavens I was not there that day, for I might have lost my position—and your good esteem."

"What happened?" Marie asked, turning to Mr. Harwood with great interest. He met her look with humorous eyes, but shook his head. It seemed he was too modest, and the admiral answered in his stead.

"My officers were on leave and were meant to keep the sailors under their regard, so that the good innkeepers, townspeople, and local society would not wish us to Jericho. This was of particular necessity, since Prince George was reputed to be in residence in Brighton Palace—or would be arriving at any moment."

Marie's quick wit caused her to say, "You might stop the story here, Papa, for I know that even if the naval officers had behaved with the utmost correctness, the sailors were probably ripe for mischief."

The admiral chuckled as he shared an enigmatic look with both Mr. Harwood and Mr. Edwards. "Well, there you would be wrong, my dear. It was the naval *officers* who started the brawl with the local yeomanry in the pub that night. Mr. Harwood, would you care to tell your part?"

Mr. Harwood cleared his throat and offered a weak smile. "I would rather let such a thing be forgotten, but of course I do not wish to disoblige you." He turned to Marie and included Sophia in his look. "The soldiers were being fractious that night and wished to have the pub all to themselves, which was not a reasonable thing to expect."

"Because the sailors were engaging in coarse behavior, I am ashamed to say. Flirting with the barmaids and innkeepers' daughters in plain sight of the militia, who were used to that privilege." The admiral's lips turned up and he gestured to Mr. Harwood. "Go on."

He paused before continuing. "A physical fight began, and some of us were in a timely position to encourage the parties involved to cease before things got out of hand."

It seemed the admiral could not let Mr. Harwood continue without including what he considered to be essential facts, for he took over the narrative again.

"Mr. Harwood is too modest. A naval officer was about to throw a punch at an enlisted soldier, and Mr. Harwood stepped between them and took the blow himself. Instead of reacting to the slight and allowing a brawl to occur, he reminded the officer of how important the navy's contribution was in defending the crown."

The admiral's eyes twinkled with approval. "Mr. Harwood went on to say that he was quite sure the navy was as devoted to keeping the shores protected as the army, and that the officer would not want to give Napoleon the satisfaction of internal altercations occurring within the British men-at-arms. He then proceeded to buy drinks for all of the naval officers, thereby winning peace for the night and my admiration for his diplomacy once I'd heard of it."

Mr. Harwood said nothing, and the admiral urged Mr. Edwards to confirm the story, which he did.

"And so, Mr. Edwards brought the matter to my attention as soon as he had learned of it, and I recommended Mr. Harwood for an assistant secretary position at the Admiralty, which he was pleased to accept."

Sophia guessed that Mr. Harwood was uncomfortable with such praise, for he gave another feeble smile and did not seek anyone's regard. However, the story could only provoke her to greater admiration. It perfectly accorded with what she had seen of him that day in Chawleigh Manor when he had simultaneously defended her and smoothed over the incident with Robert, someone known for being difficult to please.

The conversation moved on to other subjects, and Mr. Harwood asked Marie what it was like to be daughter to an admiral. She laughed and launched into a diverting list of what it meant to be his daughter for good or for ill. It made Sophia's heart ache to be in the presence of such an outstanding gentleman as Mr. Harwood, and to know that, unlike Marie, nothing about her could inspire him to return the admiration.

At the end of the evening, the guests gathered in the hall, ready to depart. Sophia was given an unlooked-for opportunity to speak to Mr. Harwood, for Mr. Edwards had stopped the

Mowbrays with an interesting piece of Admiralty gossip that he promised even the ladies would wish to know.

With firm resolve, she touched him on his sleeve. "Mr. Harwood, may I speak to you?"

There was a look of surprise in his eyes, followed by an instant attentiveness. "Yes, of course."

It was hard to push past her breathlessness, but the matter was so important she would not permit her shyness to steal her words. "I have not seen you since the day we met at St. James's Palace, and I have wished these two weeks past to thank you for your willingness to render me a service—and to offer my apologies that I was not there to receive it."

His expression eased. "I saw that you had found a gentleman willing to lend his carriage, for I returned with one just as you were leaving. Please do not think anything more of it. I was glad that you were able to receive assistance so quickly."

She nodded, knowing she should respond to this but was unsure of what to say. It was still distressing to think that he had gone to all that trouble only for it to come to nothing.

"I could see how affected you were by your sister's indisposition," he said after a brief pause.

She looked up and was once again touched by those eyes that seemed to see right into her. There was kindness there, and time. As though he had hours to spare for her and would wait until she was able to form words that did not come readily.

"I was. It is unlike her to faint. And Dorothea is with child, so I was worried."

His brows furrowed in concern. "May I ask how she is now?"

"She is well." Sophia managed to smile at him in her pleasure of maintaining a proper conversation with a man she esteemed and her relief at remembering the happy outcome.

"The baby seems to be unharmed, and apart from resting, she is going along as well as usual."

"I am happy to hear it." Mr. Harwood's eyes remained on her, and it caused a warm fluttering somewhere between her belly and her heart. She could almost fool herself into believing he was interested in her, and his next words strengthened the impulse. "My lady, please do not ever hesitate to request anything of me that you might need. I will happily carry it out." This coaxed a greater smile from her, for it seemed he meant it. He was such a kind, obliging gentleman.

But then, she reminded herself severely, it was likely just that. He was kind and obliging—to all. She had certainly not displayed any remarkable quality that would attract his interest, and she must not deceive herself by thinking he felt anything toward her but charitable disinterest.

Mr. Edwards had finished his conversation, and Marie moved forward, holding out her hand to Mr. Harwood. "I shall hope to see more of you, sir."

An easy smile lit his face as he bowed over her hand. "And I you, Miss Mowbray. Delighted to have made your acquaintance at last."

Sophia's coach was announced, and her footman and maid waited for her outdoors as she bid farewell to her hosts and the other guests and stepped outdoors. The evening had held many pleasures, and she should have been satisfied, but her spirits had plunged once again. She had carried on a natural conversation with Mr. Harwood that went beyond commonplaces, which was a signal victory for her. But she had also witnessed how enchanting Marie was in his company, and how easily they conversed throughout the evening. How could he not find her friend all that was perfect?

CHAPTER 6

In their first few weeks in London, Sophia managed to avoid several of the season's more popular balls, simply because Dorothea was not there to scold her into attending, and her mother was not passionate enough about going to bestir herself. It had been an easy thing for Sophia to appease her mother's expectations and her own conscience by attending some of the smaller dinners and routs—ones where she was confident she might largely go unnoticed.

Dorothea, however, had begun to chafe under the necessity of remaining housebound and launched a small revolt against her husband by vowing that if he didn't allow her the pleasure of attending even one ball, she would be tempted to take one of their more spirited mares out for an extended ride. This was pure provocation, but even Miles knew his wife well enough to realize he could not force her to rest against her will. Besides, she was asking for nothing more than an evening's entertainment where she would not be required to exert herself more than what was needed for conversation.

Therefore, Sophia found herself preparing for her first large ball of the season, sitting before the dressing table while

Margery set her curls with decorative sprigs of dark purple flowers sewn to small hair combs. She had chosen a pale lilac satin for her gown with beaded glass trim around the cap sleeves and bodice, and a dark purple ribbon sewn to the empire waistline. Her mother had fortified herself for an evening out by resting the entire day, and by the time she joined Sophia in the drawing room—over an hour after they were supposed to have left—it almost seemed she was looking forward to it.

Having arrived late, she and her mother were admitted into Lord and Lady Berkley's house to find the hall empty of people. Fortunately, the hosts were still greeting the last of the arrivals, so Lady Poole and Sophia had not missed the opportunity to pay their respects before the Berkleys left their post. The warmth that emanated from the ballroom was welcoming after the chill of the outdoors, but the ballroom was already dreadfully crowded, and Sophia had to fight the urge to turn around and run back to the carriage.

One advantage of this evening's entertainment was that Marie would be in attendance. A fortnight had passed since the dinner at the admiral's house, and they had met several times in their homes since. That was how she had learned that Marie had again met Mr. Harwood at an intimate supper gathering. Although Sophia had ventured to ask who else was in attendance, she could not discern whether Marie had a particular interest in him. It was a wretched feeling not to know, but she must simply resign herself to allowing fate to follow its course. If the season concluded with Mr. Harwood and Marie making a match, why then, they were meant to end up together. Nothing Sophia could do would reverse the outcome.

At least, she tried to tell herself that.

"Good evening, Lady Poole. I am so pleased you were able to come." Lady Berkley made no mention of their tardy arrival, for which Sophia was grateful. Then she touched her husband's arm. "Do you remember, my dear, when Lady Sophia and her sister came to last year's ball so newly arrived in London for their first season?"

Her husband did not, but he assured his wife that he had, and how fine they had looked. Sophia *was* surprised that Lady Berkley had remembered their attendance last year out of all the guests. It had been their very first ball and, at Dorothea's insistence, had come the same day they had arrived in London.

With the greetings exchanged, Lady Berkley informed them that, following another dance set, they would be ushering the guests into the supper room for the evening's repast, which she hoped they would find to their satisfaction. Lady Poole murmured her assurances, and they turned to enter the ballroom. They had arrived late, indeed.

In the ballroom, Sophia was swallowed up by the crowds and became distressed, fearful that someone might catch her unaware and require something of her. That a person might speak to her and find her uninteresting—or ask her to dance, only to realize she had little to offer in the way of conversation. Any dance she accepted was usually void of pleasure, for she only wearied herself in the attempts to think of something to say. To her relief, Dorothea and Miles had spotted them and were moving their way.

"Good evening, Mama," Dorothea said, kissing her on the cheek. Miles added his greetings, and she turned to Sophia. "In attending tonight, you have obeyed the letter, but not the spirit, for you are late. Were you hoping to miss all of the dances?"

Before Sophia could reply, her mother owned herself to be at fault. "We were to leave on time—or, at least only a little bit late—but I became convinced that I would grow chilled in the gown I had chosen and was forced to change."

"I see," Dorothea replied placidly. Her obvious pleasure in

attending a ball appeared to have removed all of her usual impatience with her mother. "In any case, there will be the supper dance soon. Mama, shall I take you to speak to Lady Isabelle? She is here." Lady Isabelle was Miles's mother, and the connection through marriage had allowed the two women to strike up a friendship.

"Oh, is she?" Lady Poole brightened visibly. "I should like that very much."

Sophia would have followed them, except that she saw Marie coming—a bright beacon parting the crowds on her way to her.

"I am glad you are here," Marie said after a brief clasp of her hands, "for I wished to introduce you to someone I have just met."

Sophia glanced back at Dorothea, who gave a little wave to indicate she should amuse herself, before leading their mother to Lady Isabelle. Sophia went with Marie, and as they skirted the crowds, leaned in to ask, "Who is it?"

"It is Mr. Edwards's sister, Regina Edwards. She is a delight —the most unassuming and pleasant girl, and so full of industry. You will like her, for she has the same philanthropic bent that you do."

What false praise was this? Sophia tugged her to a stop, her brows knit. "I am hardly philanthropic—no more than you are. I am nothing like Annabelle Moore." Annabelle was the reverend's daughter, who frequently visited the poor and never lost the opportunity to speak about the work she did there.

"Annabelle Moore performs her acts of service so that all may see. I would not speak ill of the reverend's daughter, for I am sure there is goodness blended in with what she does. However, your *heart* is philanthropic, impossible to distinguish from your acts. You take every opportunity your natural reserve will allow to relieve the sufferings of the poor."

Sophia had always known her friend saw the best in her, but she was touched by this glowing description. It rather made her seem like a woman whose traits included boldness, even if it was bold on behalf of the poor. Of course, that was just a friend's affection speaking.

Before they moved on, Sophia glanced over at the set in progress and caught sight of Mr. Harwood dancing the reel with energy and grace. His partner was a pretty girl who executed her steps with a bounce, accompanied by giggles.

"Mr. Harwood is here," she observed. She could not help herself.

"I know it. We have already spoken, and he requested a dance from me." Marie turned to look at Sophia. "You should dance with him as well if he asks. He would be a comfortable partner for you, for he is not difficult to talk to."

"No, he is not."

They pushed forward through the crowds again, and Sophia's feelings were painfully conflicted. A glimmer of hope had shot through her when Marie encouraged her to dance with Mr. Harwood, which could lead one to believe she was not interested in him. But then, a second, more sober thought followed the first: Marie was so at ease in Mr. Harwood's presence she could distribute his dances to other ladies and be sure he would oblige. That was more likely the sum of the matter.

"Miss Edwards, I wish to present you to my dearest friend, Lady Sophia." Marie came to a stop before a plain woman of short stature, whose features were transformed when she smiled. She did so now, as she dropped into a curtsy.

"A pleasure to meet you, my lady." Miss Edwards appeared perfectly at ease in a Society ball. Not even the introduction to someone new gave her pause. "I am thankful that my brother introduced me to Miss Mowbray, for I know few people here. I have come out only this season, and this is my first ball."

Sophia found it easy to smile back and found her even more courageous after learning it was her first ball. One would never have guessed it. "It is mine, too. That is—my first ball this season. I attended several last year."

"Ah, so you must be more at ease than I am at this one. Your gown is very pretty," Miss Edwards added.

She was spared from returning more than a thank you, for Marie spoke again. "Miss Edwards has offered to give us a tour of the Royal Naval Asylum any day that we are free. I assured her that you would be interested in visiting it, as would I."

"My father is on the committee there, and I am involved with sorting through the donations as we receive them," Miss Edwards explained. "The asylum is for children whose fathers have been killed at sea while fighting for the crown. They are given board, a place to sleep, and instruction. My hope is to bring the children's needs to Society's attention. Perhaps, if you are pleased with the good works we are doing there, you might wish to assist me in this endeavor? But there is no need to make any promises until you have seen it for yourself."

Sophia thought about how to respond. The idea of visiting it had merit. To bestir oneself on behalf of the orphans must be rewarding, although she could make no promises about promoting their needs to others. Besides, it could not be as hard to visit an asylum as it was to attend a Society function, for no one would have expectations of her there. Having needs was different from having expectations. They were easier to meet and one was not likely to disappoint anyone.

"Yes, thank you for the invitation. I would like to go with you and visit the asylum."

If Miss Edwards was put out by the length of time it took before Sophia gave her answer, she hid it well. "How delightful. I will be going Tuesday next to make a list of the number of subscriptions we must fulfill so that each of the beds are provided for. I would be delighted to have both of your company on that day."

"It is settled, then," Marie said.

A gentleman drew near, halting any further conversation between them and causing Sophia to grow tense. Robert Cunningworth towered over her, cutting off some of the scant light she'd had from a nearby sconce.

"Good evening, Lady Sophia. This is the first ball I have seen you at in London, and I am very pleased to find you here. I must not lose my opportunity to ask you to dance."

She tried not to reveal any of the dismay she felt when she answered. "I shall be delighted."

The words had been mumbled in scarcely more than a whisper, but he appeared to have heard them, for he gestured to the center of the room.

"Well, would you look? This set is ending. We might have our dance now." He held out his arm, and Sophia had no choice but to put her hand on it.

She sent a glance back to Marie, who returned it but seemed oblivious to her extreme reluctance. Sophia had told her of Robert's harassment in her childhood but had not disclosed that he had begun showing a determined pursuit of her—and that she loathed the idea. She wished that Camilla had come, for she would have deeply commiserated with Sophia's obligation to dance with Robert and might even have found a way to spare her from it. The first in the set was to be a *contredanse*, and they took their places on the sidelines.

"You look pretty, Sophia."

"Thank you." Vaguely, she considered replying with something more but had no idea what else she could say. Robert did not seem to have any further ideas for conversation either and was silent as he watched the crowds shift around him. Then he turned suddenly. "It looks like Harwood is asking your friend to dance, and they are coming this way."

Sophia glanced over and found Mr. Harwood's eyes on her. He and Marie came up to them, and she returned his greeting with a curtsy.

Robert pulled her attention back to him. "Lady Sophia, this is the supper dance, so I shall have the pleasure of escorting you into the dining room afterward. You will like that, won't you?"

She was unable to answer this. Against her will, her eyes went to Mr. Harwood. Any fantasy that he might have rescued her was routed when he turned to Marie.

"That is a capital idea. Miss Mowbray, if you will accompany me in, we might all dine together." Marie's answering smile was radiant, and Sophia's heart sank even lower, slinking between the crevices of the rocks in her stomach.

"I am still waiting for your answer, Sophy," Robert cried out with forced joviality, using the name her father had sometimes called her.

"Yes, if you wish it," she replied softly.

The music began, sending the men to the line on the opposite side of the room. The evening was going by so quickly. She had forgotten that this was the supper dance—not that she would have had the courage to refuse Robert had she known. One virtue presented itself, however. She would be near Mr. Harwood in a quieter setting, even if he were not her escort.

As the last notes of the dance died down, they made a reverence to their partners and followed the crowds into an adjoining room, where small round tables were placed close together to allow everyone to be seated. Robert claimed one and held out a chair for Sophia before taking one himself. Mr. Harwood did the same for Marie, but remained standing.

"Mr. Cunningworth and I will gladly fetch you ladies a plate of something to eat, if you will trust us with the selection."

Marie's ready smile was directed up at him. "Gladly."

Sophia was required to voice some agreement. "Thank you, Mr. Cunningworth." That would have to do, for enthusiasm was far out of reach.

When they were alone, Marie's good humor filled the space between them. "Isn't Mr. Harwood an exemplary gentleman?"

This was nothing new, for she had already told Sophia as much after her father recounted the story in Brighton. But it seemed tonight her interest had turned decidedly in his direction. Sophia had to know. "Do...do you like him, then?"

"Exceedingly," Marie said with a grin that produced an instant pain in Sophia's heart. "And I think he is not indifferent to me. I will not say that I have handed him my heart, for this is my first season and I intend to have my fun. But I should not be disappointed to know more of him, and to perhaps enter into a courtship with time."

This last bit was said with teasing that normally would have made Sophia smile, but she could only nod, her face grave. She was being even more uninteresting than usual, and her friend sensed it.

With a glance at the gentlemen still in line for refreshments, Marie turned back. "What is it, Sophia? You do not seem happy tonight. You are not upset with me, I trust?"

She shook her head. "No, not at all. Please do not think it. Perhaps I am just tired." She was quiet for a moment. "I do not know what it is."

Marie studied her with true concern, then leaned in to murmur, "I believe I know what it is." Sophia turned to her in surprise. Surely she could not have guessed? "You are discouraged to have to sit at supper with Mr. Cunningworth. I know you are not fond of him and never have been. But do you not think he has changed a little since he was the obnoxious youth always causing you trouble?"

She was unsure of what to answer. Robert had changed some, it was true. But to admit it might lead her friend to think there was still a chance she could like him. Such a thing was impossible.

She was not obliged to return a reply, for the gentlemen arrived, depositing plates in front of them. They were filled with a selection of meats and cheeses, savory tarts, sweetmeats, sugared almonds, and fresh fruit. She forced her gaze to meet Robert's expectant one. "Thank you."

"I aim to please." He sat and began eating what was in front of him. Sophia looked at hers and took a bite of the tart.

"Have you been well, Lady Sophia, since we last met?" This was from Mr. Harwood, and she looked up in surprise, a new spear of hope shooting through her to see his attention directed toward her. She was able to respond to it with a smile that did not need to be forced.

"Very well, thank you." She was proud that her voice sounded strong, with little trace of shyness. "I have been walking in Hyde Park and have attended some of the smaller assemblies. This is my first large ball of the season."

"I am glad Lady Dorothea convinced her to come to it. I had begun to fear I would have to endure the entire London season without having Lady Sophia by my side at *any* of the events," Marie added, laughingly.

"I am glad you came as well," Mr. Harwood said.

When the meaning of his words pierced her consciousness, a tentative smile grew on her face. She could hardly believe he cared enough to say it, even if he was likely being polite.

Robert glanced at Mr. Harwood with narrowed eyes. "As am I. And you may be assured that I will begin calling on you more regularly, Sophia." Along with dropping the honorific, Robert turned toward her with a look that seemed proprietary—and wrong. "I've not been able to do so before, because my father has been keeping me busy, but I have a bit more time at my disposal now."

"Mr. Harwood, do you pay morning calls?" Marie asked. As soon as the words were out, she turned to Sophia, an immediate blush filling her cheeks. That had been forward, even for Marie, and she strove to soften it. "Sometimes I sit with Lady Sophia during visiting hours, and if Mr. Cunningworth were to come, we should be delighted to see you as well."

This was untrue, but Sophia could hardly blame her. Marie had revealed a partiality that would be unbecoming if Mr. Harwood did not return it. Sophia was glad to shield her friend from embarrassment, even if she could hardly be happy about watching them make a match.

"You are indeed welcome," she said, adding her encouragement to Mr. Harwood. It was not difficult to admit that she would be glad to have him come for calls, as well, if she must endure Robert's.

"I have not been well enough acquainted with Society ladies to have made morning calls before now," he said, again with a smile that seemed in his amiable way to be just for her, although she was likely reading too much into his politeness again. "But if you are pleased—if you both are pleased to have me," he rectified, "I shall be glad to come."

Marie looked gratified, and Sophia returned his smile. She could not help it, for spending time with Mr. Harwood, even if it was to further his interest with Marie, was better than spending no time with him at all.

CHAPTER 7

The stultifying tick of the clock resounded in the drawing room, which was absent of all other noise. Marie leaned back on the reclining sofa and offered Sophia a sheepish look.

"I cannot think what possessed me to ask Mr. Harwood whether he ever paid morning calls and to follow up that piece of nonsense by assuring him I would be in your drawing room should he wish to do so."

Sophia smiled listlessly, prey to the mixed feelings of anticipating Mr. Harwood's presence in her very own drawing room, while knowing that if he did come, there was every reason to suspect he had done so to see Marie.

"And now that I've said it, I'm obliged to haunt your drawing room until he pays a visit," Marie continued. "Poor you."

This produced a genuine giggle from Sophia. "Well, as neither he nor Mr. Cunningworth have actually called these two days past, perhaps we have made a fuss over nothing. Before Mr. Cunningworth announced his intentions, I had not even given morning calls a thought, whether it was to make them or receive them. Dorothea is not here to arrange the calls as she did last year; my mother never thinks of them, and we have not gone out in Society enough to expect them."

"I feel it is all my fault," Marie admitted.

The door to the drawing room opened and Camilla entered as Sophia sighed and shook her head. "It is not your fault, for Mr. Cunningworth has promised to visit."

"You mean he has threatened to visit," Camilla said as she joined their circle.

Sophia gave her sister a reproving look but was unable to repress a chuckle. Rather than dignify that comment with an answer, she turned to Marie. "I don't suppose I would have made any effort to be at home if it were just to await Mr. Cunningworth's visit." The silence that followed this made room for her worry that she had given too much away. Did Marie take it to mean she was now staying at home because of Mr. Harwood?

Before that particular fear could grow to gargantuan proportions, Camilla changed the subject. "I told Joanna and Tilly to come down as soon as they can make themselves presentable. They have been quarreling, and we are all of us in need of some diversion."

"Even if that diversion is Mr. Cunningworth?" Sophia asked, and was instantly seized with guilt for having made him the subject of her joke. She rushed on. "Will Mother come down?"

Camilla shook her head. "Mama is feeling poorly and says we will have to do without her company today."

Marie murmured a consolation, then added, "Well, as your sister has said, perhaps we are all assembled here for nothing, for it is the third day of waiting and we have yet to receive a single visitor."

As if on cue, the rap of the knocker sounded on the front

door. Sophia and Marie both turned their heads toward the main hall to listen for the voices that would identify their callers. Joanna and Tilly entered the drawing room from the private entrance.

"Take the seat there," Joanna urged their youngest sister before sitting beside Sophia on the sofa. Seconds later, the butler entered the drawing room.

"My ladies, three gentlemen are here to see you. Mr. Cunningworth, Mr. Harwood, and Mr. Grantly."

"Show them in, please." At hearing Mr. Harwood's name, Sophia's throat went dry, but she had no time to examine this before the gentleman entered the room. He glanced at everyone present, but she felt his eyes on her. She had never been so nervous in her own drawing room before.

Greetings and courtesies were exchanged, and they piled into the remaining seats in the center of the drawing room. Mr. Cunningworth chose the seat next to Marie, which was to Sophia's left, and Mr. Harwood and Mr. Grantly took the chairs opposite.

Mr. Harwood broke the silence. "It is just as you said, Miss Mowbray. We find you here during calling hours."

"Yes." Marie looked embarrassed and, perhaps for the first time since Sophia had known her, did not have a ready rejoinder.

"Well, I hope you were not sitting here for the past three days waiting for us to come." Robert laughed heartily, causing Marie to shoot a miserable glance at Sophia, who was too irritated by Robert's comment to return a sympathetic one. For what he had said was nothing short of the truth. She had wasted three days, but it was not for him. It was for Mr. Harwood, and then only to watch his courtship with Marie.

She looked at him, and his gaze quickly skittered away as

though he had been looking at her, too. Was...was it possible he had come for *her*?

The footman and maid had been well-trained by Dorothea and entered the drawing room carrying the tea things before the guests had been made to wait for too long. The ritual of preparing tea gave Sophia something to do and allowed her to gain some mastery over her nerves. She gave instructions for where to put the trays and went over to the cabinet on the side of the room where the tea was kept. Marie, too, had seemed to regain her equilibrium, for she kept the guests amused by dissecting the upcoming social events and giving her opinions on which ones were worth attending.

Sophia had been following the conversation with hopes that Mr. Harwood might publicly commit to attending one of the events to which she might also be invited. Although he did not offer any clues to his plans, he did turn to Tilly on his right, and asked what she best liked to do in London.

She looked surprised at his having addressed her, but responded decisively. "I like to do what everyone else likes. Of course, I cannot go to balls yet, but I like to do everything else. I just don't like staying home."

"I understand you perfectly," he replied, his expression sympathetic. Sophia was touched that he had singled out her youngest sister, who was often neglected when visitors came.

"You ought to try a picnic, if one can be organized for you," Mr. Grantly said, then turned to the rest of the company. "As a matter of fact, I have come with just such an intention. With the coming of warmer weather, my aunt, Mrs. Taylor, wishes to organize a picnic on Primrose Hill and has been pestering me to add some young people to her guest list."

At his unusual manner of giving his invitation, Camilla shot Sophia a look full of humor.

"Doesn't Primrose Hill have a reputation for base conduct?" Marie asked, her eyebrows knit. "Dueling and such?"

"Not in broad daylight," Mr. Grantly assured her. "And you need have no fears that there will be anything unsavory involved—not where my aunt is concerned. As I am her only nephew, you may be assured that I will procure invitations for all of you as soon as she sets the date."

"Even one for me?" Tilly asked, causing Mr. Grantly to grow self-conscious. Joanna sent Tilly a subtle shake of her head with an added glare that told her not to speak out of turn.

When Mr. Grantly did not respond, Robert attempted to pacify Tilly with a studied look of sympathy. "Such gatherings will not usually include children, you must understand. Mrs. Taylor has never had any children of her own and therefore does not know what to do with them."

Tilly looked dismayed at the combined reproof from Joanna, their neighbor from Surrey, and the rejection. Sophia's heart went out to her, but she did not know how to ease the situation. She had often reflected that it was not easy to be in her position. Tilly was the youngest of the family, and the closest one to her in age—Joanna—was only interested in spending her time in the stables or on horseback.

"Lady Matilda." Mr. Harwood waited until he had her attention. "If Mrs. Taylor has set a limitation on the number of guests she wishes to have at her picnic, I propose that we plan another picnic together next to the Thames." He glanced at Sophia. "That is, if your mother will approve of the idea and can provide a chaperone."

"It might be difficult," Robert said, frowning. "Lady Poole is often unwell."

"Lady Matilda has sisters old enough to serve as chaperones," Mr. Harwood replied, undaunted.

Sophia looked at Mr. Harwood in surprise. Why was he

doing this? Was it to show Marie what sort of a man he was? Or was it purely to give encouragement to her sister? Or was it for some other reason? And why had Robert attempted to put a spoke in the wheel, when *he* did not have to go?

Tilly glanced shyly at Mr. Harwood, but as tears sparkled on her lashes, she looked away again. Sophia quietly willed her to answer but suspected she was unable to. After a moment of wrestling with her difficulty in speaking out, she did it for her.

"That is a gracious invitation, Mr. Harwood. I am sure my mother will approve of the plan, and I'm sure Tilly would love to go." She smiled at her sister in encouragement, then turned back to Mr. Harwood. There was warmth in his expression, and suddenly she was sure he had done it for her sister and not for Marie.

She broke the connection and looked into the teapot to distract herself. Another knock came as Sophia began to pour, and she exchanged a look of surprise with Marie. They had not been expecting any other visitors, and the ones they had been waiting for for three days were currently in the drawing room. Turton entered a second time to announce the newest arrivals.

"Lady Dorothea Shaw, Mr. Miles Shaw, and Lord Pembroke."

Movement to Sophia's right caused her to turn toward Camilla, who sat upright. Setting down the teapot, Sophia caught her attention and lifted a brow in question that asked *'was this your idea?'* Camilla's eyes widened and she gave a small shake of her head.

"Good day," Dorothea said, sailing into the room, her husband and Lord Pembroke behind her. "I see you are rather full of guests this morning. We shall not stay long, then. I wished to pay a call on Lady Berkley, as well."

"Lady Dorothea, I wish you would take my seat," Mr. Harwood said.

Sophia could not resist sending him a look of approval, having noticed that neither Mr. Cunningworth nor Mr. Grantly had thought to do the same when there were clearly not enough chairs in the circle. Mr. Harwood and Miles went over to bring three caned chairs from the sides of the room.

"It has been some time since I've come to visit," Lord Pembroke announced cheerfully, looking around the drawing room. He had a few times last season when he was still Viscount Throckmorton. Everyone had called him "Rock" then by way of abbreviation, but now the only one who continued to do so was his cousin, Miles. "It appears nothing has changed."

"Few things do that are visible," Camilla observed.

Lord Pembroke glanced at her curiously, but Camilla looked straight ahead, as though the comment had not been for him. Sophia blinked at her sister in surprise. What did she mean by that? Before anyone had time to ponder too long on this cryptic remark, Robert changed the subject entirely.

"Lady Sophia, I have not yet seen you attend the opera this season. You simply must go, for you are missing out on hearing Angelica Catalani. I have seats in my father's box when she performs next week. Why not attend with me? Our box is large enough to hold six guests."

"I…"

All eyes were on her. That Robert had chosen to ask her publicly was cruel, for she could hardly refuse him now. She would desperately have given any excuse not to go, but none came to her. Not a single word made its way to her lips, and she sent an involuntary glance to Mr. Harwood, who frowned. He must surely think her stupid for being unable to answer a simple question.

Mr. Harwood turned to Robert. "If you think your father might be amenable to the idea, perhaps I might escort Miss Mowbray and join you in your box. We can make a party of it."

Sophia had been right that he had not come calling to see her. He was interested in Marie, this much was now evident. Naturally he was, for they were so well-suited.

Marie returned a broad smile, eyes sparkling with pleasure. If Sophia knew her friend, she was not only praising her good fortune in having secured an invitation to the opera, she was calculating how she might also attend the picnic that Mr. Harwood had promised to Tilly. There was nothing wrong with such calculations, but Sophia would have liked to go with Mr. Harwood herself. It was difficult to talk to him when others were present who were more gifted at conversation.

"An excellent idea." Robert sent Mr. Harwood an approving nod. "My father will be in favor of the plan, I am sure of it."

After a slight pause, Mr. Harwood pivoted to face Mr. Grantly. "If you wish to join us, you might bring Lady Camilla." Robert's friend pulled back, his expression revealing his distaste for the idea, and an awkward silence followed. Sophia was mortified on her sister's behalf, but a rescue came from an unlikely quarter.

"You need not trouble yourself, Mr. Grantly," Lord Pembroke said pleasantly as all eyes turned to him. "Lady Camilla, if you are pleased to accept my company, I will take you. And I will invite your sister and Miles to make up the party."

By now, Mr. Grantly seemed to have recognized that he had acted in bad *ton*, for he said, "Well, it was only that I had not yet made up my mind to go…"

Camilla did not allow him to finish. "I accept. Thank you for the invitation, Lord Pembroke."

She smiled at Lord Pembroke, and looked charmingly as she did so. Camilla had always been given to plumpness but had lost some of it in the past year. Not only that, Sophia reflected with satisfaction, her younger sister was faring better than many more experienced ladies in their first season, for she had secured an invitation to attend the opera with a young and handsome earl despite not yet being out.

"Well, we must take our leave. We would not wish to outstay our welcome." Mr. Cunningworth laughed as he got to his feet, and his friends followed suit. His departure brought Sophia relief, even though it meant his friends would leave with him. However, her thankfulness at being free of him for the afternoon plunged at the reminder in his next words.

"But I shall own myself satisfied, for I have achieved the purpose of my visit." He bowed to her. "I have the pleasure of escorting you to the opera next week, Lady Sophia."

Sophia managed a wan smile, which fell as Mr. Harwood bowed before Marie. "Miss Mowbray, I will confirm the arrangements for the opera if that is agreeable to you."

"It is. Thank you for the invitation."

He took leave of all the ladies present, including Tilly, and stood before Sophia last. He bowed and smiled at her as he stood upright.

"Good day." She curtsied but was unable to respond, or even smile.

The three gentlemen took their leave, and Marie exhaled quietly. No one noticed but Sophia. However, she could not ask Marie for her thoughts or discuss anything that had transpired during the visit, for there were others in the drawing room—notably Lord Pembroke, who was not connected to their family.

Instead, Sophia gave voice to her question. "Camilla, if it was not your idea to ask Dorry and Miles to come this morning, whose was it?"

"Mine," Tilly said, surprising everyone. Sophia turned to her, puzzled, and she went on. "After all, it seemed pointless to sit around each day, waiting for callers to come. I knew you would stay at home until we finally had visitors, so I wrote to invite Dorry and Miles. How was I to know we would actually have real callers today?" This artless comment was met with stunned silence, broken by laughter.

"I have never been so set down in all of my life," Lord Pembroke said with a tragic air. "It matters not that I am an earl, for today I have learned that I am not a real caller."

CHAPTER 8

The following day, Felix received a letter from his father, who had written to tell him of an unexpected bequeathment that would provide his sisters with a respectable dowry and suggested he return home for a visit. He set off immediately with the noble intention of planning a parliamentary speech on pensions as he rode. Instead, his thoughts continued to circle back to Lady Sophia.

Visiting her in her own drawing room was like being offered a plate of sweetmeats just when he was in the mood for them. She had looked lovely in a soft yellow gown and, despite her shyness, was fully mistress of her surroundings. The only fly in the honey was Robert's persistent attempts to court her. He chose the empty seat closest to her, his gestures expansive and often invading the space in which she sat. He did not think Lady Sophia liked Robert. Her acceptance to attend the opera was not a ready one, and he was compelled to rush in with an invitation for Miss Mowbray because he couldn't bear the thought that Lady Sophia must bear Robert's attention all evening with no one to shield her. Fortunately—since it had been impulsively given—Robert had embraced the idea. And Miss Mowbray, always agreeable, was perfectly ready to assist him in coming to her friend's rescue.

There was something vulnerable and soft to Lady Sophia that appealed to a protective instinct, and he could not stop puzzling out what she might be thinking. He tried to read her thoughts and even anticipate her wishes, but seemed to fall far from his objective. The only thing he understood with any certainty was that she did not like to be the center of attention —that, and that she required time before giving her answer.

As to why Robert was pursuing her, it was perfectly clear that it came down to three things: she was above him in station and would add to his prominence; she was beautiful and wealthy, which was the only wife he would consider; he had known her the longest and had some sort of proprietary ideas about her. He probably convinced himself that he loved her, but it was clear that he loved her attributes and not *her*.

Robert may well have changed since that day Felix had had to rescue Lady Sophia from his awkward, grueling attention. After all, one could not lose a beloved mother in the intervening years and not change at least a little, becoming more staid and cognizant of what one had. But Robert's personality was bullish, and it would never be otherwise; he would not allow her the space to bloom. In short, he was utterly wrong for her. What Lady Sophia needed was a man who could be patient when it took her time to speak, a man who valued her for who she was and not for how she might elevate his position, a man who wanted nothing more than to coax the hidden gems from her thoughts.

A man like...him.

Having reached this self-indulgent conclusion, Felix was thoroughly disgusted with himself. He was determined not to reach above his station no matter how much he was drawn to Lady Sophia, and the short remainder of his journey was spent in chastisement to this end. He reached home and brought his gelding to the stable, where he handed him over to Ashly, their gardener-groom. Margaret, the eldest of his four sisters at age sixteen, crossed the stable entrance and stopped short at the sight of him.

"Felix! I did not know you were coming home."

"Good to see you, Megs." He walked over and kissed her on the top of her head. She was of an age with Lady Joanna, he guessed. And, as shy as she was with outsiders, very much resembled Lady Sophia in manner.

"Where is Father?"

"Where is he always?" Margaret answered with a quirk of her lips.

"The study, then. Walk with me?" He turned toward the house, and she matched his steps. He had not succeeded in explaining to himself why his thoughts kept returning to Lady Sophia. Was it that they both had many sisters? No. It was definitely not something so prosaic as that. That she was as shy as Meg, and so he felt an affinity for her? Perhaps his sister might have some insight into what Lady Sophia was thinking since they shared that similarity.

"Megger, if you were to allow a gentleman to court you, what traits must he have?"

She looked at him seriously without returning an immediate answer. She was like that when it required thought. They would not have time to finish the conversation before they reached the front door. They would not have time to start.

"I suppose he must be patient with me." They approached the bed of flowers that skirted the foundation of the house, broken only by the path leading to the door. "He must not talk so fast and so much that I can never say anything at all."

"*Hm*. It's what I thought." The words Felix had meant to say to himself, he spoke aloud.

"You do not have someone in mind for me!" she exclaimed, looking at him in alarm.

Yanked out of his reflections, he turned to her and laughed. "No, Megglebop. I would hardly have you married at sixteen." He didn't remember the exact moment the silly nicknames had started, but they had come from an attempt to draw her out of her bashfulness as a small girl and make her talk.

"I am relieved to hear it." Her twinkle had returned, and she was looking at him with a trusting air.

"But one day, I suppose I shall have to find someone for you. For you will never pluck up the courage to speak to a gentleman on your own, will you?" When she screwed up her lips in mock disapproval, he could not resist more teasing. "And you will have to accept whomever I bring home, now won't you? After all, Meggers can't be choosers."

This brought something between a squeal and a laugh as she pounded a fist on his arm.

They entered the comfortable stone house he had grown up in with the dark green door and large windows above the flower beds. The housekeeper, who had been in the family's employ since his birth, met him with a hearty welcome and promises to have a meal sent into his father's study. He smiled at her and inquired after her knee that was causing trouble, then went to the study.

His father looked pleased to see him and came to shake his hand. "I was just coming out to see about this commotion. You came as soon as you had my letter."

"Of course, sir." Felix took a seat next to his father's armchair. His relationship with Mr. Harwood Sr. could be described as a mix of easy affection and the expected signs of respect a son owed his sober-minded parent. His father began asking him about his life in London, inquiring into its every aspect from whether he planned to move now that he had been promoted, to what his life in Parliament was like, to how he was getting along with the Cunningworths.

Felix attempted to answer all of his questions, then said laughingly, "You have convinced me as nothing else could of my need to be a more regular correspondent."

His father smiled at this, then looked up as a knock sounded. The housekeeper opened the door then disappeared, returning with a tray of food that could feed five men, as Felix laughingly told her. They thanked her and began to serve themselves.

"So what is this I hear about a bequeathment for my sisters?" Felix asked as he tucked into the food.

"It was an aunt on your mother's side whom I had never met. We received the letter from the solicitor, and the good news is that it provides your sisters each with a dowry of two thousand pounds."

"What excellent news!" Felix said, his eyes brightening at this piece of good fortune. The lack of a substantial dowry had worried their mother when she was alive, and the anxiety had passed on to Felix, almost without his having been aware of it.

"I've only seen Meg, but I assume the others will be at dinner?" Having just taken a bite, his father merely nodded. "How have they received the news of their good fortune?"

"I haven't told them, because I wanted to speak to you first." His father paused, and when Felix looked at him, said, "Now that your sisters are situated more favorably, I was hoping you might welcome Margaret into your home next year for the London season? Put her in the way of some gentlemen of better standing than what she might find here?"

Felix's fork paused on the way to his mouth. "Father, surely you know I cannot." He smiled to soften the blow. "For one thing, I am renting a room in a gentleman's establishment. For another, she would need a chaperone to attend the parties. As I am unmarried, I cannot fathom how I am to find one for her."

"Ah, well." His father seemed to abandon the idea. They ate in silence, then he gave Felix a look. "You haven't asked how much of the bequeathment was set aside for you."

For the second time, Felix paused in the act of taking a bite. "That was because I assumed the answer was none."

His father bestowed a rare, smug smile on him. Then he wiped his hands on his napkin, stood, and went over to his desk drawer. He pulled out a paper and handed it to Felix, who opened it. He looked up at his father, stunned.

"Ten thousand? This is for me? How did we not know of this relative? And where did she amass her fortune?"

"I cannot answer either of those questions as I did not know of her existence, but as your mother had no siblings, it solves at least part of the mystery. Your mother came from a good family and was not entirely without connections. This aunt likely had no one else to leave it to. You must give me the direction of your banker in London so I can have the solicitor contact him."

Felix nodded, optimistic at his sudden change in fortune. The sum would not alter his style of living to a great degree, for he must not treat it as annual income. However, it gave him a measure of freedom he had not had before. It would allow him to lease or purchase a house in a less affluential area of London, and perhaps even to that add a small estate in Sussex.

It lessened to a degree his difference in status with Lady Sophia. A very small degree. *Not that it matters*, he reminded himself severely. Still, the news brought hope and possibilities, making it more challenging to put her out of his mind entirely. He decided he would begin looking about for a London house at once. Even if he managed to resist the idea of pursuing any sort of friendship with Lady Sophia, he would still need to marry one day, and a man needed a place to bring a wife home to.

"You must be prudent now, son. Careful with this sudden windfall that you do not develop a taste for gambling—not that I think you will—and careful in your friendship with Robert Cunningworth. His father has been a generous patron to us both, paying for your schooling and securing your first clerical position. You must not forget it and set up his back by an overt display of wealth or attempting to rise above your station."

As that was more or less what Felix had been contemplating, he frowned. "You know I have no interest in gaming, but what do you mean by not reaching above my station?"

"You have become used to mixing with Robert's crowd, and you would be forgiven for viewing yourself with a certain vainglory—although you have always resisted such temptation. You might try to live as they do, but you will quickly run through your modest fortune that way. Keep your head down, tell no one of this change in circumstances. Continue to pursue an honest career, and marry a simple gentlewoman."

"What does my marriage have to do with anything?"

"Marriage is one way to attempt to alter one's circumstances, and Lord Chawleigh will not like it if you get above yourself. As you depend upon him for your connections, as—I need not remind you—do I, you must avoid anything that displeases him. I hope you will remember that."

It was not the first time his father had warned him of what they owed to the baron, and it would be difficult to forget. Until now, the logic of this precept had made perfect sense. But he was no longer the lad he had once been, ready to bow down to the wisdom of his superiors. He had his own ideas now. The baron had sponsored his early life, and he did owe him that. But much of what he had accomplished afterward was either owing to the admiral or to his own talent and determined by his own morals. And as for marrying a simple woman, Felix had to admit the subject was not one he could even contemplate at present.

"I understand," he said, noncommittally.

CHAPTER 9

When Felix returned to London, he decided that he could lose nothing by inquiring about the possibilities of purchasing a house in London. Then he would know what was open to him at some distant point in the future. He did not dream of Mayfair, certainly, nor even of Whitehall. But his inheritance would give him ample choices if he were willing to look somewhere less central. To that end, he made an appointment with a solicitor the admiral had recommended, and was assured he would be able to find something suitable for the price of five thousand pounds.

Felix did not look too closely into the wisdom of an impulsive house purchase in London, for he thought it would be a project that would take months, if not years. However, the solicitor sent a message to him the very next day that a semi-furnished house in Bloomsbury had just been put on the market that he simply must consider. It was built according to the specifications of a wealthy nabob who had just lost his entire fortune on bad speculation. The property would not remain long on the market before someone purchased it, and he must not think he would find a deal as attractive as this.

With a sensation of being swept along by a tide, he agreed to meet Mr. Novak at the house in Russell Square to examine its suitability. One look at the front of it, and Felix had an immediate sense of rightness. It was a five-story house in yellow stone brick, with symmetrical sash windows. A shallow stone porch heralded the front entrance, and the tall windows on the piano nobile were graced with black iron balconies. What was more, the front door was painted dark green like the house he grew up in.

He followed the solicitor into the house and was charmed by the elegant curving staircase that led to the first-floor drawing room. On the ground floor, he was shown into the parlor and dining room, both of which had a marble fireplace. The view from the parlor window looked upon the garden in Russell Square, with its newly planted trees and gravel walks.

By the time he went upstairs to examine the bedrooms with fireplaces and built-in cupboards, he knew he wanted to purchase the house. It was perfect in every particular. However, remembering his father's words, he forced himself to beg for a time of reflection. He could not contemplate with any sort of ease the look on his father's face when he informed him that—despite his cautious warning—Felix had used half of his inheritance to purchase a house within the space of three days. In fact, thinking of it brought a shudder.

"It is natural that you would wish to reflect carefully before purchasing," Mr. Novak said as they were about to part ways, "but do remember that this house is likely to be bought up quickly."

"I will remember." Felix paused with his hand on his horse's bridle. "Will you inform me if someone else seems likely to make a bid?"

The solicitor promised to do what he could.

When Felix returned home, a letter waited for him from the admiral requesting he visit the Royal Naval Asylum that had opened in 1798 and was at a critical stage of needing to attract new subscriptions and donors. He must see firsthand what the asylum was about if he wished to speak eloquently on the topic; his arguments must have strength. The asylum was linked to those affected by war, and the reform Felix was pushing for. The measures involved more than just the sailors and soldiers; it involved their families as well.

Felix sent word ahead to the asylum and arrived at the gate on the appointed day, where he explained his business. Shortly afterward, the secretary came to escort him inside and asked him to wait. He was soon gratified by the appearance of the asylum's director, who had come to give him the tour personally.

"Mr. Knox, here, tells me that you are a member of Parliament, and there are things the government can do for us in terms of legislation and funding. I wish for you to have an accurate sense of how the asylum is run, so that you can better argue the case."

The director led him through the service rooms, wards, the dining area, and classrooms. He gave a thorough explanation of how the asylum functioned and what their mission was. At the end of the tour, Felix was satisfied that he had enough information to give a full rendering at the next committee meeting on the subject. He might even write one of the Positive Points reform pamphlets he had started while still in Brighton. Those had already brought about awareness that led to small changes.

"Tell me," he asked the director as they neared the end of the tour, "what is the asylum's greatest need at present? Larger one-time donations or smaller steady amounts in the form of annual subscriptions?"

The director ushered him into his office and invited him to sit. "In truth, we need both. A new ward must be built, for the old one is too small and was damaged by a roof that leaked. But our lifeblood comes from annual subscriptions, which are at a low point. I can write up a list of how many beds we will need endowed, if you would like."

"Yes, if you would, although I can make no promises. I will pass the list to Admiral Mowbray, who shares my interest in the asylum. Together, we will see what can be done."

"Very good, sir. I should also mention that physical donations in the way of wool, coal, papers and pens—that sort of thing—are very welcome."

The director jotted down the promised notes and handed the paper to him. Then he walked him to the front entrance. Felix was about to take his leave, but the director turned and caught sight of someone behind him. "Miss Edwards! I see you have brought someone to visit the asylum."

He turned and saw a plain woman wearing clothes of unmistakable quality, revealing her status as a gentlewoman and likely volunteer. Behind her was Lady Sophia. The surprise of seeing her once again so unexpectedly turned his blood to ice, only to have it chug to life again.

Miss Edwards greeted the director. "Yes, allow me to present Lady Sophia Rowlandson, sister to the Earl of Poole. I have convinced her to come and visit the babies with me."

The director bowed, and Lady Sophia dipped her head in greeting, but Felix didn't think she had seen him yet. It seemed an extraordinary circumstance that she should come to visit the asylum the same day as he. When at last she turned his way, her mouth opened in surprise.

"Mr. Harwood!"

He hastened to explain, although he did not know why he felt the need to do so. "I have come to assess the asylum's needs so I might faithfully present them in Parliament."

"But," she began, perplexed, "you volunteered with the yeomanry in Brighton. You were not in the navy."

That was true, but he guessed she did not know of his current position in the Admiralty. At first, it did not occur to him to be surprised by her knowledge, for the admiral had spoken of his time in Brighton as a military man. But watching a blush steal up her cheeks, he wondered if she was embarrassed at knowing so much about him.

Something in him went utterly still with delight. Had she been interested enough to inquire after him? "Have you finished your tour in the asylum?"

It was Miss Edwards who answered. "Yes, we have just finished. I wished to show Lady Sophia the wards, for she has promised to help me find endowment subscriptions. I believe she will be more successful at it than I, being an earl's daughter."

"Excellent news," the director said. "Your help is most welcome."

Felix could not imagine Lady Sophia launching a campaign that involved speaking to various members of Society, urging them to sign up for annual subscriptions. Even she looked doubtful at her ability to do it. He wondered if she had actually agreed to it or whether Miss Edwards had assumed her involvement.

"Have you made a list of people you wish to speak to? Or perhaps you have some in mind?" he asked.

It took Lady Sophia a moment to respond, but he was starting to expect that of her and didn't mind waiting. "I have not yet given it thought. I will ask my sister if she has any ideas."

"If you would not object to it, I should like to be of assistance to you." He held up the piece of paper the director had just given him. "This is a list of items the asylum needs. I would be happy to solicit those requests with you."

She looked at him in surprise, then replied softly, "I would like that very much."

That stillness returned—the delight—as though the whole world had stopped to enjoy this moment. Lady Sophia would like his company? Well, he would ensure she had it.

The director turned to shake Felix's hand. "I will leave you in Miss Edwards's care, for she knows the asylum almost as well as I do."

"A good day to you," he replied, and followed Lady Sophia and Miss Edwards out on the street, where they turned to face him. Wishing to prolong their time together, he asked, "What inspired you for today's visit?"

Lady Sophia's eyes scarcely met his, but she was the one to reply. "Miss Mowbray—the admiral's daughter—is acquainted with Miss Edwards, and she was supposed to come with us today, too. However, her father requested her company at some function, as her mother has gone to visit her sister, so I came alone."

Felix smiled. "I must guess the admiral did not know his daughter had also been planning to visit the asylum, or perhaps he would have encouraged us to come together." At the sight of Lady Sophia's smile fading, he could have kicked himself. With those words, he had unwittingly matched himself with Miss Mowbray.

A large horse trotted toward them, too near to the side of the road, and he pulled the ladies closer to the building. "I hired a hackney to come here. Do you have a carriage waiting for you?"

"The earl's carriage is in the mews on the street parallel to this one," Miss Edwards replied.

Lady Sophia softly chimed in, "My footman saw us come out of the asylum, and I believe he will be here with our carriage shortly."

"I see." He should heed his father's words about not reaching above his station; after all, the counsel was wise. But it was difficult to remember, for each time he found himself in her presence, he wanted to see more of her. He had thought his resolution firm concerning Lady Sophia, but he was starting to see that his will curled and disintegrated like paper to a flame whenever she was near. "I was about to propose we walk to Hyde Park from here, since it's not so very great a distance."

Lady Sophia inhaled quickly, as though she had something to say. He couldn't drag his gaze away from her as he waited to see what she would say. Miss Edwards, bless the woman, was not one to rush Lady Sophia either. And with the space to expand, she *did* speak.

"Perhaps we might take the carriage there and walk in the park itself."

His smile grew. "I think that's an even better idea. That is, if you do not mind taking me up in your carriage."

"Not at all," she assured him. These words seemed easier to get out, for she did not hesitate. She turned to Miss Edwards. "If you do not object?"

"Not in the least. Besides, it is your carriage and it should not matter a jot if I did." He liked Miss Edwards.

Once they were on their way to Hyde Park, he asked Miss Edwards about her connection to the asylum and learned of her relationship to Mr. Edwards, the admiral's private secretary. Of course! He should have thought of it. Then he turned to Lady Sophia.

"It is good of you to help the asylum's cause, even when it

means you are required to speak to people you do not know." He hoped to bring another smile and less trepidation to her face, but her response was decided and not what he expected.

"It is something I believe a woman of my station must do no matter how challenging. We are under an obligation to relieve the suffering of those less fortunate in whatever way we can—that, and to brighten their lives. It was not a difficult decision to come today—and not so very difficult a decision to promise I would seek out donations."

Felix had only time to nod before the carriage came to a stop and he helped them out of it, but an uncomfortable realization settled on him as the meaning of her words hit home. He had to consider the fact that she might be humoring him by offering her company. She might be attempting to brighten his life as one so very much her inferior. After all, a true lady was always polite. Perhaps she was only giving him such special attention because she felt it her duty. The likelihood that such a thing was true made for sober reflection.

Suddenly it became of utmost importance that she see him as an equal rather than one who required her charity. His thoughts returned to the house in Russell Square. That purchase would prove his eligibility to a degree. But he could not rush such an important decision for such a paltry reason as needing to prove his worth.

CHAPTER 10

Mr. Harwood leapt out of the carriage before their footman could open the door, and he held out his hand to each of them, even Margery, her maid. Sophia conferred with the driver, who promised to wait for them within eye's distance of the entrance. As they crossed the gates into Hyde Park, she was conscious of a bubbling happiness from being in Mr. Harwood's presence. It mattered little that Miss Edwards was also with them, for as much as she was comfortable chatting away, she was equally comfortable with silence; it was easy for Sophia to make herself heard in Miss Edwards's company. In the intemperance of spring, the brief bouts of sun they'd seen earlier in front of the asylum seemed to have disappeared. Grayish clouds brought a cool breeze that whipped the ribbons of her bonnet as they followed the path that branched away from Rotten Row.

"Do you think it will rain? Perhaps we should not travel too far within the park." Miss Edwards continued to march forward, her actions belying her words of caution. Sophia glanced behind her at Margery, who returned a bolstering smile. If no one else seemed to mind the threat of rain, she was not going to deny herself the opportunity to walk with Mr. Harwood. It was he who expressed his hope that the rain would hold.

"When shall we begin approaching members of Society on behalf of the naval asylum?" Miss Edwards asked. "Mr. Knox has informed me that without an act of benevolence, they will have finished their stock of textiles in a month's time, and there are no fewer than twenty beds that require subscriptions."

Despite the urgent need, the thought of approaching anyone at all caused Sophia's breath to leave her. It occurred to her that she was about to reveal how few people she knew in London. She was not someone of significance, her title notwithstanding.

When she did not answer immediately, Miss Edwards—kind as she was—was ready to fill the silence. "I suppose I might apply to my father for whom to approach. With his connections in the Admiralty, he will be able to recommend people. He just requests to be left out of the discussions so there is no conflict with his work on the board."

Sophia walked between Mr. Harwood and Miss Edwards, with Margery following at a respectful distance. It was her turn to contribute something to the conversation.

"If you are able to discover from your father whom to approach, then I will take it upon myself to visit them." Perhaps she could convince Dorothea to come with her, although her sister was supposed to be staying at home as much as possible. It must be Marie, then.

"Although I don't have many connections in Society," Mr. Harwood said, "I might be able to speak to certain members of Parliament and ask if their wives would be amenable to receiving a visit from you on the subject of subscriptions."

He pivoted slightly to catch her eye, and she offered a feeble smile back. He had likely noticed how daunting she found it to call upon persons unknown and was doing what he could to help.

"Oh, but look." Miss Edwards pointed. "There is Mrs. Nickleson. I have been wishing to speak to her about donating a portion of her late husband's library to the asylum, for I have learned she does not know what to do with all of those books. Would you please excuse me?"

"Of course," Sophia and Mr. Harwood replied at the same time.

Miss Edwards hurried off, her short stature forcing quick, small steps. Before reaching her object, she turned and called back, "I shan't be long. If you continue in the same direction, I will find you."

The path was not as crowded as the Row, but it was still strange to see it so empty of people. The only sounds were their footsteps on the gravel path and the rustle of leaves in the wind above. Sophia realized that at last—*at last*—she was walking alone with Mr. Harwood and would have her chance to know more about him. She did not know how long the uninterrupted time would last but hoped she might think of something interesting to say. Something he would call to mind after they had separated. How dreadful it would be if he found her insipid and wished himself elsewhere. Their elbows brushed, and the touch sent a shock through her, increasing her awareness of his presence. Out of the corner of her vision, she saw him begin to lift his arm to offer it to her. Then he dropped it.

"Miss Edwards seems wholly devoted to the concerns of the asylum. She is an admirable woman," he said.

Their steps had slowed, and she guessed it was so they would not leave Miss Edwards too far behind. As though Margery understood her mistress's wish for private conversation, she allowed her steps to lag.

"I, too, admire Miss Edwards." She almost added *she is able to do what I cannot* but stopped herself. Mr. Harwood would already know that.

She had not walked on this path before, which was lined by a row of hedges on one side separating it from the Serpentine River. On the opposite side of the path, plane trees and oaks grew at steady intervals, offering shade. The ripple of leaves overhead revealed glimpses of a gray sky, and the light wind caused a swath of bluebells under the trees to dance.

It was so peaceful, she forgot her resolution to engage Mr. Harwood in conversation. She was simply enjoying the moment. A movement from the hedgerow caught her eye, and she paused. Mr. Harwood drew to an immediate halt.

"Look!" she said, pointing. "A bird has made her nest in the hedge, close enough for us to see."

She went up on her toes to see if it was a hedge sparrow as she thought. He followed her movements, leaning over with her, and the warmth of his arm next to hers traveled to her heart. The bird cocked its head warily from the short distance, and she felt Mr. Harwood's eyes on her.

"Is it a robin, do you suppose?"

She forced herself to look at him, but it was difficult to remember how to reply when he was looking at her so intently. "I do not think so, for it has no orange breast."

A series of notes emanated from the hedge and was repeated. At the flute-like song, Sophia smiled. It seemed the bird was trying to introduce himself. "It is a song thrush. I can tell by its trill."

"Is it? I shall put my trust in you," he said, smiling down at her, "for I confess I do not recognize the sound. I have never stopped to pay attention."

Sophia listened until the bird had finished its aria, feeling it deserved their attention. Mr. Harwood made no move of impatience, waiting until she moved forward again before taking his place at her side.

"I once found a book on ornithology in my father's library and grew curious. I was first captivated by the illustrations, but then I began to listen and observe the birds near me."

"Well, your time spent studying the species has served you well, for you were certainly able to identify that one." She could hear the smile in his voice, and the compliment warmed her. He spoke of studying and achievement—attributes that were not usually applied to her.

Mr. Harwood crooked his elbow again in what seemed an unconscious gesture before dropping his arm. She searched for other things she might share that would interest him.

"Lady Sophia—" In a quick movement, he placed his right arm around her waist and his left hand on her arm. "I fear the path here is too muddy for you to tread upon it. Might I suggest we walk to the edge, where the ground appears firmer?"

An answer was not required, and he led her that way, gently. She did not mind it, for she could not remember a time when someone took such care of her. Every step, encircled in his arms that way, filled her with raw awareness. It was such an odd and reassuring sensation that every nerve, and even the air around her, was flooded with it. For once she did not feel pressured to speak. The silence was enough.

At the other end of the muddy patch, he removed his arms, leaving her unmoored. It had been a delicious moment, one she would relive again and again in the privacy of her room, but of course such intimate contact could not continue. She glanced behind her and saw that Margery had navigated the muddy spot with perfect ease. In turning forward again, she spotted a rider approaching them.

"Admiral Mowbray," Mr. Harwood called out.

The admiral greeted them from horseback. "You two are

taking a great risk to go walking in weather such as this. I suspect the skies will open before long."

"You are very right, sir. We had best turn back." He glanced behind them. "We have come with Miss Edwards, your private secretary's sister. I met the ladies by chance when visiting the Royal Naval Asylum this afternoon."

The admiral raised his brow in surprise. "Did Marie go to the asylum today? I know she had intended to, but if she did, she did not tell me."

When Mr. Harwood met Sophia's eyes, she saw mirth in his, along with an expression of awkwardness. She understood that she was meant to make the explanation and gathered her courage to do so.

"Marie said she could not come today because she was to accompany you on a call." She hoped she was not putting the admiral on the spot, although she knew that Marie never lied so it must have been the truth.

The admiral laughed loudly, and his horse sidestepped underneath him. "And so I did. But the visit was canceled by the other party at the last minute. I had forgotten. Poor Marie. I am sure she would have liked to go with you"—he focused on Mr. Harwood as he added—"and will certainly have regretted missing out on your walk."

Sophia darted a curious look at Mr. Harwood, wondering if he regretted it, too. It was impossible to read his thoughts, and he answered only, "There will be other opportunities."

He did plan to walk with Marie, then. She must not step ahead of herself and assume he was interested in her. After all, a gentleman as considerate as he would have helped any woman over a muddy section of the path.

"Well, I shan't keep you," the admiral said. "I'm too old to enjoy being caught in a downpour. And Lady Sophia, I am sure you are too delicate to wish for it. Harwood, you had better see her to shelter."

Although Sophia did not think of herself as particularly delicate, she dared to hope the admiral did not object to her walking with Mr. Harwood—that perhaps he might even admit that she was a good match for him.

There was no time to build on these hopes, for Admiral Mowbray said, "I know I need have no fear for you, Harwood, for you are a hardy chap. When it comes time to settle upon a wife, choose one with a constitution as hearty as yours, for she will need it. I hear that quite as much debate is done in the MP's drawing room as in Westminster." The admiral laughed at his own jest.

"Yes, sir," Mr. Harwood responded with a polite smile.

The admiral rode off, his horse picking up its pace, and Mr. Harwood led Sophia back in the direction they had come from. He carefully navigated her around the spot of mud but avoided putting his arm around her waist. He was likely heeding the words the admiral said and did not wish to give her false encouragement. After all, she was in no position to host political gatherings when she could scarcely speak to a person she did not know. It was a painful reminder that she was creating castles in the air when it came to Mr. Harwood.

Before they had walked much farther, the rain began coming steadily down. Mr. Harwood removed his cloak and held it over her for extra protection as they ran over to the spreading branches of a thick oak. Her maid rushed behind them and stopped several paces under the protection of the tree from where Sophia and Mr. Harwood stood. Sophia turned and saw the sodden form of Miss Edwards hurrying to meet them from the other direction, still some ways off and dodging the rain between the trees.

The rain picked up in strength and began to wet them even

through the heavy canopy of leaves. Mr. Harwood guided her backward to the thickest part until she was resting against the strong trunk of the tree, and she felt the heat of his nearness, felt him looking down at her. She lifted her eyes, and his expression intensified.

"I wish I might offer you a better shelter. One you deserve," he said.

With her head tilted upward, a raindrop landed on her cheek and trickled down. "I am not as delicate as you might think." A flash of something lit his eyes—intrigue or attentiveness. She could not be sure.

Miss Edwards arrived, laughing. "Well, we did not have enough sense to turn back when we should have. But rain never melted anyone, did it?"

The thundering of hoofbeats approached from the same direction the admiral had come from, although the rider was not yet visible. The rider slowed when he came to them, and Mr. Harwood turned, giving her a view of him. Of all the people in London, it was none other than Robert Cunningworth.

Robert reined in fully. "You were caught in it, too, were you, Harwood? I'm just coming back from Bloomsbury and have cut through Oxford Gate." His smile fell when his gaze landed on Sophia. "The two of you are out walking together?"

Sophia did not like his accusatory speech. She knew Mr. Harwood was in some debt to Lord Chawleigh, but that did not give his son the right to look down on Mr. Harwood or control his steps. Although thoroughly drenched, she stood upright and lifted her chin to Robert.

"We met by chance at the Royal Naval Asylum. Miss Edwards and I were visiting there, and Mr. Harwood had gone for his own purposes. As the weather still seemed fair, and we were going in the same direction, we came to Hyde Park together."

She had said more than she meant to. It almost sounded like an excuse, or an attempt to cover an assignation. And she knew from experience, the more words one uttered, the more chance one could be mocked for them. The heavy rain that had come so quickly was already tapering away, and Robert looked up at the sky, then over to them.

"Well, I will take advantage of this lull in the rain to head home, and I recommend you do, too. Lady Sophia, I will see you on Thursday." He tipped his hat and rode off, but not before she had a glimpse of his look of displeasure.

No more than a nod was required in return. The rain had stopped, and Miss Edwards led the way back to the path. She carried on a cheerful conversation that required only small contributions from her and Mr. Harwood. This was fortunate, for although Sophia had enjoyed an extended period in Mr. Harwood's company—the first time such a thing had happened—she was less certain than ever that he might one day come to admire her.

CHAPTER 11

On the night of the opera, it was decided that Marie would come with Sophia in Lord Chawleigh's carriage, and Mr. Harwood would meet her at the King's Theatre. She confessed that although she would miss the intimacy of riding in a carriage with such a dashing man, it solved the problem of her own chaperonage.

The baron had invited Lady Poole to join the party, but she was too unwell from a lingering sore throat to stir from the house. Sophia could only feel relief over this constraint, for she had begun to feel his neighborly interest might develop into courtship and she had no wish to begin calling Lord Chawleigh "Papa." The baron therefore engaged Mrs. Heathrow as chaperone, a Society matron and widow who had recently put off her blacks.

It was with mixed feelings that Sophia dressed for the opera. She would be with Mr. Harwood all evening while not being *with* him. That honor would go to Marie. Thankfully, as the footman helped them into the carriage where Mrs. Heathrow was already waiting, chance placed Marie across from Robert instead of Sophia, and she was not disturbed by his knees pressing into hers. At the opera house, Lord Chawleigh led the way to his box and held the door open to allow the ladies to enter.

Mrs. Heathrow waved her fan as she peered over the balcony to see the stage below and the audience. "It looks like all of London is here tonight."

"The only reason one truly comes to the opera," Robert said, raising a quizzing glass to the box seats on the far side.

She could not agree. There was something about the rich and soaring music of opera that made her soul tremble. That was why she came.

Sophia became aware of Mr. Harwood's arrival by Lord Chawleigh saying, "Ah, Felix, there you are."

"Good evening," he said, bowing generally to the party. His eyes landed on Sophia, and it seemed to her they lingered there for a moment, sending a spear of happiness through her. They then quickly shifted to Marie, and he smiled and bowed. "Good evening, Miss Mowbray."

"Mr. Harwood." Her return smile was beatific, and it seemed plain how smitten she was with the gentleman who had invited her. Sophia's heart felt raw and pained at witnessing it, at the reminder it brought. Lord Chawleigh placed his hand on Mrs. Heathrow's arm.

"We were just choosing our places. Mrs. Heathrow, won't you take this seat beside me? Miss Mowbray, yes that's it. You may take the one near you, with Felix at your side. And Lady Sophia, you will have a very comfortable seat in the front next to Robert."

Obediently, she sat where he'd indicated and fixed her eyes on the pit below, striving for something to ground her. Robert sat in the chair beside her, spilling over it, his elbow brushing hers. She pulled her arms inward.

"This is nice, is it not?" he asked her, smiling.

She nodded, unable to smile back at him. The seats were arranged in a semicircle, with Mr. Harwood on her left. It was possible to look into his face without too much difficulty if she wished to do so, but she refrained.

Mrs. Heathrow filled the box with light teasing that was mostly harmless, except for her comment that sometimes the best matches were made in the box seats at the opera. She leaned forward to address the younger set in a conspiratorial tone.

"One is lost in the romance of the moment. The music stirs the finer feelings and allows affections to form and deepen. And one never knows if the person you came with is the one with whom you wish to leave." She laughed loudly, tapping Lord Chawleigh with her fan. "You agree with me—you know you do."

Sophia wanted to sink beneath her chair, embarrassed both at how vulgar the comment was and how true. She very much wished to leave with a different gentleman than the one she had come with. Robert fidgeted at her side, and she could almost hear him say to his father, "Why did you invite her?"

Mr. Harwood asked Marie whether the admiral would be at the opera, and she replied that he would not. Then, after a pause, he touched Sophia's glove. "Did you take cold after being caught in the rain?"

The fact that he had addressed her when he was there with Marie restored her smile. "No, for as I mentioned, I am not overly frail."

"How can that be?" Robert demanded, determined not to be left out. "You are the shyest thing I know. A breeze could knock you over."

Marie leaned forward enough to catch Robert's eye. "One would think it, but you would be surprised, Mr. Cunningworth. Lady Sophia may show some reserve, but she is stronger than what her appearance might lead one to think. She can walk for hours without being fatigued."

"I heard this opera when it debuted last year," Mrs. Heathrow interjected. "It is about a woman who goes to great lengths to save her husband from prison; she even dresses as a boy."

She laughed again, and Robert, who seemed to be in a particularly contrary mood, muttered under his breath, "That is ridiculous."

"Oh, I don't know," Marie said, addressing Mr. Harwood. "I find it noble. Heroism is not reserved for the stronger sex. I think true love can cause somebody to do heroic things, and it matters little whether one is a man or woman."

"You are right, Miss Mowbray," he replied.

Sophia could not say anything to this. She privately agreed with Marie, but the sentiment ran too deep to be able to express so glibly. She also knew that Marie would go to great heroic lengths for the man she loved; surely Mr. Harwood would perceive this and admire her for it.

The chandeliers were lowered, and metal cylinders were placed around the candles, causing the house to grow dim and the stage to take on a greater brightness. For the first time since she'd attended the opera, Sophia had been more conscious of the drama going on in her own box. Now she turned her eyes to the stage.

The backdrop was painted so that it looked like stone walls with a window, and the opera began with a maiden sweeping the floor and a young lover attempting to convince her to marry. Sophia listened, tears already springing to her eyes, which she would not allow to fall. Her mind placed a different scenario over what was being sung below. It was Mr. Harwood stretching out his arm, saying, "When will you give me your consent? It could easily be today."

But the young lady was interested in another man named Fidelio. Now, Sophia felt from the depth of her soul Marzellina's love for Fidelio when she sang:

> I wished we were united yet
> And I could husband call you!
> A girl may never what she thinks,
> Tell anyone aloud.
> But when I never have to blush
> From kisses of a loving heart,
> When nothing ever will us part—
> And hope already swells my chest
> With untold sweet desire,
> How happy shall I be then!

It was as if the words were written to express her own heart, her story, and Sophia was lost imagining herself in it. It was only in the third scene that she figured out that Fidelio was actually a woman—the wife in question—which made Marzellina's infatuation ridiculous. The disguise was thorough, and she had thought the singer to simply be a male tenor with a particularly high voice. The surprise was so great, she covered her lips with her fingers to hide her laugh and received the lesson from it. Perhaps she should not allow her own emotions to be so consuming.

Robert leaned in close to whisper, "What have you found amusing?" She only shook her head in reply.

But when she felt Mr. Harwood's eyes on her, she was compelled to lean in and whisper, "Fidelio is Leonore." He nodded, and she felt his slight shake from laughter. Marie turned inquisitive eyes in their direction, a smile on her face, but she did not attempt to inquire into what they were saying.

It seemed to Sophia, not for the first time, that not all operagoers attended the opera to listen to the music, for the audible discussions around her produced a continual rumble. She did not know how the singers could bear this—to sing before an audience who did not appreciate all they poured into their performance. The box seats were lit, their occupants providing as much interest as what was happening on the stage. When the final notes of Act One were sung, the cylinder was removed from the chandeliers, and the theater became light again.

"A nuisance that the opera is sung in German," Robert said, getting to his feet.

"And yet, the words were translated for you right in your libretto," Mr. Harwood retorted with a teasing smile. "You are too particular."

Lord Chawleigh invited Mrs. Heathrow to take champagne, and they exited into the corridor, where the sounds of people milling spilled into the box.

"Would you like some champagne, Lady Sophia?"

She looked at Robert, and then ahead as she thought about it. It would require mingling with crowds and perhaps being surprised by meeting someone she would be required to talk to. She might not know what to say. And yet, it would not be comfortable to stay in the box with Robert either.

Robert. It was a shame that the man she loved was a mere Mr. Harwood to her, for she had been given no right to address him in more intimate terms and did not dare to do so, even in her head. All the while, the man she had known since childhood and referred to mentally by his Christian name was one she could never love.

"Well, Sophia?" Robert had a strange look on his face.

She blushed, knowing she had taken an unseemly amount of time to answer. "I think I would like to stay here."

"Of course," he replied, resuming his seat. It felt like he was saying, *of course you would*. She knew he was frustrated with her, for he would rather drink champagne, stretch his legs, and meet people. Didn't he see how wrong she was for him?

"Mr. Harwood, if you don't object, I would very much like to have some refreshment. Sophia, you don't mind, do you?" Marie asked her with a look of concern. She was a true friend and worried about leaving her in Robert's company alone, but naturally she, too, would desire to move about and see people.

Mr. Harwood's glance in her direction was quick before he turned to Marie with a smile. "An excellent idea. Let us go."

FELIX WALKED beside Miss Mowbray plagued by a sense of dissatisfaction. He did not like to leave Lady Sophia behind with Robert; she had the appearance of a small animal trapped by a predator. But what could he do? He was here to escort Miss Mowbray, and his obligation was to see to her comfort.

"The soprano is as wonderful as everyone has said," she observed, as they wove around the operagoers to where the champagne was being served.

"Madame Catalani? Yes, she has a rare talent." It took everything in him to pay her the attention she was due, but his mind was still in the box with Lady Sophia. Was Robert taking undue advantage of their time alone? Was he pressing her to return his feelings—was he *proposing*? Certainly, he was a better match for Lady Sophia on paper. Even if his status as the son of a baron was not on par with the daughter of an earl, he was heir to a title and the Chawleighs' wealth was not to be scoffed at. And there was no other heir but him.

He forced his attention back to Miss Mowbray. "Let me fetch a glass for you. If you'll wait right here, I think you will not be troubled by the crowds."

"Thank you, Mr. Harwood." She gave him an unaffected

smile. It was a shame he could not give her his heart, for she was a perfectly agreeable woman. But one could not control such things.

As he waited for the person in front of him to be served, he thought back to the day in the park with Lady Sophia as he had often done since. He remembered guiding her around the muddy patch and facing her as he shielded her under the oak, although he could do little against the drops that fell from above. The small space between them buzzed, and it felt like they were inhabiting an island of their own, despite her maid and the eventual presence of Miss Edwards. He supposed it was then his heart was lost to her. He no longer wanted to pretend that his feelings were disinterested. But his father's words, and his own sense, dictated that he had no right to pursue her.

When it was his turn, he held up two fingers, and the servant handed him two glasses. "Here you are, sir." He paid and forced his mind back to his companion.

"Your champagne, Miss Mowbray," he said with a dip of his head. He would not be a cad and make her feel she was uninteresting just because his heart was elsewhere. That was not her fault. "I was surprised not to see your father tonight. I know how much he loves the opera." He chuckled, adding, "And any party and entertainment one might propose to him."

She chuckled. "He and my mother are dining with old friends, and it was planned before he knew of tonight's performance." After a pause, she looked over her glass. "I heard you met Lady Sophia and Miss Edwards at the naval asylum."

"Yes, quite by chance." Another memory washed over him of Lady Sophia facing him under the oak tree—a different expression on her face, something other than shyness. He lifted the champagne to his lips. "We went to Hyde Park afterward, but it was an unfortunate decision, for we were caught in the rain."

"Yes, so I have heard. Sophia said you have offered to assist her in soliciting subscriptions for the asylum. If I know her, she will make every effort to be successful at finding donors, even if it is difficult for her to approach strangers."

Lady Sophia had confided much to her friend. About their chance meeting, the walk in the park, the rain—she had even told her about his offer to help. Was it because women talked to each other about everything? Or did she talk about him because her mind dwelled on him?

"I did indeed. I do not know how much assistance I will be, but I will do my best to find members of Parliament with generous-minded wives. Kind ones," he added.

"Oh yes, you appear to understand that about Lady Sophia. She will flee from anyone who will not receive her with kindness." The words were warmly spoken and showed true affection, but Miss Mowbray's eyes were on him. From the intensity of her focus, he suspected her interest went beyond mere friendship. He had no wish to lead her to believe something of that nature lay in his own heart, but how did one pass on such information without being unkind?

This produced in him a desire to escape, and he spoke without thought. "Shall we return to our seats?"

"But, Mr. Harwood...we have not finished our champagne." She looked at him, perplexed.

He considered the glass of champagne in his hand, noting that he had scarcely touched it. "Oh, how right you are." He smiled feebly and took a large swallow. Although her smile remained fixed, something in her eyes faltered. A small group was descending on them, and they both turned.

"Good evening, Marie. Good evening, Mr. Harwood." Lady Dorothea had approached with her husband, and they were flanked by Lady Camilla and Lord Pembroke, who Felix remembered had offered to escort her to the opera. Lady Camilla's cheeks were flushed and her lips stretched in a smile, showing how much she was enjoying the evening.

They exchanged greetings, and Lady Dorothea asked, "Where is Sophia? Is she not with you?"

"She stayed behind in the box," Miss Mowbray answered. "I think the masses assembled in the corridor was probably more than she wished to face this evening."

"Very likely."

Lady Camilla turned to Miss Mowbray, her brows now furrowed. "She stayed behind in the box with Mr. Cunningworth?"

There was something about the way she said it. Perhaps she knew how little her sister liked being in Robert's company. It made Felix even more eager to return to the box. He had learned his lesson, however, and would not appear rushed. "Are you walking back to your box? Shall we go together?"

"We are," Lady Dorothea replied, taking Mr. Shaw's arm.

Felix checked that Miss Mowbray's glass was empty. In an excess of caution, he asked, "Finished?"

She smiled and handed him the glass, and he returned both to a servant. They returned to their seats, bidding farewell to the others, for Lord Pembroke's box was situated above the stage. The last few steps were difficult to maintain at the same calm rhythm, but Felix forced himself to do so. When they entered the box, Robert was leaning into Sophia as she shrank back.

He took a hasty step forward, and Miss Mowbray said in a clear voice, "You were very right not to have gone, Sophia. You would have disliked the crowds."

Robert pulled away and turned as Felix stepped around his chair and met his expression with a shuttered one of his own. Watching Robert bully a woman like Lady Sophia made him incensed. It was infuriating not to be in a position to shield her from it. He waited until Miss Mowbray was seated before sinking into his chair.

"It was a crush out there? I daresay it was." Robert looked behind him at the door to their box. "Perhaps there's enough time for me to have a glass of champagne—that is, Lady Sophia, if you do not mind?"

"Not at all." It was difficult to make out, but Felix had been listening for her reply and caught it. That was all it took for Robert to get to his feet and head to the opening of the box, just as his father and Mrs. Heathrow entered it.

"You had best stay put, son. All of Society is returning to their seats." Lord Chawleigh spoke in an imposing manner that would have been difficult to disobey. Robert hesitated for a moment, then returned to his seat.

The activity on the stage increased as actors took their place for an intermezzi ballet and the chandeliers were lowered again. Felix wished he could ask Lady Sophia what she was feeling, wished he could reach over and lay a comforting hand on her arm. But wishes were just that. He hoped he wouldn't have a life made up only of wishes.

CHAPTER 12

Three days after the opera, the infection in Lady Poole's throat had descended into the lungs, and Sophia was just bidding farewell to the doctor who had come to examine her. As she settled into the drawing room, Turton brought her the morning post that included an invitation to Mrs. Taylor's alfresco picnic that Mr. Grantly had promised during his morning call. Marie arrived shortly afterward to inquire after her mother's health, and Sophia was able to relay the pleasing news that the doctor did not think her in any real danger. After exhausting the subject of treatments and necessary time for convalescence, their conversation turned to the picnic. Marie pulled out her own invitation and was able to confide that Mr. Harwood would be in attendance. She knew this because he had come to collect from her father a list of widows from various coastal towns whose husbands had died at sea. He was to go and gather petitions from them and present these in Parliament.

Having her best friend with her in London produced contrasting sentiments in Sophia's heart. On one hand, it was all she had wished for when she imagined spending her season with Marie. They were together almost daily and enjoyed the same pastimes. Since Marie had no siblings, she came to Grosvenor Square often and was fond of her whole family. Their conversation was comfortable, and Sophia never felt pressure to be someone other than who she was. Such were the blessings.

These pleasures were mitigated by the fact that every time Marie mentioned Mr. Harwood, Sophia was reminded of how well-suited her friend was to him. Marie's father esteemed him enough to serve as his patron, and it was only natural that the admiral would welcome him as a son-in-law. As for Sophia, she had only fleeting moments to latch on to that suggested he was interested in more than friendship. Mr. Harwood was known to be congenial and friendly to all, which meant that she must weigh every interaction cautiously.

It was only at certain times that she suspected some deeper affection existed between them. It was those fleeting glances or the lingering regard when he thought she was not looking, the occasional touch. The way he seemed to gravitate toward her. But she could not even rejoice when she observed these promising signs, let alone dream of building anything in the way of a courtship with him. That would mean being disloyal to her best friend, and she could not hurt her that way. From a purely objective standpoint, Marie would be a better fit for Mr. Harwood. She would certainly be capable of hosting his political dinners. Yet Sophia was prisoner to the affection she had for Mr. Harwood; it was not something she could put aside like last night's gown.

The day of the picnic dawned bright, and the earl's carriage brought Sophia, Camilla, and Marie to the rendezvous spot at the base of Primrose Hill. They stepped out of it into a festive atmosphere where other carriages were depositing guests, none of whom she knew. They all appeared to be older. Scores of servants carried rugs and baskets up the hill while others returned to fetch more items. From the evidence before her, it would be a feast.

She looked around for a sight of Mr. Harwood, but instead saw Robert. He was not looking in her direction, so she steered Camilla to where they were hidden by the carriage. Perhaps, if she were in luck, he would not attach himself to her this afternoon.

He had grown bolder at the opera. When they were left alone in the box together, she was almost breathless from fear that he would declare himself. Thankfully, he did no more than insinuate, but she had no confidence that he would just fade from her life. It would likely require a firm rebuff in order to shut down his intentions. Such a confrontation was what she dreaded the most.

"There is Mr. Grantly." Marie indicated the gentleman with a nod.

Sophia had never really taken Mr. Grantly's measure. He had been at Chawleigh Manor that day when she first met Mr. Harwood, and she knew he was Robert's friend from school, but he seemed a distracted sort of gentleman and not at all warm-hearted. As though he could change one company for another without suffering any loss. But then, she could not know any such thing with certainty.

At his side was an older woman she deemed to be his aunt directing the servants up the hill the way a sergeant might direct his troops. It appeared she was not allowing any of the guests to ascend until everything had been prepared.

"Shall we go and greet our hostess?" Marie glanced at her then Camilla, who nodded. They led the way to Mrs. Taylor and Mr. Grantly, with Sophia following behind.

"It was kind of you…" Camilla began, her words trailing away when Mr. Grantly turned abruptly to address a servant. Whether he had snubbed her sister accidentally or on purpose

Sophia could not guess, but it was the second time he had been rude to her. Camilla turned back to Mrs. Taylor with a bright smile. "...to have invited us."

Sophia had begun to notice a change in Camilla now that Dorothea was no longer with them at all Society events. Whenever they went somewhere together, she tended to take on the more vocal role that Dorothea had held before. She was certainly more at ease in that role than Sophia would ever be. Another reason why she would make a terrible wife for an MP.

"It is a pleasure to have you here." Mrs. Taylor's greeting was welcoming but brisk, like a woman used to having things her way. The embellishments on her hat trembled in the breeze as her eyes surveyed the comings and goings of the servants. "When Pierce spoke to me of inviting some of his young friends, I was immediately in favor of the idea. There's nothing more tedious than a picnic made up of nothing but old people."

"Robert!"

Sophia recognized Mr. Harwood's voice, and Marie must have, too, for she turned to it, her smile at the ready. Sophia's heart sank. It was no surprise that her friend would be glad to see him. They watched while Robert spoke to Mr. Harwood, and she thought he seemed more friendly and approachable somehow when Mr. Harwood was present. She didn't know why she was so opposed to Robert's presence. He was likely not a monster—in fact she knew he was not. It was just that he was not a good match for her, and it was painful to be forced to endure his attentions because he thought she was. If only he could be convinced they did not suit.

Camilla leaned in to murmur to Sophia, "If you had to choose between the two of them, I believe I can divine which one you would prefer to be seated by."

Sophia darted a look at her. Had Camilla truly guessed where her heart lay? She turned to see if Marie had heard

Camilla's comment. Marie had and was smiling, her eyes sparkling with amusement.

"I daresay I can guess, too. I may have to share Mr. Harwood."

Marie's unaffected laughter submerged Sophia with a flood of guilt for holding the same man in affection as Marie, especially when all logic pointed to her being a better match for him. She was grateful to have a friend so guileless and kind. Marie was not of a competitive nature, but somehow that made the guilt even sharper. Then there was the growing suspicion that Camilla knew of her secret longing. As Sophia was unused to sharing the deepest part of her heart with others, she did not know what to do with that possibility.

"Lady Sophia." Robert had caught sight of her, and he raised his hand in a wave as he came over. Mr. Harwood had managed to put him in a good humor, for his smile was genuine. He greeted Camilla and Marie with a polite bow and cordial tone. Sophia could not help but risk a glance at Mr. Harwood, who upon catching her look, strode over and bowed deeply.

"Good afternoon, my lady."

"Mr. Harwood," she replied, curtsying. His face was flushed, and it hadn't been when he was talking to Robert. Was it her imagination, or was he overly conscious in greeting her? He seemed…flustered, but surely that could not be.

The servants had finished carrying up the rugs and accoutrements for the picnic, and Mrs. Taylor invited the guests to climb the hill. Robert leapt forward to hold out his arm.

"Lady Sophia, the path will be difficult for you. Allow me to assist."

She was unable to hide the frown that came to her brow. If he found her so infirm, why on earth did he wish to marry her? Besides, it was not as though she *were* infirm. Sophia glanced behind her, miserable in the knowledge that she must accept.

She would have much preferred Mr. Harwood's company. Besides, now Camilla would have no one to walk with.

"Miss Mowbray, Lady Camilla, allow me to walk with you, so I might be of assistance to either of you, or both—whomever might require it."

"You are too kind, Mr. Harwood." Marie's smile sounded in her voice behind Sophia, and she understood why. His offer was gallant. He did not declare that the women needed his help—only that he would be there if they did.

"Thank you," Camilla added, and Sophia heard their steps and light conversation as they climbed the hill. In truth, the path was not always easy to manage, for it was slippery in places. The knowledge that Mr. Harwood had been gallant to her sister warmed her heart.

"You look very lovely today, Lady Sophia," Robert said as they walked, patting her hand on his arm.

"Thank you, Mr. Cunningworth."

He cleared his throat. "We have known each other nearly our whole lives. Sometimes I slip into saying Sophia rather than Lady Sophia as I ought. I hope you have forgiven me when I do. I blame it only on our longstanding connection and not on a lack of respect due to you. But...you might call me Robert if you wished."

She sensed his regard from her side, waiting for her answer. To her relief, she was not required to give one because they were near the top of the hill, and Mr. Grantly waited there, leaning down to give the final tug to bring Sophia to the flat land on top. *That was gallant of Mr. Grantly; perhaps I have wronged him*. Her thoughts swung back to Robert. She knew it would be better to end his push for intimacy right away, but with the moment lost, she could not bring herself to do it. Instead, she watched Marie and Camilla crest the hill, waiting half-turned until they arrived to where she stood. Robert exchanged a few words with Mr. Grantly, but she felt his uneasy glances in her direction and knew it was because she had not answered. Still, there was no reason she must continue walking with him, and she slipped her arm through her sister's.

Camilla surveyed the flat expanse on top of the hill. "Shall we go and see the view?"

Marie agreed to it, and the three of them walked toward the edge. Sophia was acutely aware of Mr. Harwood's presence as he followed, and she heard Robert's voice, revealing that he was behind them as well. When she reached the edge of the sloping hill, the sight there sent Sophia's troubles flying. Before them was an unhindered view of the vast city of London, its roofs and spires jutting across the expanse, with some squares and parks visible between them.

"Magnificent," she breathed.

"It is, isn't it?" Mr. Harwood had come beside her, and leaned in to speak. He appeared to be the only one who heard her. She turned and sent him a shy smile.

All of the guests had arrived by then, and Mrs. Taylor called everyone over, directing them where to sit on the rugs that had been spread out. The other guests all seemed to be particular friends of Mrs. Taylor, while the younger guests had come at Mr. Grantly's invitation. At some distance was a family with children and another young couple who were not attached to their party.

"Lady Sophia, why don't you sit on this rug with Lady Camilla on your right?" Mrs. Taylor was momentarily distracted by a servant gesturing to one of the footmen that carried bottles of wine. In the distraction, Robert took the opportunity to sit on her other side. Sophia's mood sank at the knowledge that she would have to endure his company throughout the meal.

Mrs. Taylor turned back and saw what had transpired. With a firm smile and shake of her head, she said, "Mr. Cunningworth, I had quite pictured you here on this side next to Miss Mowbray. Pierce, you may sit next to Lady Camilla, and Mr. Harwood you must take this place here."

Sophia tried to show indifference when he sat next to her, but it was difficult. She was astonished that things could turn out so favorably for her after all, for that *never* happened. She glanced at Marie to see if she was disappointed, but her friend was too good-natured to show it. Instead, she began to draw Robert into cheerful conversation. He grumbled an opinion about matrons with high-handed ways, but Marie was charming enough to turn his mood in a different direction.

Camilla sat with her feet tucked behind her, leaning on one arm. She looked up at her neighbor with a bland expression. "Mr. Grantly, I regret that you are obliged to sit at my side. We shall hope that you might be spared from having to partner with me afterward should there be any games."

Sophia could not believe what she was hearing and looked at her sister in horror. One did not provoke a person like that, even one whose manner was not particularly cordial. Mr. Harwood quickly averted his face, and she could only conclude he thought ill of her sister. Would he also think ill of her?

Mr. Grantly furrowed his brows, his color rising. "I cannot divine what you mean, Lady Camilla."

She smiled at him, appearing as complacent as if they were discussing the weather. "It is only that you were bent on escaping having to accompany me to the opera, and the fact that you should now be relegated to spending the afternoon at my side seems like a cruel and unjust punishment. Not that you will need to stay with me for the whole picnic, mind you, for I am sure I will wish to go walking."

"Camilla," Sophia murmured, anxious about what Mr. Grantly must think, her own cheeks seared with embarrassment.

"I assure you, Lady Camilla, I am not looking for an excuse to escape from you." This was said stiffly, and Sophia feared he was offended beyond repair.

"Thank you. But I give you leave to do so should you wish it."

Mr. Harwood leaned in to whisper, "Your sister is amusing."

She turned to him in surprise and saw his eyes twinkling with humor. So he had not turned away in dislike?

"Do you think so? I fear she has offended him."

"If he had a better sense of humor, he would see she was giving him back his own for snubbing her in your drawing room," he said quietly. When their regard held for seconds longer than what was casual, her breath seemed to disappear.

A servant brought dishes over to where they sat, placing them in the center of their blanket, then returned to bring more. There were small sandwiches, meat pies, slabs of ham, fruits, cheeses, sweetmeats, and a beautiful array of tarts for them to choose from. More servants did likewise for the other guests. Once everything had been brought, Mr. Harwood prepared a plate of choice items—a sandwich, some cheese, a fruit tart. Sophia eyed it, thinking that these were just the sorts of things she particularly liked and wondered if he was preparing it for her. Across from her, Robert was doing the same, but in a more hurried manner than Mr. Harwood. He heaped the plate to overflowing for Marie, then stood and brought it to Sophia instead. Her mouth fell open in dismay. How could he do this when Marie was his seated companion?

She was obliged to speak. "Thank you."

When Mr. Harwood turned back, he saw the heaping plate in front of her and glanced down at his own. "I see that you have already been served, my lady."

"Zealously," she murmured under her breath, but Mr. Harwood shot her a look of amusement, showing he had heard it. Robert filled another plate, this time for Marie, who took it with thanks and acted as though he had served her first. Marie was so good.

Mr. Harwood put his plate to his side, saying quietly, "This was meant for you."

"I fear this one might be too much for me," she murmured, nudging her plate in his direction. He smiled and took a sandwich from it. She was careful to choose something from the plate Robert had prepared for her, so as not to offend him. Then she took something from Mr. Harwood's offering, relieved that the tense moment had passed.

The conversation grew easier as everyone enjoyed the delicacies. Even Camilla and Mr. Grantly spoke more naturally, and she asked him questions about his father's estate that he seemed to enjoy answering. Sophia was content to listen and enjoy the feeling of the sun on what was proving to be a most agreeable afternoon. The weather was balmy, and the only young women present were ones she was close to. She even had the privilege of sitting next to Mr. Harwood, enjoying simple, cheerful exchanges of absolutely no consequence that made her feel they could truly be friends. That he had passed from the phase of someone she loved from a distance—for no more rhyme or reason than a bolt from the heavens—to a friend whose qualities she could say she was coming to know.

Afterward, by general consensus, the younger set decided to walk about the hill. It was not cold, by any means, but at this height the wind picked up. Sophia, having worn a favorite bonnet decorated with flowers and ribbons, had not considered that as they were not well attached, it was a poor choice for the excursion. Just as she was thinking this, one of the small decorative flowers attached to a ribbon was caught by the wind and flew away. She saw a glimpse of the red from the corner of her eye and ran after it, but Mr. Harwood was quicker. He darted ahead, giving her a glimpse of his athletic form which she would tuck away in her memory for later. The wind brought the flower directly into the path of a bush, where it caught. He seized it, and walked back to her, holding it up with a grin. She could not help but smile at his triumphant expression.

Robert intercepted their path from the right. "Good, you've caught it. Hand it over, Harwood. I will tie it back on her bonnet."

"It is not necessary," Sophia tried to say, but her words carried no weight against Robert's determination. Mr. Harwood could do nothing against Robert's demand and the sight of his imperious hand reaching for the flower.

Robert, with flower now in hand, bore down upon Sophia, and she stood still as he attempted to tie it back onto her bonnet. She could feel his fingers, clumsy and ineffective, as she stayed prisoner to his unwelcome ministrations.

Camilla walked over and held out her hand. "Mr. Cunningworth, I helped trim this bonnet, so I know the trick of getting it to stay. May I?" He looked relieved and handed it to her, stepping away. Marie, ever diplomatic, pulled both him and Mr. Harwood into conversation, and Camilla leaned in to whisper, "This flower won't be attached without needle and thread, but I will hide it. He might have stayed here forever otherwise." Sophia sent her a grateful smile, ready to hug her.

Mrs. Taylor called them over to where a stool was being set up between blankets and an older woman was opening a wooden box with paper, charcoal, and scissors.

"Mrs. Sandhurst is skilled at cutting profiles, and she will make some for us today." Mrs. Taylor looked around. "I think we all agree that the most interesting profiles will be those of the young people, is that not so?" This was met by general assent, and she went to take Sophia by the arm. "My lady, you will be glad to sit for your profile, I am sure, for it is such a pretty one."

Sophia submitted to it. She did not like to be under scrutiny but did not wish to offend her hostess. No sooner had she sat than Mrs. Taylor had a servant bring another stool. "Would it not be lovely to have paired silhouettes? Mr. Cunningworth, I saw you rescuing the flower to Lady Sophia's bonnet. Why don't you pose together? You may sit here and face Lady Sophia."

Mr. Cunningworth hastened to comply, and Sophia brought her eyes to Camilla in a desperate plea. Her sister returned it, eyes lit with sympathy, but she was powerless to help. Sophia's gaze then shifted to Mr. Harwood, who had folded his arms and was watching them. When Marie walked up to him to say a few words, he smiled at her and offered his arm. She placed her hand on it, and they returned to the edge of the hill to admire the view. Sophia, left with the trial of suffering Robert's stare from inches away, blinked and sat upright.

CHAPTER 13

Felix led Miss Mowbray away from the crowd collected around the artist and two people sitting for portraits, a helpless anger building up inside of him. He was able to read people to a certain degree, and although he could not convince himself that he was a worthy suitor for Lady Sophia, he firmly held to the idea that she should have a husband of her choosing. And he was nearly certain she did not choose Robert.

He did not fully understand why Robert persisted in pursuing Lady Sophia in the face of so little encouragement and went through his likely reasons for doing so once again. To Robert, position and prestige were important. It would therefore be essential that he select a wife who brought something to the marriage of equal or greater value than what he already possessed. She must be of a noble family; in this case, Lady Sophia was even his superior. She must be wealthy, and although Felix knew nothing of Lady Sophia's dowry, he had no reason to believe her family lacked wealth. It went without saying that she must be a well-looking woman for that was generally important to all men—a man must find his wife attractive. For Robert, it would be particularly important, for he would only be happy if others envied him his prize.

Felix considered all of these factors, but what he thought was really driving Robert in this instance was something deeper. As Lady Sophia's neighbor, he would feel he had a prior claim and would expect her to respond to the flattery of his interest. The fact that Robert had set his mind on someone who did not return his regard would cause him to push harder until her resolve was worn down. It would be a matter of pride.

Miss Mowbray did not immediately pull him into conversation as they walked, allowing his thoughts to wander. As soon as he realized it, he searched for a suitable topic of interest. By this time, they had approached the place where the land sloped downward and stopped to stare once again at the skyline. She turned slightly to address him.

"Are you achieving your aims in Parliament, Mr. Harwood? You must not fear discussing such matters with me, for my father is in the habit of speaking to me almost as an equal. He has always shared freely his naval exploits, and more lately, his effort at reform."

"Your father is an estimable man." He believed her claim, but even if her father did speak to her of his affairs, Felix did not want to bore her by expounding on his own.

"The Naval Inquiry Commission is taking form in a way your father finds satisfactory. Perhaps he has told you that?" She nodded for him to continue. "Most MPs appear sufficiently aware that appointment should be based on merit rather than rank, and they support the inquiries into situations where that does not seem to be the case." He sent her an apologetic glance. "You understand I cannot speak of any specific incidents, for that would be divulging confidential information."

"Yes, I would not ask you to do such a thing."

She looked at him as she said this, and as much as he saw

friendliness in her expression, he observed a hint of expectation that made him pull back since he could not return it. He faced the view and allowed his gaze to roam over the London skyline. He liked living in it much better than he would have imagined. He was fond of the village where he was raised, but there was something exciting about being in a place where things happened, one where he had a part of making them happen. Miss Mowbray turned to face forward, and he continued.

"So, in one sense I am satisfied. I continue to participate in the committee meetings to provide for the wounded sailors and the families of the dead and add my voice where I think it is needed. But since I am in my first year, my aim at this stage is more for support and voting than it is for eloquent speeches."

She lifted a brow playfully. "Perhaps you underestimate yourself."

"Perhaps." He smiled at her, unconvinced, and another silence fell between them. He scarcely noticed it, both because his mind was elsewhere and because she did not force herself on him.

"As for the widows' pensions we are hoping to achieve," he went on absently, more in an attempt to keep up the conversation than a desire to speak about it. With his mind on Lady Sophia, he seemed to forget what was so important about the active reform he was attempting to bring about.

"There is sympathy in Parliament for the fallen soldiers and sailors, and many supportive institutions such as the Royal Naval and Military Asylums. However, I am finding that it is easy to offer sympathy when all it requires is words. It is more difficult to offer it when one is required to give up coin." He shot her a wry smile, and she returned it.

"Yes, the two are very different." She allowed the silence to fall, and he knew he wasn't giving her his best. His heart was tied up with an impossible choice, for he should not aspire to

Lady Sophia and yet could not help his attraction. He had no wish to give Miss Mowbray the wrong idea either.

He turned back to the area where their large group and other smaller ones were gathered. More had arrived since they had begun their picnic. His eyes settled on Lady Sophia, who perched stiffly on the edge of a stool facing Robert. Although Robert's eyes were fixed on her face, hers stared somewhere around his cravat.

"Mr. Grantly is a fellow I cannot at all make out." Miss Mowbray was looking in a different direction, and he pulled his eyes from Lady Sophia. "Perhaps Lady Camilla should not have teased him, but I assure you, when we first arrived, he turned away from her as soon as she began speaking in what seemed a decided snub. And, if you'll recall, during your morning call, he seemed visibly against the idea of escorting her to the opera. It is all so awkward. What do you make of it?"

Felix observed Lady Camilla and Grantly still speaking together, appearing slightly more in harmony. But without a doubt, Mr. Grantly looked as though he wished to be elsewhere.

"Ever since I have known Mr. Grantly, he has been excessively awkward around women, for maintaining a conversation does not come easily to him. I would not be surprised if he ends his days as a bachelor, for he prefers just about anything over attempting conversation. Believe me when I tell you that he is quite a different gentleman when in the clubs, or sparring, or going to watch a race. You would not recognize him."

"That makes me like him a little better," Miss Mowbray admitted. "For at least I know he is not insulting Lady Camilla specifically."

"Not at all, I assure you."

She turned suddenly in what felt rather like a surprise attack. "If you return to the naval asylum—that is, I have not yet seen it, and I would be interested in going." She left the rest unsaid, but Felix knew she was hoping for an invitation.

"I hope you will have a chance to see it, for the work they are doing there is inspiring." He smiled at her in a way he hoped was kind. "At present, I am unable to get away for a second visit, unfortunately. I am sorry to disoblige."

She flushed. "Oh, it is of no matter. Miss Edwards and I will go. Or I shall see if Lady Sophia wishes to return to it." She shrugged. "Shall we see how the profiles are coming along?"

He nodded and walked beside her, conscious that he had probably relayed, no matter how awkwardly, that his heart was not unengaged. She seemed to have accepted it, and he silently sent her thanks for being so gracious.

When they returned, Mrs. Sandhurst was holding up two cut profiles, independent but still joined at the top and bottom of the paper. Felix found one of them very pretty and wished he might have it.

"As you have seen, I have kept them attached in these two places, but there's no reason you have to keep it that way. I am not forcing a match," Mrs. Sandhurst announced with a titter.

Robert stood. "We shall take them like this"—he looked at Lady Sophia—"for now. Perhaps we will separate them and perhaps not."

Lady Sophia looked as though she wished the ground would swallow her. Felix wanted to rescue her but stopped short, reluctant to perform an act in obvious opposition to Robert.

Miss Mowbray leaned in to say, "If you will excuse me, Mr. Harwood, I will join my friend."

"Yes, of course." At least she was in a position to rescue Lady Sophia from Robert's ungallant advances.

After folding the profile on the connected border and tucking it into his waistcoat, Robert sauntered over to where the servants were serving drinks. Felix remained in place, watching Lady Sophia as Miss Mowbray stopped at her side. He saw her put her hand on Lady Sophia's arm and lean in to say a few words to her. He watched them longer than was wise, but it was how he caught Lady Sophia's expression of alarm.

His gaze shot in the direction of hers to the edge of the hill. The little boy who belonged to another party was wandering near the edge of it unattended. It was a sloping hill rather than a cliff, but he was too young to be steady on his feet. If he fell and began to roll down it, he might truly be hurt.

Lady Sophia broke away with a cry and started to run. Without a thought, Felix took off at a sprint in the same direction. The toddler stood looking down the hill and pointing, and his father finally noticed and shouted at him from a distance. Just as the child was about to take a step on the sloping grass, Felix threw out his arm and scooped him around his waist, spinning him in the other direction as Lady Sophia reached his side. She had run much faster than he had thought possible.

"You have saved him," she gasped, out of breath. She held out her arms, and the child went into them without hesitation. "You gave us a scare, young man." She smiled at him as the father arrived at their sides.

"Thank you," he said to Felix, his breath also coming fast. "We had thought him playing with his bigger cousin and were not paying attention as we ought. We are much obliged to you."

"You have Lady Sophia to thank," he said, smiling at her. "She was the one who saw the danger and began running."

"Much obliged to you, my lady," the father said, as she handed the boy over to him.

Felix glanced at Lady Sophia as they both turned to face the other guests, some of whom had seen what had happened. Camilla and Marie were walking toward them, and Lady Sophia gave Felix a grateful smile that blinded him for a moment.

"I am amazed that you saw the danger, too, Mr. Harwood. I thought I was the only one who did and that I would not reach him in time."

"I was watching you," he said before he could check his words. "It was your expression of alarm that alerted me."

"You—"

Then Lady Camilla and Marie were upon them, and she was not able to finish her sentence. Her tone held a question. Felix's chest pounded, for he had revealed his interest in that one sentence. In a way, he was glad she was not forced to return a response right away. He did not want her to be pressured into returning his feelings, although he hoped that someday she would.

The picnic soon drew to a close, and they were given no further chance for a private exchange. But as they mingled with the other guests, he saw her looking his way more than once. It almost didn't matter that Robert insisted on leading her down the hill again; the picnic had given him something to hold on to. It led him to hope that perhaps she was not indifferent to him.

Felix was at home the next day when a servant knocked and handed him three letters. With no plans to attend Parliament that afternoon, he sat to look through them. The first was a letter from his father.

Dear Felix,

I am required, as the executor of Mr. Thurlow's estate, to come to London and prove the will to the PCC at Doctor's Commons. I have taken a house on Searle Street and Margaret will accompany me on the journey. It will be a pleasure to have her company, and I think she might amuse herself with you in London. Mrs. Macklesby has assured me she is perfectly capable of caring for Elizabeth, Susan, and Anabelle while we are gone. It will do our Margaret good to have her first grand adventure and perhaps give her some of the confidence that disappeared when we lost your mother. I hope you will be able to spare some time from your parliamentary duties to entertain your sister—and perhaps, for the sake of your old father, you might even consent to dine. You may expect us on Tuesday next.

Your father,

T. Harwood

Felix was touched by his father's letter and did not miss the affection that read through his words. Then he cocked his head, grinning, as he imagined Margaret in London. She would be petrified by the crowds, unable to utter a single word. He would have fun drawing them out of her.

A new thought entered the realm of possibilities. Perhaps he might introduce her to Lady Sophia. They were alike in some ways, and his sister would certainly benefit from meeting someone who was higher in Society but also struggled with shyness.

He sat down with the letter in his hand, then folded it back up, absently stirring the air with it. One such opportunity might be the picnic he had invited Lady Matilda to go on. What if he were able to arrange it so that it occurred while his sister was here? It would give him more reason to ensure Lady Sophia was a member of the party. He spent a moment imagining this pleasant outcome before looking at the rest of his mail.

A second letter came from his solicitor proposing three possible houses on the market that might be of interest to him should he decide against the one in Bloomsbury. As for the one he had visited, so far no offers had come, but one gentleman was extremely interested and was applying to his father to assist him in making the purchase. Felix was also still weighing his decision, for although he was very tempted, his father's caution weighed with him and he was loath to rush in with an offer to purchase. He decided to think the matter over a little longer.

The other letter waiting for him brought no pleasure. It was from Lord Chawleigh, requesting he come to Grosvenor Square, and Felix had an inkling of what the interview would be about. The baron was likely going to ask him if he had made any headway with the admiral about getting his son the position he desired. It occurred to him then that Robert had never approached him directly about the favor. Did he know about it and not care? Or did he assume Felix would carry out his father's request without raising a fuss? Well, there was nothing for it but to face the meeting and get it over with.

At 20 Grosvenor Square, the footman opened the door and admitted him into the drawing room, where Robert was waiting for him.

"You came. I was thinking to go and visit you myself and would have done this afternoon if James had not informed me of your arrival."

The words sounded agreeable enough, but Robert did not look happy, and Felix grew uneasy. His mood likely sprang from one of two things. It either had to do with Lady Sophia, or the matter his father had called him to discuss. No, it could not be that, for that would not make him look thunderous. It must concern Lady Sophia. Well, Felix would delay the confrontation if he could.

"Your father sent me a letter, requesting that I come, and here you have me, all obedience." Felix strove for a light tone.

Robert stood and went over to where a side table held a decanter of brandy. "Care for a glass?"

Felix was not in the mood for it, but he thought it would be more polite to say yes. "Thank you."

Robert poured the drinks, handed one to Felix, and sat across from him. He drank, his eyes not straying from him. Felix leaned back, refusing to cower under such scrutiny. He had done nothing wrong. Besides, he'd learned at an early age that he had to stay strong with Robert, or with their social disparity, he would become nothing more than his lackey.

"It seems you are growing cozy with Lady Sophia."

Felix set his glass down carefully. He would not deny it; nor would he offer anything more than was needed. "Lady Sophia is an admirable woman."

"Her family is our closest connection. She is the woman I've had my eye on for many years. You are not ignorant of the fact," he reminded Felix grimly.

Felix flicked his hands, forcing himself to relax. "I am aware of your interest and intentions. I was able to see it for myself. However, I am not aware of hers."

"What's that supposed to mean?" Robert shot back.

"It means," Felix said carefully, "that I cannot say that I have detected any partiality on her side."

"And so you mean to step in and attempt a bid for her hand, do you?" Robert was poised on the edge of his chair, looking ready to mill him down.

Felix shrugged and looked away. This was direct, more direct than he was ready to own. It was one thing to tell Lady Sophia that he had been watching her, which was how he was able to come so quickly to her assistance. It was another thing to admit to Robert that he was fully pursuing the lady because he could not stop thinking about her. How humiliating it would be should she turn him down with a reminder of their difference in wealth and status, of which he was readily aware.

When Felix did not answer, Robert downed the rest of his drink. "You are far beneath her in Society. I did not think I would need to remind you of that. I hardly think her family would agree to such a match."

Felix leveled his eyes at Robert. "And since I am not

proposing a match at present, I hardly find this discussion to the point."

Robert stood, and Felix watched him. He knew Robert well enough to know that he was extremely put out, but that he wouldn't likely begin a physical altercation.

"Just stop interfering where you don't belong. Since you cannot hope to win her, don't hinder my courtship. I'll tell my father you are here."

He did not wait for Felix's reply and left the drawing room. Felix sat there for a long moment. He was glad he had not been forced to give an answer, as he did not know what to say. The conversation sat ill with him, for it brought into light the conundrum he was facing. His friend wished to make Lady Sophia his wife. She did not appear to return his regard. Felix, on the other hand, was hopelessly caught by her gentle manner and heart and would likely be the sort of husband she needed. But he was in some doubt of being in the position to advance his cause.

He did not wish to be at odds with Robert, but nor would he simply accept Robert's orders and ignore the direction of his own heart. The moment of solitude went on long enough that his mind returned to his reasons for visiting. And just as he thought he would have to go in search of Lord Chawleigh, the baron entered the room.

"I was informed that you had arrived but was meeting with my man of business. I'm sorry to have kept you waiting. I believe Robert was here to entertain you for some of that time?"

"He was indeed." Felix pointed at the two glasses. *If it could be called entertaining.* "I received your letter, and I have come."

"Good, good." The baron sat down and crossed one leg over the other.

With a sudden desire to put off the inevitable, Felix took control of the conversation. "I have just today received a letter from my father. He will be in London next week for the probate of Mr. Thurlow's will and is traveling with my sister."

"Is he? I was unaware Thurlow had made your father the executor of his will." He glanced at Felix as though he could find the answer to his puzzle there. Then he relaxed his pose. "Your father must come and pay us a visit. You will let him know that I have invited him?"

Felix nodded. "I will."

A beat of silence fell before Lord Chawleigh came to his point. "I have not brought up that matter I had written to you about concerning Robert's future. I had hoped you might come and see me of your own accord with good news. What progress have you made on this matter?"

Felix felt ill. He should have responded right away that the request would be impossible to honor, but it had seemed too difficult a thing to do. He took a breath. "To own the truth, I have done nothing, for I don't believe the matter will succeed."

Lord Chawleigh looked at him strangely. Clearly it had not occurred to him that he might refuse. "Why ever not?"

"The admiral is for reform, which I think you know," he said. "He used his influence outside of Parliament to make sure the Commission for Naval Inquiries was founded. He can hardly go against everything he believes in and render me a favor by giving a position to Robert based on connections rather than merit."

"It is not a favor," Lord Chawleigh said carefully, "so much as an obligation, wouldn't you say? After all, your family owes much to me. Your father his living. You, your start in life."

"And I am not insensible of that, nor is my father. However, I beg you will leave my father out of this matter, for he is not in any way connected with it." Felix attempted to think how he might convince the baron and decided on the truth. "I know

Admiral Mowbray, and he won't go against his principles on this."

Lord Chawleigh stared at him for a long moment. "Then approach someone else in the Admiralty."

Felix slowly shook his head. "I truly do not wish to disoblige you, but I *know* no one else. I have no connections there apart from the admiral." He knew Mr. Edwards, but he was only the private secretary to the admiral, besides sharing the same convictions for reform.

Lord Chawleigh pressed his fingers together and took a weighted moment before replying. "I must express how disappointed I am in this outcome. I suggest you discover if there might be some other way to make this appointment happen. I shall expect to hear a more positive response soon." He got to his feet.

Knowing he was at an impasse, Felix stood. It was cowardly, perhaps, but he had no more opposition inside of him after his interview with Robert. There were too many obstacles to overcome, and he was unable to push back as decidedly as he should. He merely nodded, then bowed and took his leave.

"I wish you good day, my lord."

As he left the baron's residence, he let his mind dwell again on whether he could possibly approach the admiral with such a request. He turned the question over, but no matter how he looked at it, he knew that it was simply impossible. One did not throw one's principles away at the slightest pressure, and the admiral would not do it.

Felix must not either—he would have to stand firm. He just wished there was not so much at stake.

CHAPTER 14

Sophia sat quietly in the drawing room working on a pretty piece of embroidery she hoped to do something special with. She would set it aside for her wedding trousseau, except that she had a secret fear she might never marry. The only thing she added to with any regularity was her memento book, which now had pressed flower petals that had been in a vase the day he had come to call, and the beribboned accessory he retrieved that she never did sew back on her bonnet. The libretto from the opera had also gone in the book, although it carried painful memories along with the happier ones.

Marie and Camilla sat with her, Marie engaged in untangling a mass of colored threads and Camilla tapping her fingers on the armrest of her chair. The subdued atmosphere was partially owing to Marie's depressed spirits. She had explained them away by saying she had not had enough sleep.

Sophia was filled with sympathy for her. Her affection for her friend remained undimmed, even though it had been painful to watch her walking with Mr. Harwood and conversing in such intimate posture. It was all her own fault for not having told Marie of her interest in Mr. Harwood from the beginning, and now it was too late. It would be impossible to tell her anything now when her friend had expressed her own interest first. Because of her secret, a distance seemed to have sprung up between them that had never been there before. And besides, as often happened when she was not directly in Mr. Harwood's company, she convinced herself that there was every reason he would choose Marie over her.

At least that was what she had thought until the picnic. But there, he had admitted to watching her, and his eyes had been alive with warmth when he had said it. His statement had surprised her so greatly, she was not sure what she would have said had she been allowed to finish her sentence. But surely, he would not say such a thing if he was not interested? His revelation left her more confused now than ever.

Camilla finally stopped drumming her fingers and picked up her tea. The cake on her plate was only half-eaten. "Evo should be here soon."

They had been waiting for their younger brother to come, now that he was on school holiday. He was to spend two weeks with them, and Sophia could not wait to see him.

"I shall be glad to have a glimpse of him, too, for I am sure he is much grown," Marie offered. "But then I shall leave you to your family. I should not wish to impose."

"You will not impose," Sophia protested.

"You are generous to say so, but it is best that you be allowed a private family dinner to catch up on everything. Besides, Papa has invited Mr. Edwards this evening for dinner. And he brings news that Papa thinks will interest me. He is very droll and well-connected," Marie said dully, quelling any hopes Sophia might have that she would fall for him instead.

"I am sure it will be a very pleasant evening," she answered cautiously.

Tilly entered the room carrying a tray of paper cuttings and scissors. She sat on one of the chairs and placed them on the table, picking up one she had cut into the shape of a flower.

"What's that, Tilly?" Sophia leaned forward and picked up another sample of her cutting. "How pretty! You are skilled at this delicate work."

"Miss Cross showed me how to make the extra layers. She learned it from her sister on her last visit." She smiled at Sophia. "It's to decorate the table for Evo's return. I have made something else, as well, as a surprise."

"I am sure his spirits will be lifted by the paper flowers," Camilla said gravely. Sophia was sure she was teasing, but there was no malice in her tone so she refrained from comment.

"You appear to have ended on good terms with Mr. Grantly when last I saw you at the picnic," Marie said. She had been unnaturally quiet on their return that day and made few observations on the afternoon. "Has he redeemed himself?"

"I believe I understand him a little better. He told me he does not converse well with ladies." Camilla paused, adding with a smile, "So I encouraged him to go on ignoring me, if that will make him feel better."

Marie and Sophia laughed. "I would protest that you did no such thing," Sophia said, "except for the fact that I am sure you did."

Camilla chuckled. "He does have some surprises in him, however, for he admitted—quite by accident—to developing a subscription program for a local school so that the village children might have literacy. Perhaps you ought to see if he is willing to subscribe to the naval asylum, Sophia."

She knew from her sister's tone that she was teasing, but she repressed a shudder at the thought of approaching someone so intimidating. "I dare not approach a gentleman on such a matter—*especially* one who does not enjoy conversing with ladies."

"I will send Regina Edwards to him," Marie said with a laugh. "She is not afraid of anyone."

A familiar rap sounded on the front door, and Sophia stood in anticipation.

"It's Evo," Tilly said, hurrying to the door. The others followed, spilling into the corridor where the young earl, now fourteen, stood proudly.

"Halloo," he exclaimed, taking off his hat with a cheeky grin. "It's the hounds."

Sophia was accustomed to his desire to shock, but this could not slide. "What is this expression, Evo? Every time you return to us from school you have grown more savage." Despite her severe expression, she held out her arms. "You should greet us properly."

He came and dutifully offered her a kiss on the cheek and allowed her to hug him back. He then bowed before Marie and greeted her, gave a sweeping but ironic bow to Camilla, and hugged Tilly from the side and shook her. "And here is the pup."

She frowned at him, but Sophia could see she was not angry. Tilly had always looked up to her older brother, even at his most exasperating.

"Well, I must be going," Marie said.

Sophie called the butler to her. "Turton, can you fetch Miss Mowbray's bonnet please?" He nodded and disappeared into the cloak room.

Marie inhaled suddenly. "I almost forgot to tell you. There is to be a masquerade ball at Vauxhall in a fortnight, and there are to be fireworks! Papa said it is to be announced soon and that the Duchess of Wexcombe has reserved a supper box and will be in attendance. I have always wanted to attend a masquerade. My father and mother adore them, but this will be my first."

Sophia glanced at Camilla, her brows knit. "That does sound amusing. Perhaps we might mention it to Mother?"

Camilla nodded, clearly not opposed to the idea. Although the mention of Vauxhall would give Lady Poole pause, Sophia hoped she would accept if the duchess was also in attendance. She had heard it possible to reserve a supper box to avoid mixing with any unsavory members of the crowd. However, the real difficulty would lie in convincing Dorothea of the idea, for she was the greatest stickler.

"Farewell," Marie said, addressing them all. She looked at Sophia, and some of her smile returned. "We shall speak more about the masquerade. I will own myself surprised if we do not already have costumes stashed away in trunks for both you and I—and Camilla, too, if you wish to come."

Sophia agreed to this and caught a glimpse of Marie's face as she turned. Her smile had vanished as soon as it was not on display, showing that she was still not herself. Sophia wondered if it was because Marie had guessed of her feelings for Mr. Harwood and was hurt by her duplicitous nature. There was every reason to think she knew, for Sophia felt utterly transparent whenever she was near him. If only she knew exactly how he felt about her. She turned to her brother, who had been twisting the knob on top of the stairwell that had come loose.

"Evo, we will be eating in three hours. I am sure you will wish to clean up and have some sustenance before then."

"You have set it in the wrong order, but you are precisely right."

She smiled and turned to the butler. "Will you...?"

She did not need to finish her sentence before their two footmen—both named George and called George One and George Two—came into the corridor to bring Evo's trunk to his room. She put her hand on her brother's shoulder and gave him a little push.

"You go with them, and I will have something sent up to

you. Mind that you dress properly for dinner. Mama has not seen you in a while."

"Where is she now?" he asked.

"She is recovering from an illness and preferred to dine with us rather than wait for your arrival and be too tired for it." She hoped their mother would be well enough to come down for the dinner hour.

He seemed completely unaffected by the news of his mother's illness as he mounted the stairs, but it was more likely his confidence that nothing was seriously amiss with Lady Poole than it was a lack of affection for her.

Before dinner, Sophia entered the dining room and glanced around the table to check that all was in order. It was set for the entire family for the first time since last season. Tilly's paper decorations were in front of every plate, and there were sugared violets on little dishes next to each glass to add color and sweetness.

Their dinners were often subdued without two members of their family—three if one counted their father. But tonight everyone would be here, including Dorothea and Miles. She looked up as the door opened and Tilly came in carrying more decorations, this time branches of rosemary tied with ribbon.

"You have done well with decorating the table," Sophia said. "The sugared flowers are exquisite. It is just what our dinner needed."

Tilly beamed under the praise and turned as their mother entered the room, followed by Joanna.

"Mama, let me help you to your seat," Sophia said, coming to lend the countess her arm. She had spent every morning with their mother during her convalescence, reading to her and watching over her anxiously. She did not wish to lose her mother as well as her father. "Are you feeling well this evening?"

"Yes, quite. A sore throat followed by an infection of the lungs must take some time to fully heal, but I believe I am truly on the mend." She sighed. "You may guess how it affected me to be struck with such an illness, with your father having been carried off in nearly the same way."

Sophia murmured words of encouragement, ignoring the fact that he had been riding in altered spirits when he had fallen from his horse. Lady Poole had remembered that he'd had a cold before the shooting party and was determined to think that was the cause. Not wishing to see her mother fall into a dejected state by dwelling on this, Sophia attempted to turn her mind to more cheerful things and was relieved when a knock at the entrance heralded the arrival of Dorothea and Miles. Before the butler could possibly have allowed them entrance, the door to the dining room flew open, and Evo entered.

"How do you do, Mama?" He came over and gave her a kiss on her cheek in his casual manner that no one seemed to be able to train out of him.

"Evo," Lady Poole greeted him fondly. "I am well, now that you are home."

Sophia was glad to see the pink tint to her mother's cheeks —hopefully of health and from the joy of having her family gathered together. The reunion was a happy one for them all. Joanna reached down to sample one of the sugared violets just as the door opened again.

"Good evening. Everard, welcome home." Dorothea walked toward him. When he tried to duck out of her embrace, she grabbed him by the ear and planted a kiss on his cheek. "Not so fast."

He turned and made an exaggerated expression of surprise. "Dorry, is that you? You are beginning to look like a barge. I thought it was just your belly that was supposed to expand, but it looks as though your lips are, too."

Miles stepped forward and placed a hand on Evo's shoulder, pinning him with a steely look. "It is good to see you, Evo. I know we are due for another round at the gym, and I should not like to accidentally mar your handsome face with a direct strike."

Evo's face lit up, clearly enjoying the thought. "We shall go, then. Will Rock come with us?"

"Until you are an adult—and probably afterward—it is Lord Pembroke to you." The earl just grinned.

"Let us all sit," Sophia said, gesturing to the table.

Everyone chose the seat that was closest to them, and Evo, finding himself somewhere in the middle, looked around, frowning. "Should I not, as head of this family, be seated at the head of the table?"

"When you act like you are the head of the family, you may do so," Dorothea said, as she placed her napkin on her lap. She then shot him an affectionate look. "I've missed you, Evo."

"Fie! Do not grow *maudlin* on me." He looked at Miles. "Is this what it is for women to be in the family way? My sympathies." Miles laughed.

As the servants brought in the first course, Sophia thought it the right moment to bring up the masquerade. She had been worried all afternoon that perhaps if she did not go to the ball, it would be another opportunity for Marie and Mr. Harwood to become more closely acquainted. If that were to happen, she would not try to hinder it, but it was difficult to resist attempting to direct fate when nothing was yet decided. Besides, there was something freeing about the idea of a masquerade that appealed to her. Disguised as she was, she would not be recognized as the shy daughter of Lord Poole. One could be anything one wished when one's identity was hidden. This gave her the courage to speak.

"Mama, this afternoon Marie told us there is to be a masquerade ball at Vauxhall."

"I do not think a public masquerade is at all the thing," Dorothea said. It was, however, spoken less categorically than it would have once been. Her look told Sophia she was not trying to ruin her fun but was merely concerned.

"Marie said that the Duchess of Wexcombe has reserved a supper box," Camilla added. "It is being publicized so that the *ton* will know of its respectability. If she goes, surely we might reserve a box and go as well."

Sophia looked in silent entreaty at her mother and then Dorothea, hoping they would approve. A moment of quiet followed Camilla's statement, except for the clink of cutlery. Finally, Lady Poole addressed Miles.

"If you are able to reserve the supper box for us, and also come as our escort, then I think we might attend. If Her Grace deems it correct, I do not see why we might not enjoy the masquerade, as well."

"You may depend upon it," Miles said easily, then turned to Dorothea. "My dear, you may decide if you wish to come or not. Perhaps I will invite my cousin to join us in case I need to return early." He turned to Lady Poole, adding, "If that is acceptable to you."

It was agreed, then! Sophia sent Camilla a quick smile. She could hardly believe they had won their mother and sister over so easily.

"May I go as well?" Tilly asked.

Their mother seemed to consider it, and even Joanna looked hopeful, waiting for the answer. Although she had stated she did not anticipate her debut into Society parties with any enthusiasm, an outdoor masquerade ball with fireworks was a different matter.

"I think we might all go. But Matilda, you will not leave the box. And Joanna, you will not do so either. I will permit Sophia and Camilla to dance, but every other one of my children must stay in the supper box we have reserved unless accompanied by Miles or Lord Pembroke."

Evo lifted up his fork, a bite of pigeon on it. "Mother, surely you will not tell the head of the family that *he* must stay in the supper box."

Their mother sipped her wine and set down the glass, saying softly, "Oh no." A rare mischievous look came over her as she added, "You may dance as well." Camilla smothered her laughter in her napkin.

"You may laugh," he said, glaring at his sister, "but I will have you know I excel at dancing. I just…choose not to do it."

"I am sure you do," Sophia assured him.

"What are you learning at school?" Joanna asked, drawing his attention to a more worthwhile topic of discussion. She tolerated dancing but did not enjoy it.

"Oh, the usual. Latin, geography…"

"I would like to learn geography. I've been reading the journals of Captain Cook's adventures." Her eyes shone as she looked around at her family. "Did you know that in New Holland, there is a creature the size of a greyhound, the color of a mouse—and that he hops on his hind legs like a rabbit?"

"That is not true," Tilly said, determined not to be gullible.

"It *is* true," Evo countered. "And he has a pocket to put his babies in—*here*." He pointed to his midsection. "Imagine if we could stuff you in there. I would do it."

Tilly went red. "You wouldn't dare."

"Children," their mother interjected mildly. "I am not sure that strange animals are the proper subject for dinner conversation."

"What else are we to talk about?" Joanna protested. "You have already told me I cannot talk about horses all of the time. I wish *I* could go on an adventure like Captain Cook. Why are women not allowed to go on grand adventures?"

"Because girls cry all of the time."

She looked at Evo, outraged. "I *never* cry."

He raised his brow skeptically, then shot a look at their youngest sister. "Or, perhaps that's Tilly."

Dorothea sighed and sent her mother a look of affection. They had grown closer over the past year, especially since Dorry had become with child.

"Well, Mama? Happy to have all of your children around the table again?" Her lips quirked upward.

Their mother's smile encompassed them all. "How can I not be?" When Dorothea shot her a look of doubt, she added, "You will see."

CHAPTER 15

It was a quiet hour on a particularly quiet day, and Sophia reveled in it. There had been a flurry of activity since Evo's arrival two days before, and she had had little time to compose her mind. The drawing room of 42 Grosvenor Square received a generous share of afternoon sunlight in a way her bedroom never did, so she sat reading a green leatherbound book by Frances Burney and attempted to ignore Evo's occasional sighs.

At last, he scooped up the spillikins and shoved them into the container. "Shame Harv is not in London. I shall die from boredom."

"Have you no other friends in London, dearest?" She looked over in sympathy. He shook his head, shaking the fruitwood canister and prompting her to protest. "Careful. You will break the sticks."

"Fitzroy is at Ashbourne and will return to Eton from there. Charley had to go to Bath." Evo's tone spoke his opinion on that scheme.

"Why not take George Two out? You can go to the Serpentine and try and see if you can skim rocks there." George Two was the younger footman who had been brought on over the summer, and Evo tolerated him better than most.

He scoffed. "He just does whatever I say."

"I should hope he does," she replied gently, trying to turn his humor.

"But he is not amusing—"

They were interrupted by a knock echoing in the hall. It was early for calling hours, and Sophia would have preferred to escape visitors altogether. She sighed as the butler opened the door.

"Mr. Cunningworth is here to see you, my lady."

This was worse than expected. In desperation, she looked at Evo as she folded a bookmark into her novel. "Do not feel you must go."

He rolled his eyes. "Stay here with that bore? I hardly think so."

Mr. Cunningworth stepped into the room, his eyes lighting on Sophia, his smile broad. It faltered slightly when he spotted Evo. "My lord, I had not realized you were home, but I suppose I should have expected it. I hope you are enjoying your Easter holiday so far."

"Vastly. *Tempus fugit*—except during calling hours."

Lady Sophia glanced at Robert, suspecting he did not follow —hoping he did not. She shook her head at Evo.

"I had hoped to speak to your sister privately," Robert said with a dignified glance Evo's way. Sophia's heart sank. This was precisely what she had hoped to avoid, and she tried to tell Evo so with her eyes. He either did not read her urgent unspoken message or did not heed it.

"I see how it stands," he said, coming to his feet. Grinning at what he likely thought was a capital joke, he turned to Robert. "You have come to *veni, vedi, tormentavi*, I suppose," he said.

"Something like that," Robert said, looking uncomfortable.

"I suppose you are here to make an offer for Sophia, but she won't have you. Dorry married beneath her, so it's up to Sophia to establish the proper line." A sardonic twist of his lips made an appearance.

"Everard," Sophia said quietly, shrinking with shame.

"Well, if I were to offer for her—not that it's any concern of yours—I should tell you that I am hardly beneath her. As for..." He stopped, glancing at her. "But I shall say no more."

"Wise." Evo bowed carelessly. "Well, if you succeed, summon me, by all means."

He crossed the room and exited as Sophia closed her eyes. They really needed to do something about Evo. His upbringing had had the unfortunate recipe of too much coddling and too much neglect. Who would take him in hand? Miles was best at it, but he did not live with them. Much as she loved him, Evo was unpredictable, like a savage animal ready to strike out for no other reason than whim.

"Sophia, your brother was right on one thing." Robert turned, and the skin above his cravat had grown red. "I am here to make you an offer. I think you know of my feelings for you."

He stopped and stared at her as though willing her to confirm it. She looked away, unable to answer him. He had been giving subtle hints in those years before his mother died, and broad hints ever since the season started. Although she was certain Robert would make a fine husband to somebody who loved him, she was no candidate for the role. A woman of more fortitude would not be crushed by his brusque ways, but she would.

Sophia had been silent for too long, and he continued his course of persuasion.

"Well, I have always admired you, as you must have known, although your modesty prevents you from admitting it." She inhaled silently as he continued, seeming to fear any silence that might permit her to refuse him.

"I do not think there will be any objection between our two families. Yours is higher in status, to be sure, but my family's wealth is not to be discounted. And it is not as though I am merely of the gentry, for my father is a peer, as yours was. I've known you your whole life and will not expect you to suddenly become talkative or stand up to people with a stronger temperament. That is what I will do for you. I can stand up for you when you cannot speak for yourself."

Sophia should stop his flow of eloquence, but it seemed impossible to interrupt when he had not directly asked the question. At her continued silence, he looked slightly less sure of himself, but soldiered on.

"I know it is the highest wish of my father, and given how well our fathers rubbed along together, I am sure yours would have wished for the same." Another pause, and then, "So, I...will you do me the honor of becoming my wife?"

It had been fair in the way of proposals. He had offered his heart in the way he was most capable. It was painful that she could not give a favorable reply. She clasped her fingers together tightly, attempting to draw strength from the gesture.

"I am sorry, but I must disoblige you, Mr. Cunningworth. My heart is not engaged." It had been blunt, but she had got the words out. Only after she had spoken them did she dare to lift her eyes.

He sat across from her and leaned forward. She saw the mix of hurt and anger in his eyes. "I think you cannot have thought this through. My father might not be an earl," he began.

With sudden clarity, she knew he would continue to press her if given the chance. He would not leave until she was reduced to a mere pulp and had no more resistance in her. She summoned every ounce of courage she had and cut off his flow of speech.

"Mr. Cunningworth, we do not suit. It is not because your father is of a lower rank than mine. Such things do not weigh with me. It is because you deserve someone who thinks the world of you, and that woman is not me."

After a stunned moment, he stood abruptly, his face mottled with color. "I allow that the shock of my proposal might have prompted a hasty answer. You must have time to reconsider. I shall not entirely despair."

She stood as well. "I would not dream of telling you what to do, but I hope you will give it up. I am quite, *quite* resolved."

Robert stood for the space of three seconds, then bowed sharply. He strode toward the door but halted steps away from it as he turned. "You will come to regret this decision." He left and shut the door hard.

Sophia sat, trembling. It had been her first proposal and her first rejection. His words that she would regret it would continue to haunt her, even if she did not think it was true. It was astonishing to her that she had found the strength to turn him down, yet that was precisely what she had done. Love for someone else had perhaps made her strong. But she knew that even if she had never met Mr. Harwood, she could not have married Mr. Cunningworth.

When Felix received a request from the admiral to pay him a call at a specific hour, an odd fear struck him that the purpose might pertain to his daughter. He didn't think so, but the last time he had been to the Mowbrays' home, the admiral had purposefully left the two alone so they might talk, causing Miss Mowbray to be as uncomfortable as he was. After their conversation at the picnic, he thought she was astute enough to see that his heart was not free.

His fears proved unfounded, however, for when he was escorted into their sitting room, Mr. Edwards was already occupying one of the seats.

"Harwood, good of you to come," the admiral said. "Our news will interest you."

"I came as soon as I saw your note," Felix said, choosing an unoccupied chair facing them.

Admiral Mowbray reached for a printed advertisement that sat on the table in front of him and handed it to Felix. "I imagine you have some familiarity with the balls and parties that go on at Vauxhall? This is for a masquerade ball that is to be held there."

Felix read the advertisement. He had seen them posted in two public places, but he had not given them further thought. He knew only that Vauxhall could quickly descend into a gathering that only the less respectable guests would enjoy. He set the paper back on the table.

"Only a vague knowledge of it, nothing more."

"Well, the Duchess of Wexcombe is offering her patronage for the masquerade ball. It is being done in an indirect manner, but by reserving a supper booth, she has made the event respectable. It will encourage others from Society to purchase a supper box and to attend the ball." The admiral exchanged a glance with Mr. Edwards. "What has not yet been announced is that the funds collected will go directly into supporting the Royal Naval Asylum for building a much-needed ward there. Mr. Edwards had this from his father, who is on the committee."

"Is that so?" Suddenly the event held interest. "How generous of the duchess."

"Her Grace's brother was a captain in the navy; I knew him.

His ship sank in Gibraltar, struck down by enemy privateers." The admiral studied his clasped hands. "I believe, in her quiet way, she is honoring her brother by sponsoring the ball."

Felix nodded thoughtfully.

"I shall hope for your presence at the masquerade, for I have reserved a supper box for us all. My wife and daughter, Edwards here—and your sister, too, is that not so?—and the First Lord and his wife will sit with us. You may dress simply in a domino and mask if you wish, but on the chance we make Her Grace's acquaintance, it would not go amiss if you were to put more care into your costume."

Felix had not counted masquerade balls as one of his objectives for London Society, but he was not going to ignore his patron's expectations. His only preoccupation was how to find a more elaborate costume than a simple colored hood and mask. "You may count on me. I will see what I can find. When is it?"

"It is on Friday, the twenty-fifth of April." The admiral stood, went around the sofa, and dragged a trunk into view. He looked at them with a sheepish air. "I, myself, enjoy a good masquerade, and I have taken the liberty of asking my servant to bring the characters from past balls."

He opened the trunk and pulled out a crimson mantle and plumed helmet and handed that to Mr. Edwards, who accepted it gamely. "Here is the cloak. I have a decorative shield somewhere in the house, and I am sure you will have a sword. Once I locate the shield, you will be perfectly suited for Achilles."

Edwards thanked him, and the admiral dug through the trunk again and pulled out a long white robe and what looked like a rustic blue shawl embroidered with stars and a moon. He held them out to Felix. "When I first married Mrs. Mowbray, I was Endymion, and she went as Diana. You will make a perfect shepherd if you can find a staff somewhere. And with this shawl, you will easily be recognized as Endymion. Besides, you have the hair for it."

Felix agreed to this meekly, feeling a bit like he was swept along in a current. He would rather be something a bit more manly than a sleeping shepherd, visited by Diana at night, only to spend his days miserable and moping.

Once the costumes had been distributed, a tea tray was brought, and the conversation shifted to how to stir the sympathies of the *ton* over the very real plight faced by the dead sailors' families. Felix had not had time to gather a list of signatures from the widows in coastal towns, so Mr. Edwards offered to go and accomplish the task. They agreed that the best way to meet the widows' most pressing needs was to apply to prominent sponsors and create a subscription fund. The move would be complementary, for the petitions would show the need and the subscription fund would demonstrate Society's support. Felix could bring both before Parliament to enact legislation.

"And I will be the first to put my name on the subscription list for the widows' needs," the admiral said, slapping his armrest in satisfaction.

When Felix felt the conversation had drawn to a natural end, he set his hands on his knees. "If you will excuse me, I must be on my way to visit my father. He has come to London, for he was required to appear in the Prerogative Court of Canterbury. My sister Margaret has come with him."

With a glance at the helmet sitting on the table in front of him, Mr. Edwards said, "If your sister and father are in London, perhaps they will wish to attend the masquerade."

Felix bit back a laugh at the thought of his father dressing for a masquerade or allowing his daughter to come to one. He shook his head.

"It is most kind of you, but as vicar, he is overly cautious in the invitations he accepts. He fears to be seen as loose on morals by the stricter members of his parish." He softened this by saying, "But you may depend upon me. I will look forward to it."

He flagged down a hackney to Searle Street, where his father and sister had taken rooms, conscious that he was arriving later than had been expected. His sister opened the door at his knock.

"Felix!" She hugged him. "London is something to be wondered at. I did not expect it to be so big. How ever do you manage life here without always feeling overawed by it?"

"I believe *you* are too easily awed." He was teasing, for he could remember his own first view of London and how much it had overwhelmed him. "I shall take you to see everything—even the royal menagerie, where you may cower before the tigers."

She shuddered in earnest. "Oh no, anything but that."

"A presentation to the queen, Megeween?" he proposed, cocking his head with a grin. She went pale and he went on teasing. "You needn't fear, for she is not likely to speak to you. You need only worry about not tripping over your gown."

He finally relented when it looked like she would faint. "Have no fear, Megs. Only those invited to visit the queen may do so. The rest of us are spared that honor." He thought back to his own visit to the king's levee, remembering how heartily glad he was to have been ignored after his initial reverence. He would not tell his father and sister about that, for they would likely make a bigger deal of it than was warranted.

Their father entered from another room. "Forgive me. I heard your arrival, but I was struggling to open the trunk I had brought with me. The clasp must be broken."

"Do you need my help?" Felix asked, but his father only shook his head.

"If you are free at present, I wish to have some time to

prepare my case before I must meet with the proctor. Might you escort Margaret out to see some of London?"

"Certainly." Felix hesitated, wondering if he should mention the house he was contemplating purchasing in London, for he had not stopped thinking of it. But he felt unaccountably reluctant, and besides—his father was occupied. He glanced at his sister. "If you are ready?"

She nodded and fetched her bonnet and cloak from a peg near the door. He decided they would begin by going to Hyde Park. There was much to see with Society strolling about at this hour. A pleasant scenario struck of him running into Lady Sophia by chance. He had not forgotten about the picnic he'd invited her younger sister to and was determined to deliver the invitation, perhaps securing approval for his own sister to join as well.

They spent two hours walking in Hyde Park, where he impressed his sister by returning the acknowledgment of two gentlemen and a lady at separate intervals, then by providing her with her first taste of strawberry ice under the plane trees next to Gunter's. His only disappointment was in not having seen Lady Sophia or another member of her family. On a whim, he glanced at Margaret.

"There is a family I know a very little—the daughters of the late Earl of Poole, and I met some of them for the first time when visiting Robert. They are his neighbors in Sussex," he explained.

Her eyes grew wide. "You never told me you knew an earl. You must truly be important."

He smiled at her naivete. "I don't know an earl precisely. I've not met the heir yet. But I promised the youngest sister that I would arrange a small picnic, for she was disappointed at being excluded from a larger one. I thought we might go and see if they will receive us so we can fix a day."

His sister looked at him with large, worried eyes—a feeling he was not far from himself. It seemed like an audacious thing to do were it not for the fact that he thought the invitation a justifiable excuse to call. Taking his sister's arm, they went on foot to Grosvenor Square, where he knocked on the front door. Margaret looked up at the facade and then at him mutely. The broad row of immaculate houses fronted by an expansive carriage road were grander than what they were accustomed to seeing.

A footman opened the door, and Felix mustered a confidence he did not feel. "Good day. If you would be so good as to present my card to Lady Sophia, or any of the young ladies of the house, I will wait to see if they are at home to visitors. I have come with my sister, Miss Harwood."

The butler came forward at that point and seemed to recognize him, for he did not betray any sign of shock at the presumption of an unannounced visit. After disappearing with the card, he returned. "Lady Sophia will receive you, if you would be so good as to wait. I will return in a moment."

"Thank you." Felix tried to settle his fast-beating heart, and Margaret was staring with open wonder at the bright corridor leading from the entrance hall. They waited in silence, and when the butler returned, he led them toward the drawing room.

"Follow me, if you please." He opened it and announced, "Mr. Felix Harwood. Miss Harwood."

Lady Sophia was the only one in the drawing room, and she stood as they entered. Signs of distress were discernable on her face, but he did not think their visit the cause of it for she was smiling. As he advanced to greet her, the private door to the drawing room opened, and Lady Camilla entered.

He bowed first to Lady Sophia and then to her sister. "Good day. I hope we have not called at an inconvenient time. We do not intend to stay long. Allow me to present my sister, Miss Margaret Harwood."

Lady Sophia's face transformed into a welcoming smile and she advanced, holding out her hand. "How do you do, Miss Harwood? I am Lady Sophia, and this is my sister, Lady Camilla."

Meg looked like she was ready to sink into the floor and, blushing furiously, she managed to curtsy.

Felix saw understanding dawn in Lady Sophia's features, as she seemed to grasp that his sister was even shyer than she was.

She clasped Meg's hand, then indicated the sofa. "Will you both sit?"

"We truly do not wish to trespass upon your time," he assured her again, "but I remember my promise to plan a picnic for Lady Matilda. As my sister and I were nearby, I took it upon myself to come and propose a day. I also wished to present my sister in hopes that she might come as well."

Sophia turned to her, her smile still in place. "You are very welcome to come, if you wish it. It would be lovely to have you." She turned her eyes back to Felix, and her expression had relaxed, as though the distressing occurrence had faded from mind. "What day do you propose?"

Felix had not thought that far ahead. But the desire to have the picnic sooner rather than later propelled him to say, "I thought Saturday would be ideal, if that suits you."

Lady Sophia glanced at her sister before replying. "I think I can speak for all of us when I say that we are free."

"Excellent. I propose to hire a waterman in Richmond. He will take us to a meadow I know of along the banks, and at the end of our picnic, he will row us back." He hesitated. "The only thing we must consider is that the carriage ride to Richmond might be as long as two hours, which means a full-day excursion. Does that sound like something you…your sister would wish to do?"

If he had had any fear that this constraint would make the picnic unpalatable, her expression dispelled it. "It sounds like a perfect way to spend the day. I think I can speak for Tilly and say yes."

Lady Camilla exchanged a glance with her sister. "My brother is home on holiday, and I am sure he would be glad to join us."

"Wonderful."

His smile felt like it might split his cheeks, and if anyone cared to read the direction of his thoughts, they might easily do so. When they left, however, Meg had an entirely different subject occupying her mind.

"Oh, Felix! We are to picnic with an earl. How ever will I find anything to say?"

CHAPTER 16

Pen, their maid-of-all-work, carried the picnic basket from the kitchen and set it near the front door next to other provisions for the picnic. "Cook said this is the last of it."

Sophia glanced at the pile, wondering again if they should bring a servant to help. But Mr. Harwood had sent a note, saying not to concern herself with preparing for the picnic, for he would take care of all that was needed. She trusted him, but could not help but wish to contribute.

"Thank you. Have George One bring this to the carriage." The maid nodded and went off to find the footman.

Tilly came downstairs, carrying a sketchbook, her stuffed reticule dangling from her arm. Sophia looked her over and said, "You will need a bonnet. Go up and fetch your brown poke with the large rim."

Her sister turned without protest and hurried upstairs. She had spoken of nothing else but the picnic since they had received the invitation. Camilla moved to the side for Tilly as she descended the stairs, tying her bonnet under one ear. She had joked that morning that she was not interested in attending another picnic and would much rather sit inside and be lazy. Then, with a look of innocence, added that instead she must play duenna to Sophia and Mr. Harwood.

Sophia had sent her a look of mild reproof, hoping Camilla did not truly know the way of her heart. Her feelings were so full and large and raw, and the fact that they were hers alone was her only comfort. Besides, there was no reason to think he was organizing the picnic for her, when he had specifically stated that he was fulfilling his promise to Tilly.

Joanna would not be joining them, for their groom had told her that Mr. Cushings, known to be extremely wealthy and an excellent judge of horseflesh, was bringing home the new black chestnut he had bought at Tattersall's. Joanna would not miss that for the world.

Apart from Mr. Harwood and his sister, it would be Sophia, Camilla, Tilly, and Evo—if he did not change his mind at the last minute. *Where is he?* She went into the drawing room, where she found her brother, flipping through a book at a pace too quick to read anything.

"There you are. Did you still wish to come?"

Lately, Evo had been making himself scarce for hours at a time and gave only vague answers when asked where he had been. Suspecting her brother was getting into mischief, Sophia was making more of an effort to invite him to accompany his sisters on any outing he might find pleasurable. Today, however, she did not push him into attending, for after his display in front of Robert, she had no wish to have him embarrass her in front of Mr. Harwood.

He stood and grabbed a walking stick leaning on the chair next to him. "I found this in the room in the attic that's filled with boxes. Thought it might come in handy."

Sophia's thoughts had returned to Mr. Harwood. She was too nervous at seeing him to respond and followed Evo into the corridor.

She had debated whether to invite Marie to join them, and in the end, did so. For one thing, she had not seen her friend lately and missed her. For another, she was determined not to be mean-spirited. If Marie and Mr. Harwood had a shared affection, she would not put herself in the middle of it. It had been a difficult decision to reach but she was satisfied with her choice, for it was the right one.

However, Marie sent her regrets and offered no reason for it. Sophia was not given a chance to fear that their friendship was in danger, because Marie had come the next day to invite them to come to her house before the masquerade and choose amongst the selection of Greek and Roman characters her parents had accumulated over the years. Before leaving, she mentioned in passing that Mr. Harwood would be sitting in their supper box at the masquerade.

Sophia had never before considered herself a volatile creature, but her spirits plunged at the image of Mr. Harwood sharing a supper box with Marie, knowing all the while that her feelings were not just—or reasonable. In one breath, she had been determined to include Marie in an outing with Mr. Harwood; in the next, she was jealous because her friend would attend the masquerade with him. Her only comfort, meager though it was, was that Mr. Harwood *would* be at the masquerade. That was something she had wondered about but did not —could not—ask. It would be too forward. And besides, if he were to be there, she was not sure she wanted him to recognize her. To what purpose, she could not explain to herself. So she could observe him without his knowledge?

The sounds of the carriage pulling up outdoors alerted her to the fact that Mr. Harwood and his sister had arrived. Their own carriage was being loaded with a blanket and large basket of food, and in her hand she carried a parasol. Sophia was about to go in search of Tilly when her sister ran up from the kitchen carrying a smaller basket.

"I helped Cook make tarts," she explained.

Sophia nodded and turned to Pen. "Tell Mama when she awakes that we will be home well before dinner, and that she must not worry about us, for we are accompanied." Then she greeted Mr. Harwood, who was helping his sister out of the carriage.

Miss Harwood was as shy as she had been at their first meeting and seemed even more so to meet Evo and Tilly for the first time. Mr. Harwood, whose curls looked burnished in the sunlight, held out his hand in an uncharacteristic act of gallantry, and when she placed hers in his, he bowed over it. As he lifted his eyes, that same open-natured smile she had admired all those years ago reappeared and sent the same quivers through her.

"I will give instructions to your driver to follow my carriage to the boathouse in Richmond. We will take a wherry there."

"Very well." She could feel happiness leak out through her grin and the sparkle in her eyes. Surely he must divine her feelings when she was with him, but she was powerless to hide them. She watched him go and speak to her driver, then they all piled into their respective carriages and were off.

The ride to Richmond was accomplished in only an hour and a half, and as soon as the carriages came to a stop, she heard Mr. Harwood shouting a greeting to someone. George One opened the carriage door for them, then went over to untie the heavy basket and carry it over to the bank. Sophia's face was protected by the large rim of her bonnet, but she could see the sun dancing off the ripples in the water in front of her.

Long flat boats rocked gently in the river, tied to the shore with thick ropes, and boys carrying hot pies or stone jars of drink ran from one waterman to another as two dogs sniffed along the bank. Mr. Harwood entered her vision on his way to one of the watermen in patched breeches and a simple shirt, standing inside of a wherry. A second waterman soon joined him carrying a long pole. Evo, eager to miss nothing, hurried over to Mr. Harwood.

"Have you traveled on a boat like this before?" she asked Miss Harwood, who stood beside her taking everything in.

"Not like this. Merely a rowboat on our neighbor's pond." A brief smile appeared, then she turned forward again.

"Lord Poole, if you would be so good as to assist your sisters into the boat, I will help the footman with our baskets." Mr. Harwood went to his carriage, and Evo broke away from staring at the boats like one transfixed and moved forward to carry out the task.

The wherry wobbled as they stepped in, but the two watermen held it steady, and Evo's grip was firm. They sat on benches in the middle, then lay the baskets at their feet as Mr. Harwood handed them in. Once it was loaded and Mr. Harwood and Evo had climbed in, the two watermen pushed off the bank with their long poles, steering the craft upriver.

Sophia was lulled by the gentle rocking on the water and the sensation of gliding as Evo, seated at the front end of the boat, kept up a steady stream of questions: Had he capsized the boat before? How long would it take to arrive at the meadow, versus how long the return trip would be, considering they would then be riding with the current? Was it too deep for the poles in the middle of the river?

Joanna would have enjoyed the day for the boat ride alone, and Sophia thought it a shame she had not come.

She glanced at Mr. Harwood and found that his eyes had been on her. He now turned them to Tilly.

"Lady Matilda, I hope you will be satisfied with your picnic today."

She beamed at him and held up her sketchbook. "I mean to record everything that happens so I might remember it."

"An excellent idea." Mr. Harwood tugged his sister's arm. "As we did not think to bring your sketchbook, you will just have to keep it all in your head and draw it later, won't you?"

She sent her brother a fleeting smile, then glanced at Evo and the three sisters before turning away, a blush on her cheeks. Sophia could understand her movements and reactions so well. The idea that Mr. Harwood might have a family member who was so similar to her had not occurred to her. She allowed her regard to settle on him again now that he was looking ahead.

"Have you returned to the naval asylum?" she asked, astonished at the courage she possessed in opening the conversation.

"I have not had a chance to, but having visited once enables me to speak on the subject more eloquently. I am on a committee where we are arguing for pensions to go to the families of fallen soldiers." His eyes rested on hers for a prolonged moment, and she felt the interest in them. "And you? Have you returned?"

Before she could respond, he clapped his hand to his head. "I have completely forgotten that I promised to inquire on your behalf for members' wives who might wish to donate—and to assist you in arranging the visits."

Sophia had not forgotten it. She had nobly agreed when Miss Edwards asked it of her because she thought it the right thing to do, but she had not yet found the courage to seek anyone out and begin. "Yes, I have not yet fulfilled that promise."

"I will not forget again," he vowed, then swiveled in his seat to point. "That is the meadow I had in mind for us."

Sophia trained her eyes on the pretty stretch of grass. There was a stone walkway on the bank with an iron hook that made it easy for the wherry to pull up alongside it. The grass sloped gently upward where they could set their picnic. Farther ahead was a true meadow, and if one continued along the river, the path disappeared into a wooded area. A spreading oak provided shade nearby, and the area was empty of pleasure-seekers. One of the watermen pushed the boat over to the bank and threw the rope over. The other leapt out, but before he could secure it, Evo landed on the walkway, dropped the big stick he had brought, and wrapped the rope around the iron ring.

"May I hand this to you?" Mr. Harwood lifted up a basket, which Evo took and set to the side, and they repeated the process until all the baskets had been transferred to land. Then Mr. Harwood helped Sophia, her sisters, and Miss Harwood to alight from the boat. He did not release her from his firm grasp until she stood on solid ground and smiled at him in thanks.

As each carried an item over to the shaded spot, Mr. Harwood conferred with the watermen about the time to return, then grabbed the largest basket and followed in their wake. Despite some of the protruding roots under the tree, there was space enough in the shaded area for soft grass, and they had a perfect view of the river. A family of ducks paddled by, undisturbed by the progress of a passenger barge.

The setting was idyllic with the sounds of lapping water and the chirping of a wagtail, and Sophia thought she had never been so happy in her life. When everything had been set out, she sat, and Mr. Harwood immediately took the seat at her side. She tried not to put meaning to the gesture and busied herself with setting out the food and admiring the sandwiches, which Miss Harwood quietly admitted to having prepared.

"Excellent," Evo said, taking one. "*Fiat lux!*" When Tilly looked at him confused, he took a bite of his sandwich. "It's Latin for, 'Let there be luncheon.'"

Miss Harwood smothered a laugh, and the corner of Mr. Harwood's lip tipped upward. "To any Roman citizen from antiquity, they would have thought it to mean, 'Let there be light,' but I might like your definition better."

Evo returned a genuine smile, and Sophia was touched to see it. The only other gentlemen he had ever seemed to like were Miles and his cousin, Lord Pembroke. His easy manner with Mr. Harwood was in stark contrast to his antagonism toward Mr. Cunningworth.

"Would you care for some lemonade?" Mr. Harwood asked, and Sophia smiled and nodded. He served everyone a glass as Camilla set the plates out.

Evo filled his plate quickly and immediately tucked in to his food, causing Camilla to utter a reproach. "*Do* try to eat as a gentleman and not as a mongrel."

"I will if you allow me the use of your sleeve." Without looking up from his ham he added, "Looks more like a napkin, that gown you're wearing."

Embarrassed by his behavior, Sophia shook her head at him. "A gentleman does not put aside his manners, even when in informal company."

"My excuses," he mumbled without looking at anyone.

Sophia asked Miss Harwood questions about her life at home, while Mr. Harwood examined each of the sketches that were already in Tilly's book. Two swans glided by in front of them, and she was almost too happy to eat.

She had barely touched her lemonade, so when she went to drink some, was surprised to find her glass nearly empty. At the same time, Mr. Harwood lifted his, spilling some as he brought it to his lips. He pulled away in surprise.

"I'm not sure this is my glass. I had thought I'd drunk more of mine."

Evo was clutching his sides in laughter. "I switched them. I'm sure you will not mind sharing a glass, since you appear to share a regard." This crass jest was met by an awkward silence, and Sophia felt her face turn crimson.

"Not at all," Mr. Harwood said smoothly, recovering the situation. He gently took his glass from Sophia's hands and handed hers to her. "However, I do not want to deprive your sister."

It was inevitable that Evo would embarrass her, but the fact that he had thought them to share a partiality gave Sophia pause. Did he really think so?

Does Mr. Harwood?

If Mr. Harwood felt any self-consciousness at Evo's teasing, it did not show. He was at ease, even giving Evo back his own before turning to encourage Tilly and his own sister. It was as though he were already part of the family. One could almost say like a brother, except that her feelings toward him were anything but.

CHAPTER 17

It was a glorious day, one as perfect as Felix could have imagined it to be. Megs was conversing naturally with Lady Sophia; to all appearances, they might have been friends for a long time. He enjoyed an unhindered view of Lady Sophia, admiring the way she ducked her head when she smiled and the way she spoke firmly to her brother. He thought his attention had gone unnoticed, but the earl must have caught on to his interest or he would not have played such a prank.

Felix felt sure he had a glimpse of Lady Sophia's true nature when surrounded by her family, and it only increased his admiration. Despite his desire to impress her, which he tried to rein in, his prevailing feeling was that of contentment. Whether she remained silent or spoke a few gentle words, he wanted nothing more than to sit beside her. He noticed her skill in smoothing over quarrels that sprang up between siblings and thought that some of the MPs could benefit from her talent.

When they had finished eating, Lady Matilda gasped. "I have forgotten about my tarts!" She went over to a basket that sat tipped onto its side and set in the center of the blanket, tentatively removing its cloth. "Oh no, they have been ruined." She swallowed hard.

Felix leaned over and peered into the basket. "Are those rhubarb tarts? They are some of my favorites. Might I have one?"

Lady Matilda nodded with a trembling smile and used a spoon to serve the crushed pieces of tart onto his plate. Felix made a show of eating it, smacking his lips loudly, and declaring it delicious. The others followed his example, and she smiled broadly when he asked if there was enough for him to have a second.

After the meal, they left their picnic in place and went to explore what looked like a path stretching along the bank. At first, the trail was near nonexistent, but the earl ran ahead to see where it would lead and called back that it was a true path. As this portion of the bank was on a sharp incline, Felix walked below Lady Sophia to make sure she would not topple down the hill, only to suddenly remember there were three other ladies. He motioned to Margaret to draw nearer to him, then called out to Lady Sophia's brother.

"My lord, will you walk at the side of your sisters, so they do not slip? After all, you have brought that staff, and you may as well put it to good use."

Lord Poole turned back. "I will, if you agree to race me as soon as we all reach the path."

Felix narrowed his eyes and found where the path began, and as he considered the challenge, a bubble of laughter grew inside of him. Being with the earl reminded him of an age when the greatest worry in life was sports and diversion. "Where to?"

The earl shaded his eyes, then pointed. "That split oak just ahead."

"What does the winner gain?" Felix asked, entering into the spirit of it.

"It is not what we gain." Lord Poole grinned, waggling his brows. "It is what the loser must *do*."

"And what must the loser do?"

"He must kneel in the dirt and rub each lady's boots until they shine, then lay down his handkerchief so they might walk over it." His tone showed what he thought of such indignity.

To the earl this might seem like punishment, but Felix laughed. "Agreed. Now come and escort your sisters. The price of our race is that you must also assist them on the return." The earl did his part dutifully until they had all reached the path, where Felix halted. "We will need someone to signal the start."

Lady Camilla came up behind him and lifted a small blue reticule attached to her wrist. "I will do it." Once he and Lord Poole were in place, she lifted it high and looked at them both. "On your marks. Go!"

Her reticule came down and Felix found himself running next to a very agile young man. However, he was not so far beyond youth himself and was determined not to do the earl any favors. Despite his noble intentions, at the very last second, the earl sprinted ahead and touched the oak first.

He laughed, pointing a finger at Felix. "It is a particular trick of mine. You thought I was running as fast as I was able, but I always save up my strength for the very end."

"I will remember that." Felix was out of breath and doubled over, leaning on his knees. "You are good at running. I shall not deny you your prize."

"Well, I must say that for someone old, you acquitted yourself well."

"Thank you," Felix replied meekly.

They walked back to where the ladies stood, and Lord Poole wasted no time in folding his arms. "Mr. Harwood, you must now shine the ladies' boots from the youngest to oldest."

Felix nodded gravely. "You are very right. I have lost this

round and must settle up." He bent on one knee and whipped out his handkerchief, indicating for the youngest to step forward.

"Lady Matilda, with your permission?" He lifted his eyes and smiled at her, determined that he should not embarrass any of them. She kept her eyes fixed on the toes of her boots, peeping out from the hem of her skirt as he studiously shone the tips. "Is it to your satisfaction?"

She nodded and smiled at him. He lay down his handkerchief so she could walk over it, then shook the dust out of it. Next in line was his sister, and he repeated the procedure, much more at ease since he did not fear impropriety with her. "Is it acceptable, Megaboots?"

"They're very shiny. I am sorry you must demean yourself so, but I must say you should have run faster." With a twinkle in her eye, she curtsied primly and walked over his handkerchief.

Lady Camilla allowed him access to the tips of her boots, managing to retain modesty while showing her usual ease of manner. "What did you call your sister?"

Felix looked up at her, having forgotten about the nickname and belatedly regretting any embarrassment he might have caused her. "In this case, it was Megaboots, was it not, Megs? I make up silly names for her."

"Hundreds of them," Margaret agreed, laughing. So she had not been embarrassed. "He began it years ago as a way to encourage me to talk."

"Very clever." Lady Camilla smiled at his sister, then turned to him. "I am satisfied."

She moved away before he could lay down his handkerchief, and Lady Sophia stepped up. He looked up at her, conscious of a desire to shower her with every form of gallantry, even kneeling before her and wiping the dust off her boots.

"Your brother must have been a great encouragement to you," she said to Margaret.

"He is the best brother I could have asked for, and I know my younger sisters would say the same."

Felix carefully applied the handkerchief to every corner of Lady Sophia's boots, while she kept her eyes studiously on Margaret. "And how many sisters do you have?"

"I have three, all younger. Felix is my only brother."

Lady Sophia looked down just as he raised his eyes. As their gazes crossed, his heart went still. "You are very fortunate," she said, and he felt her smile go right through him.

In some confusion, he busied himself with laying down the handkerchief, but she carefully stepped over it. Then, he shook the dust from it, although it would be good for nothing but the wash. He stood and dusted off his pantaloons, then turned to the young earl.

"Do you declare yourself satisfied?"

"I am, sir. You are a good sport." The earl saluted him and turned to walk forward, assuming everyone would follow. They did, and Felix found himself at Lady Sophia's side. After a slight hesitation he asked, "May I give you my arm?" She nodded and slipped her hand around it.

"I wonder if I would not be so shy had I an elder brother to tease me like that. But my father was intimidating, and Evo is much younger."

Felix looked ahead and saw that Evo had remembered to walk with Lady Matilda. Lady Camilla and Megs were talking together and appeared to need no assistance. Although Lady Sophia's arm felt slender and her touch light, there was strength in the way she held herself that he admired. He suspected it extended to her character.

"Megs is still rather shy, as I am sure you can perceive. I remember her being more talkative as a girl, but she was only six when my mother died. She changed after that. It deeply affected her."

Lady Sophia nodded, silent for a moment. "I understand. She is delightful. I am glad she was able to join our picnic."

"*I* am glad she was able to meet you," he said, unable to resist giving her some clue of how he felt. He might not be her equal, but nothing in the way she treated him suggested she regarded it. Instead, she made him feel that he was not only her equal, but even someone of value to her.

She had not responded, and he shifted to look at her. Her cheeks were pink, and a smile trembled on the corners of her lips, showing that she had received his words as encouragement. He wanted to say more but even if the temptation to begin an open courtship was strong, common sense dictated he go about it properly. It was time he made a decision about that house in Russell Square, for a man did not pursue a woman to whom he had nothing to offer. He was a cautious man and must first review his finances and possible unforeseen expenses one more time to be sure he was making the right decision.

The sight of the watermen standing beside the wherry brought him back to the moment. Lord Poole had run ahead and was now holding his hand next to his mouth so he might be heard.

"It is time to return. Sophia, you had best hurry. You never know if Cunningworth is going to call and press his suit again today. You wouldn't want to miss it."

As if by reflex, Felix dropped his arm, somewhat stunned. She allowed him to release her without looking at him. Was she still receiving Robert's addresses? If she was, then perhaps he had mistaken her kindness for interest. On paper, Robert's was the better suit, so it should not surprise him if she were seriously entertaining his proposal. The thought sent a frown to

Felix's brow. They had arrived at the blankets, and he bent down and reached for it without looking at her.

"Your brother is right. All good things, no matter how delightful, must come to an end."

The return trip to the boathouse was smoother and quicker, since they traveled with the current. Felix's mood had plunged after Lord Poole's offhand comment, and the thought of Robert still pursuing Lady Sophia cast a pall over an otherwise delightful afternoon. But then, he tried to remind himself, even if Robert called on her and attempted to persuade her into a match, it did not follow that she must accept it. Perhaps she was *not* interested in Robert.

When they reached the boathouse, Felix went to help Lady Sophia and her sisters and his out of the boat. Their carriages were waiting for them, and he sidled up to Lord Poole as the servants came to secure the baskets.

"My lord, I was wondering if I might borrow this wooden stick of yours for a short spell? I promise to return it to you before long."

The earl handed it to him without a fuss. "It is yours for as long as you need it."

"Thank you." Felix was a little surprised that his request garnered no questions but was thankful that Lord Poole did not ask why. He wished to keep his character secret for the masquerade. He handed the staff to the servant he had hired for the short trip and went to assist Lady Sophia and her sisters into their carriage. When he did so, he held her hand in his.

"We will ride beside you to Grosvenor Square and see that you are safely returned home."

She murmured her thanks, and he went to help his sister into the carriage, leaning back against the squabs as the driver directed the horses forward. He closed his eyes, refusing to dwell on Robert's intentions toward Lady Sophia. His sister was quiet beside him.

"Well, Meg-pearl, you can now say you have met an earl. What do you think of him?"

He heard her soft laughter. "He is not intimidating in the least!" After a short pause, she added, "Although, I could not say the same if he were a man grown. Even if we had already become acquainted, I think he would intimidate me if he were much older."

Felix smiled, his eyes still closed, and did not return a comment. His thoughts continued on their own trajectory, an unlikely, though hoped-for, scenario presenting itself. *But would he still intimidate you, should he be your brother-in-law?* he wondered.

CHAPTER 18

Marie stood in the middle of her sitting room with textiles spread out on every available seat.

"I have laid out the possibilities I thought were best suited for your costumes," she said, gesturing to coordinated Greek-apparel habits, modified for modesty. "My mother has collected one from every masquerade she and my father have attended."

Camilla was drawn to a costume with color, but the sight of a quiver of arrows set on top of one of the gowns caught Sophia's eye, and she walked toward it.

"That is Diana, of course," Marie told Sophia with a smile. "My father wishes for me to wear it, but I am more interested in dressing as Juno."

Sophia lifted the quiver and pulled out one of the arrows. Although the quiver was a prop and would be easy to carry, the arrow appeared to be real. The idea of going as Diana appealed to her. The goddess of the hunt was fearless, something Sophia could never be.

"I think I shall be Minerva," Camilla said, lifting a loo mask decorated like an owl with real feathers.

"Will there be an unmasking at the end of the evening?" Sophia asked. "Might we remain anonymous if we wished to?"

Distracted, Marie dropped the habit she was holding and turned her eyes to a simple gown with wings sewn to it.

"Or I might play Psyche. I would enjoy confounding Cupid." She turned to Sophia, the question apparently just registering. "There will be an unmasking, but there is no reason you have to remove yours. You may simply disappear when the fireworks begin."

"If it encourages you to move and speak more boldly," Camilla added over her shoulder, "then I advise you *not* to reveal your identity. The knowledge that you are truly hidden will give you freedom you don't generally have."

Her sister's comment was astute, for that was precisely what Sophia longed for. Perhaps she might discover which costume Mr. Harwood wore, and she would allow herself to compliment him in a bold way. She would be free to do so if he did not know her.

At the picnic, he had given her signs that he was interested —at least she thought it was interest. He said he was glad she and his sister had met, suggesting the introduction held some significance. But perhaps he was just being polite. She wished she understood the male sex better.

"Or you may cast a gentleman into despair by remaining anonymous," Marie countered. "He may wish to know who the mysterious huntress is who has bewitched him and will expire from not knowing." A servant entered the room carrying a tray. "The tea is here. Let us have some, then sort out how to complete each of the characters."

The tea was brewed and set out and each helped herself to cake. Sophia's mind still revolved around the idea of remaining hidden, which would have the added incentive of ensuring that

Robert, who was likely to attend the masquerade, would not find her.

"I suppose if I were to wear a domino as well, that would keep my hair hidden," she said.

"Yes, but it would hide an elaborately made costume." Marie glanced over at the huntress dress. "Do you intend to go as Diana, then?"

Sophia paused before answering. "You did say your father wished you might. Would you not consider wearing it?"

Marie shook her head. "If you wear it—and I think you should—I believe you should have your maid style your hair in the old way, the way our mothers did. She could give it height and add powder and curls, even leaves. You will look charming."

"The matching loo mask extends low enough and will reveal only your lips," Camilla added. "I hardly think anyone will recognize you. And then you can decide if you wish to reveal yourself at the end of the evening. I, however, am decided to stay for the unmasking."

Sophia ruminated over this and glanced back at the costume. It was the only one that caught her eye, and although the thought of wearing it seemed daring, the impulse was strong. "I shall go as Diana, then, and although I do not know whether I will participate in the unmasking, I will do as you say and style my hair rather than covering it."

THE CRESTED CARRIAGE deposited the earl's family at Whitehall, where a crowd was gathered to take sculls across. Dorothea and her husband soon joined them there, and Miles flagged down two watermen to carry them across. As Sophia stepped into the boat, memories of her picnic with Mr. Harwood returned. Her thoughts grew unsteady whenever she thought of him. In one instant she was sure he was engaging in a subtle courtship and felt all the delicious heart flutterings that went with it. In the next, she was sure he must be destined for Marie.

The more time she spent away from him, the more she became convinced that he could not seriously be considering pursuing her. Even if he was interested in her—and why would he be when she was deficient in so many ways—he would not take a step so injurious to his political future as to propose.

Daylight held as they entered Vauxhall Gardens, but inside, paper lanterns dotted the path leading to the center, where a large area held tables and chairs for public dining. It was still early enough that one might easily admire the decorations, including the elaborate Greek scene painted at the rotunda reserved for dancing. An unspoken thrill of nighttime masquerade and anonymity seemed to permeate the air. Miles walked ahead confidently in a simple domino and half mask, and Dorothea sported a loo mask and crown of braided wheat as Ceres, but otherwise wore a simple gown. "It was rather half-heartedly put together," she had said laughingly.

It was Sophia who had dressed with the most extravagance, shocking everyone. It was all due to Marie's influence, but she was glad she had done so. It felt like she had taken on the character of strength and aloofness when she donned the costume.

Having told her maid she did not wish to be recognizable, Margery teased and powdered her hair into an elaborate style with curls and leaves. Her mask was silver, and she allowed her lips to be painted a dark red. When she looked into the mirror at the final result, she gasped. No one would know her for Lady Sophia Rowlandson. Now, as they walked toward their supper booth, men and women turned to stare at her, and only the knowledge that she was in disguise allowed her to face the scrutiny without fear.

"The box I reserved is here, waiting for us." Miles led them around to the back, where a sign appeared on the door, proclaiming, "Mr. Miles Shaw."

"Famous!" Evo declared. "Joanna and Tilly, you should sit on the sides, since you are the least in character." Joanna scowled at him, but Tilly followed his orders without demur.

It was not until they had stepped inside that Sophia realized how visible they were in the lighted booth. It was like being on display. One of the chairs in the front was tucked behind the pillar, and she slipped into it. It did not matter that she was determined to be courageous; it would serve no purpose if everyone attending saw her with her family and recognized her.

Lady Poole had fully recovered from the ailment that had kept her abed for several weeks and appeared to be cheerful and ready to enjoy the evening.

"You must remain in the central alleys that are well lit." She then pointed to one of the more shadowy, narrow alleyways. "Avoid those at all costs, for you are in mixed company, and not everyone has good intentions."

"We have no inclination to stray from the areas that are well lit," Sophia assured her mother.

Evo had come as a Roman senator, his eyes keen as he looked around. Miles placed a hand on his shoulder and said a few words to him, which reassured Sophia. Dorothea's husband would keep him in line this evening. More guests streamed into the gardens, as the lanterns that floated gently in the breeze shone more visibly with gradual nightfall. Robert, easily recognizable in a simple mask, walked by their box, and Sophia shrank back out of sight.

The rotunda meant for dancing was visible from their booth. The orchestra had started early, its lively notes filling the air. Although the dancing had not officially begun, some of the guests broke into spontaneous country dances. The smell of roast meat and punch promised that dinner would not be long in coming, and with the sounds of laughter and talking from all quarters, Sophia was blanketed in the festive atmosphere.

However, she could see why one would be cautious in coming to Vauxhall. Some guests had already had too much to drink, and it was equally evident that not everyone in attendance was Quality.

Marie came along the path in front of her with a shorter woman in a plain domino whom she recognized as Miss Edwards, and she guessed the older couple with them to be the admiral and his wife. Immediately, she perceived a gentleman of Mr. Harwood's height following behind in a bright red cloak and plumed helmet over his domino. She was sure it must be him. He turned when passing their booth, then looked away just as quickly, proving that her disguise was good.

Either that, or it was *he* who did not wish to be recognized —or was not interested in knowing her tonight with Marie there. Not in the way he had at the picnic. The thought depressed her.

Marie turned and spotted their party. She said something to her father and let the others continue on before running over to Miles's box and tiptoeing up to where Sophia stayed hidden. "You look stunning, Diana." She winked at her. "This habit seems to be made for you."

Her friend's praise warmed her. "As do you. I must thank your parents for the loan of such elaborate outfits."

"Let us meet at the rotunda when the dancing begins. Mr. Edwards has come, but I have not yet seen Mr. Harwood."

"Very well," Sophia said, squeezing her hand and feeling lighter. So, it had been Mr. Edwards who looked at her, then turned away, and not Mr. Harwood. This was followed by the sobering reminder that Marie had commented on Mr. Harwood's absence, which meant she was waiting for him.

Their booth was situated next to Lady Berkley's, and they had the Duchess of Wexcombe in their view. Sophia guessed Miles had arranged it thus to make her mother feel comfortable. Lady Berkley invited Lady Poole to come and sit with her party until the dinner was brought, and Camilla turned to Dorothea.

"You will not mind if Sophia and I visit the rotunda? It is just to see what is there. I promise we will not walk down any dark alleys." This last bit was said with dry good humor.

Dorothea smiled at her. "I know you will not." She turned to Evo. "This is your chance to walk, too, if you go with them. I do not intend to move, and I hardly think we will let you out of our sight tonight."

"What a dull evening *this* will be," he retorted. "If I'd been told I would have to trail my sisters around all evening, I might've thought twice about coming."

Miles took out a deck of cards. "That is why I ordered plenty of food, and I brought cards, so you will not be bored if such a thing is possible. Lord Pembroke is to join us, too."

"Is that so?" Evo looked more cheerful at the thought, and even Camilla turned back briefly before slipping her arm through Sophia's.

"Let us go," Camilla said. "We will just have a look, for the servants are starting to bring the food." Some had already begun depositing plates in the supper boxes that lined the path.

"You really do look perfect. I would not have thought you to wear such a bold costume, but I am proud of you." Camilla, rather than choose a complicated hairstyle, had worn a red domino to cover her hair and the brown and gray owl mask to cover her face.

"There *is* something freeing about nobody knowing who I am." Sophia laughed and clutched Camilla tighter. "I saw Robert, and I was *spared*." She had not told Camilla about his proposal, and although she hoped he had let go of his pursuit for good, she could not be sure.

On their approach to the rotunda, they passed by the admiral's box, where Marie and Miss Edwards stood within talking to Mr. Edwards. As she watched, another gentleman of similar height stepped into the box with them wearing a silver loo mask, a white chiton, and a dark blue scarf across his chest. His were the unmistakable light curls of Mr. Harwood, and when she noticed the wooden staff in his hand that Evo had brought to the picnic, her heart gave a little leap.

She allowed herself to look longer than she might otherwise have and to smile in his direction. He turned and stood still when he saw her, and Marie turned as well. With a guilty start, Sophia moved forward again, but not before noticing that Robert and his father had rented a supper box close to Marie's. She stepped on Camilla's other side before he would see her.

"There is not as much room to dance as I had expected," Camilla said, looking at the circular area enclosed with curved barriers that were cut off at regular intervals to allow access. "It will be a crush."

"Do you intend to dance?"

Camilla hesitated for a moment before shaking her head. "I will not put myself forward. I am sure there will be no shortage of beautiful women wishing to have their chance."

Sophia turned to peer into her sister's face. "Why not you? You are beautiful."

Camilla's lips twisted up in irony. "It is kind of you to say so, but you know very well that I am the least favored of the family where looks are concerned."

Sophia stared at her in confusion. "Where in the world did you come up with that notion?"

It was some time before Camilla answered, and the intervening silence was filled by the din of good-humored conversation. She faced ahead, watching a group of revelers going through the exaggerated movements of a minuet.

"Oh, I don't know. Perhaps because Papa said I must attempt to learn some of the womanly arts since I was not to be thought of as a beauty."

Sophia let that piece of knowledge settle in, as indignation on her sister's behalf rose up in her. Before she could say it was untrue, Camilla went on.

"And Mama is always telling me to pay more attention to what I put in my mouth, for I have a tendency to plumpness. Joanna lets out snide remarks that show what *she* thinks of my figure, and even Dorothea does not seem to view me as one who might secure a husband—clearly the only trait that properly denotes a woman's worth."

It was too much to respond to at once, but she did protest at the one concerning their sister.

"Dorry has changed. You must see that she has. Miles is good for her. And just the other day, she complimented your figure to me. She said you were becoming quite pretty."

"Did she?" Camilla faced Sophia, the crease in her brows showing her disbelief but the vulnerability in her eyes how much she wished to believe it.

"She did," Sophia said firmly. "Not that you need anyone's confirmation to know yourself to be *very* lovely. Tonight you shall dance and amuse yourself to your heart's content. And then you will set your mind on believing how truly wonderful you are."

Camilla gave Sophia's arm an affectionate squeeze as they walked back to the supper box. Again, they passed by Marie's booth, and Sophia looked out for the silver mask, disconcerted to find him staring at her. She turned forward, attempting to appear unconscious of his regard, comforting herself that he could not know it was her.

Lord Pembroke had arrived in the supper booth in their absence, and he stood to greet them with extravagant courtesy as he bowed over their hands. Plates of food were laid out on the tables, and no one had taken Sophia's place out of view. She only hoped Robert would not cross their booth often, or he would know to look for her there. Viewed together, her family was easy to make out in their costumes. But then, he had not visited her again. Might he have given up his suit after her firm rebuff?

"Goodness! Look at this ham," Dorothea said, lifting a piece on her fork. "It is sliced so thin you can almost see through it."

Miles poured a glass of warmed orange-flavored negus for each of them, and Sophia ate sparingly of the ham, a cold slice of roast duck, some strawberries, and a sweet bun. She found it difficult to eat in her anticipation of seeing Mr. Harwood again —to speak to him and discover whether he would know her— what he would say.

The dinner conversation was lively even if the food was sparse. When they had finished, Camilla turned to Dorothea. "Do you not wish to walk around? If you do, we will accompany you—if you feel well enough."

"I do wish it, if my bear of a husband will permit it." Dorry's lips quirked in a smile.

"I will permit it," Miles replied in fine humor. "Perhaps I will take your two younger sisters and brother for a walk before Evo gets the fidgets."

Camilla and Dorothea stood, preparing to leave, and Sophia got to her feet to go with them. Lord Pembroke nudged Evo to stand, which he did begrudgingly.

"That's the way, Evo," Lord Pembroke said. "Show them you are a gentleman."

Dorothea laughed as they exited the box. It had grown cooler and fully dark in the time they ate their meal, but the paths and rotunda were well-lit with the excess of paper lanterns. Sophia could not resist another glance into the admiral's box when she went by but was disappointed to see that it was empty but for the admiral and his wife and another older couple. She followed her sisters to one side of the rotunda, outside of the stone barriers, where two things happened at once. A man in a plain domino and loo mask came and bowed before Camilla. She looked at him in surprise.

"I hope I might have the honor of dancing with Minerva and trying my wit against hers," he said. It was impossible to guess who he might be, but his speech was that of a gentleman.

She curtsied. "You may. Although Fortune cannot hope to win against strategy, so you must not allow your hopes to soar too high."

He laughed and swept her away as Dorothea spotted a friend who had made little effort to disguise her identity. "Anne," she called out. "I have not seen you this season."

It was Dorry's friend Anne Kensington, and Sophia did not begrudge them a chance to catch up, even if it meant waiting on the sidelines with no one to talk to. She stood straight, as regally as Diana herself, and watched the flash of color and movement of the dance in front of her. She felt a presence at her side and turned. Her gaze snagged on the blue scarf draped across a gentleman's chest with suns and moons embroidered on it.

Then she lifted her eyes and found herself looking right into those of the man in a silver loo mask. He was close enough that she saw his eyes fixed on hers through the holes in his mask. His lips curved into a smile, but he did not speak, as though the moment had held him captive, too.

Mr. Harwood. He had come to her—had sought her out. Did he know it was her? She did not think he could. But it was time to be bold whether or not he did.

CHAPTER 19

Although Felix felt himself obliged to attend the masquerade, his motivation for going was to see Lady Sophia. It had been four days since the picnic and he had not been satisfied with his leave-taking, for once they had arrived in Grosvenor Square, their surroundings were too public for him to ask to see her again. One point in his favor was that young Lord Poole did not seem to despise him. But it all progressed too slowly, and he was determined to pursue Lady Sophia with more intention—to persuade her to begin a serious courtship.

It inspired him to take the one step he had too long hesitated over and purchase the house in Bloomsbury. It was still available, and he had an appointment with his solicitor to sign for it the next day. There were no longer any doubts about the rightness of this purchase, and he dared hope the house would please Lady Sophia should he be so lucky as to win her for his wife.

He was glad to have Miss Edwards's company, for she was just as pleasant and unaffected as she had been on the day of Hyde Park. Miss Mowbray and Mr. Edwards had found a common subject of humor in one Admiralty clerk who was forever spilling ink over important documents or losing his spectacles only to sit on them. Their laughter was not unkind, for Miss Mowbray began to think seriously about which young lady might suit him since he was clearly in need of a wife. Miss Edwards, on the other hand, was pleased to follow Felix in a discussion much more suited to his own interest—Lady Sophia —even if the conversation concerned subscriptions for the asylum and the best way to secure them.

Shortly after arriving in the admiral's booth, Miss Mowbray leaned in to murmur that her friend, Lady Sophia, was crossing in front of their supper box at that moment. She had borrowed her mother's character disguise of Diana and did it not suit her fetchingly?

That was all it took for Felix to grow distracted. Was that vision of bold loveliness truly her? He had caught sight of red lips and hair that was thick and piled high with curls that escaped down her back. She disappeared from his view where the path turned and led to the rotunda, but he kept his eyes peeled for her. After a short time, he was rewarded. She returned with her sister, and this time directed her attention to their box—at him. Perhaps it was her shyness, but she turned away before he could give any sign of recognition. She should know him, should she not? For he was clearly standing with her friend. But then, was that not what a masquerade was? A chance to pretend one was *not* acquainted, thereby being free to express all that was on one's mind. Very well, he would play that game.

If Miss Mowbray had not pointed out her friend, he would not have known her. Lady Sophia generally wore discreet gowns, it seemed with an aim to blend into the room, clearly not realizing that her beauty did not permit such a thing. But tonight her chiton, although modest, allowed a glimpse of her figure. With red lips and hair cascading down her back, she revealed an entirely new, bewitching side to her.

Politeness compelled him to remain in the box while they ate and to stay afterward to partake in the conversation. With his eyes continually on the crowds passing by, he did not miss it when Lady Sophia passed in front of him again. Shortly thereafter, Robert and Grantly left their supper box, and Miss Mowbray invited them into hers. Miss Edwards drew Mr. Grantly into conversation with surprising ease, and at the first opportunity, Felix excused himself by saying he wished to walk around. He did not care whether Robert suspected his true aim or not; he had to see Lady Sophia.

The crowds had grown thick around the rotunda, making it difficult to spot her. He walked around it, craning his head to look, and then…she was there. Heart pounding, he approached and bowed, willing himself to fall into character and not propose to her on the spot.

"Do I have before me Diana, the goddess of the hunt?"

Her answering smile was arch and so unlike her in its teasing, his mind threatened to turn sluggish. "How ever did you guess?"

"Why, your legendary beauty." He watched dimples appear in her cheeks below her mask, and she seemed to be fighting the smile that sprang up at his words. He reached around her, allowing his arm to brush hers as he touched the quiver strapped to her back. "And, of course, your weapon."

"You must take great care, then, not to displease me," she responded with mock severity. "And what are you, sir?"

It was then—only then—that the harmony of their costumes came to him. Endymion was the shepherd whom Diana loved; he loved her in return, although he could only meet with her in his dreams.

He affected a look of hurt. "Why, Diana, I am your Endymion. Can you not tell?"

It took a moment, then her eyes lit up, first in surprise, and then a laugh escaped her. "I see it now." She then quelled her humor by scolding. "But should you not be sleeping?"

"You should not wish for me to sleep, my fair Diana, for it is our chance to break the eternal cycle. If we are meeting while I am awake, then it means we are destined to celebrate our love and not mourn its loss."

She shot him a surprised look, and the way her mouth opened and closed let him know she did not miss the truth he had infused into his words.

"How is that so?" she asked, her voice now feeble.

Her return to shyness did not deter him. Instead, it made him long to confess both his identity and his love, but he refrained. It would be breaking the rules of the masquerade, and he might frighten her away. He needed to pursue her in a faithful, open manner, and not give her cause to think him volatile. So he answered as lightly as he could.

"Why, Endymion's story is a tragic one that we should not wish to reproduce. He is hopelessly in love with Diana." He paused and allowed himself to give her a significant look before going on. "She can visit him only when he sleeps and at no other time."

"So true. I had forgotten. Ah, tragic." Lady Sophia sighed and, falling back into character, matched his light tone. "So we are destined to meet only in a dream."

"I fear that is true." His voice was deep, revealing more of his feelings than was wise. The introductory notes for the cotillion began, saving him from slipping his arm around her. "Since we are dreaming, shall we make it a pleasant one and dance together?"

"Yes." Her face tilted up, and she set her hand on his.

They took their places on the crowded floor, and Felix remembered the part of her disguise that might be a constraint during the dance. He had left his staff in the supper box.

"Shall I hold your arrows for you?"

She tilted her chin and pursed her red lips. "You must not, for they belong to me. How will I be a huntress if I have no arrows?"

He swallowed over a dry throat at this bold version of Lady Sophia. The music began, and he turned at her side to pace the steps with her as he answered.

"Pierce with your gaze, with your voice"—they circled around others in the dance and returned to each other, coming face to face—"pierce with your lips."

Lady Sophia's red lips parted, her eyes widening under her mask, and as they were separated again by the dance, his heart beat in his chest—with excitement, but also with trepidation. He had gone too far, revealed too much. And yet, he could not help himself.

"Sir, you do not know me, and yet you dare speak such words," she said as the dance brought them back together. Her character voice had returned—playful and aloof—and he knew he had not gone irreparably too far.

"How can I not know my Diana, since she is the one I am destined to love?" he answered back. "I must seize this occasion to speak the words, for I might never speak them in waking hours." They stepped apart, then the music brought them together again.

"Well, then, speak," she replied, boldly meeting his eyes through their masks. "For when your dream is over, you will have no chance."

He truly was in a dream, and the words went through him as easily as any arrow. The evening had cast a spell on them both, it seemed, so that they were neither who they truly were.

There was no difference of station, no risk of losing patronage, of alienating friends. The evening had woven its magic, and he would take his chance.

"Then I will speak of my love." He caught the look in her expressive eyes when they parted and came back together again. "The woman I love is pure of heart, incorruptible, and not like lesser mortals."

She remained silent as they separated, and he looked into her eyes when they came together again. "The woman I love is strong and able to raise her voice to defend the weak. She settles the disputes of the proud."

He saw doubt in her expression. She did not think he was speaking of her; he gave her hand a squeeze when they met again.

"She is graceful and elegant, and no other mortal can compare to her beauty."

There was still uncertainty in her eyes when the music reunited them for the final chord. He stood as close as he dared —close enough to pull her into an embrace though he refrained. He held her eyes for a long moment, and when he spoke his voice had gone husky.

"The woman I love has pierced my heart and made me unfit for anyone else."

The dance was over, and the partners gave their reverences. Felix bowed deeply, and when he rose, saw that she had remained frozen. He took a shaky breath.

It had been bold. She could choose to pretend he had been speaking in character if she did not return his regard. Or...she could reveal her knowledge and allow him to speak in earnest. One look at her, and he feared she was not ready. To spare her the embarrassment of having to decide, he took her arm and led her outside of the rotunda as people crowded on to the floor for a reel.

He did not wish to end their time together but *did* wish to avoid the very real temptation of inviting her to sit on a bench in a darkened alley where he might kiss her. The lure was strong, particularly after the words he had poured into her ear. He saw Grantly leading Miss Edwards to the rotunda and feared that Robert would come their way. He did not wish for him to mar what was for Felix a moment of perfection.

"Shall I bring you to your friends?"

Lady Sophia was still quiet; perhaps she, too, was attempting to sort through whether they were dreaming or awake. She inhaled and shook her head. "No, that will not be necessary."

He knew he should release her to her family, but any struggle his conscience had put up was gone, and he abandoned the attempt.

"I feared to monopolize the hours of the prettiest lady at the ball, but I cannot, in good conscience, release you without protection into this crowd. It appears my dream is to go on a bit longer." He smiled at her, feeling the truth in his own words.

Dimples made an appearance in her cheeks, and the way she leaned into him gave him hope that she felt at least something of what he did. A loud *boom* caused them both to start, and he looked around before recognizing the smell of gunpowder followed by another *boom*. A flash and crackle in the air caused them to turn their focus upward, where the sky filled with bright lights like a starburst that faded into darkness.

"Oh," she said, her lips parted in amazement.

"Fireworks. Is it your first time to see them?" he asked, leaning close to be heard and catching the whiff of bergamot in her hair. She nodded, and another *boom* sounded, followed by another flash of light. He felt her flinch and took her hand, putting it on his arm to steady her. He watched her face as the white and gold tones of her loo mask and the powder in her hair sparkled in the light.

"Beautiful," he said, looking at her.

She turned and their faces were close—close enough to kiss. After a brief, charged moment, she gently slipped her hand from his arm and looked up. He longed to recapture the moment but knew it would be pressing his luck. It was unfair to say so much in the character of someone else and not in his own skin. She needed to know that it was he, Felix Harwood, who spoke these words of love to her, Sophia Rowlandson—and that he meant them.

As soon as the lights from another starburst faded, he turned to her, accepting the added distance and returning to his light tones. "The unveiling is to be soon. Will I be allowed to see your true face, Diana?"

Her expression was mixed—part panic and part daring and playfulness that was her in character. "Perhaps." Her lips turned upward. "If you are not sleeping."

He smiled back, but his attention was diverted by the admiral escorting his wife to the rotunda, and he stepped back to make way.

Catching sight of him, the admiral turned with a bright smile. "Why, if it is not our dear Endymion! Was I not right to have kept every one of these costumes? They have certainly come in handy."

Mrs. Mowbray's reply was swallowed up as another *boom* sounded, followed by a flash of light. He turned to see whether the admiral had recognized his partner but was met with empty space. He looked around him, and there was no sign of her. It was as though she had melted out of sight.

"Oh," he murmured to himself, disappointed. "It appears I have been dreaming after all."

"Felix!"

Robert strode toward him, his displeasure evident. "Where did Lady Sophia go? I saw her with you just now."

Felix turned to face him, irritated at the proprietary way Robert spoke of her. "I do not know. She did not inform me of her movements."

"But you did know that the character of Diana was her. How? There is no similarity to how she usually looks. I would not have known if Miss Edwards had not mentioned it." His gloved hands were fisted and a muscle quivering in his jaw showed how tightly it was clenched.

Felix was suddenly assailed by doubt. *Did* Robert have reason to be jealous?

"Have you an understanding with Lady Sophia?" he asked, his voice carefully controlled.

Robert looked away, frowning. "It is not an understanding in the classic sense, for nothing has yet been agreed upon between her man of business and mine. But it has long been understood that we would be paired."

"By whom?" Felix asked. When Robert did not immediately answer, he pressed him further. "Does Lady Sophia accept this understanding?"

A giggling pair, dressed as a satyr and a beribboned courtesan, tipped into Robert from behind before joining the rotunda. He turned and scowled at them.

"My affair with Sophia is none of your business. I've said this before, but you had best leave her alone. There are thousands of other women in your sphere to choose from. Do not set your sights on her."

"I will not remove Lady Sophia's right to choose her own husband," he shot back.

Felix could scarcely contain his fury. While he once might have agreed with Robert—conscious of what his own father was apt to remind him was all he owed to Lord Chawleigh—the constant suggestion that he was from a lower sphere began to grate. It was not as though he were a common laborer. He was a gentleman, a junior assistant in the Admiralty, and a member of Parliament. He had made an appointment to purchase a house in an area of London that was not to be scoffed at. Besides, he was fighting for reform—for people to be recognized for their merit rather than their birth—and did not the same apply to him?

Another fireworks shell burst as if in sympathy, and Felix used the distraction to turn away. He would not prolong the fight with Robert. Nor would he stop pursuing Lady Sophia.

CHAPTER 20

At the sight of Robert walking her way with purpose, Sophia did not stop to think and hurried back to their supper box. If Mr. Harwood had guessed who she was, then there was no reason to think she had stayed incognito, especially if she remained standing beside him.

What did Robert want? Was he coming to press his suit again? Trembling, she dodged partygoers, some who turned to watch her path and others who ignored her; fortunately all left her alone. Even if Robert had been the inducement to send her away, her flight was spurred on by her fear of remaining in place and letting Mr. Harwood confirm her identity for a certainty at the unmasking.

She needed time to think through the things he said to her —the things he had said about her. She could not believe he truly viewed her in such a light, while still daring to hope that the words he spoke were true. There had been enough evidence to believe they were, but the desperate fear that he had been mistaken in who she was continued to haunt her. In her more sensible moments, she could not doubt that Mr. Harwood *knew*. A man did not speak such words of love to a stranger without having any idea of who she was. But the niggling fear persisted that he had been speaking of someone else... Did he care for Marie after all? Was he letting Sophia know that it was her friend he admired?

She reached the door to their booth and lingered in the dark outside, sounds of female conversation reaching her through the thin board. Tortured, she shook her head, remembering all he had said, the words spinning through her mind again and again. She should take heart, for surely he had been addressing those words of love to her! But in the end, any courage she'd found in playing at someone else deserted her. Robert approached, the admiral drew Mr. Harwood's attention, and she'd slipped into the crowd and disappeared.

Her mother and Dorothea sat alone in the booth talking comfortably and ignoring the excitement of the garden without. Apart from offering Sophia a smile and asking whether she had danced, they returned to their conversation about what qualities Dorothea should look for in a nurse, and Sophia was left alone with her thoughts.

A small tap came on the door to their box and Marie slipped into it, coming to sit beside her. After greeting Sophia's mother and sister, she leaned in to whisper, "I saw you dancing with Mr. Harwood. Why did you not stay for the unmasking? Now that the fireworks display has ended, let us return."

Sophia stared at her in surprise and consternation. Marie had seen her dancing with him and was truly not angry? After a small pause, she answered, "I do not wish to have my identity revealed."

Her friend stared at her. "Why ever not?"

She tried to decide how to answer. It was cowardly, but she gave only a partial truth. "There are too many faces, and the idea intimidates me."

Marie accepted her excuse with a nod and sat back, apparently surrendering to the fact that she would not change her mind. That was one thing Sophia loved Marie for. She never pushed her to do something she did not wish to do.

"I shall leave you, then. My parents will be waiting for me at the rotunda, and there are some I would like to see unmasked, for I could not make them out at all." She reached over and gave Sophia's hand a squeeze. "I shall visit you tomorrow so we can discuss everything. Wasn't this famous? I now understand why my parents attend masquerades whenever possible. I shall very likely end up just like them."

Sophia smiled and watched her go. Voices came from every direction outside of their box, and she was content to sit alone with her thoughts, for they were mostly pleasurable, even when the doubts crept in. From the rotunda, she could vaguely hear the prompt to remove the masks, and the laughter and exclamations as everyone participated in the game. Shortly afterward, streams of people crossed in front of their box to return to other parts of the gardens, and Miles and Lord Pembroke returned with Evo, Joanna, and Tilly.

"The Prince Regent was there," her brother announced.

"Was he?" Dorothea asked with interest. "In character?"

"Apollo," their brother vouchsafed. "He had a laurel and a golden lyre."

Miles came and placed a hand on Dorothea's shoulder as he addressed Lady Poole. "My lady, I hope you will not mind if we retire early. I am concerned for Dorothea and wish to see that she does not overtire herself."

Lady Poole shook her head and stood. "That suits me perfectly."

Lord Pembroke had found friends and decided to stay on, and he bid them good night. They filed out of the box and made their way toward the gate leading to the river. It was still early enough that only a few partygoers waited there, so it was a simple matter to find two sculls to take them across to Whitehall to their carriage, and from there—home.

Marie came the next afternoon as promised. Sophia, equal parts tortured and hopeful, had been waiting for her. She stood as soon as Marie entered the drawing room.

"I was thinking we might go out to the garden on the square. We seldom go there, but the sun has a pretty light today, and there are benches where we might sit."

Marie agreed to the plan, and Sophia slipped the key to Grosvenor Square's private garden into her reticule. They crossed the carriage road when traffic allowed it and went to the closest gate. Inside, they found a stone bench in a quiet corner.

"I should have asked if you wished for anything before we left the house, but I was so anxious to be outdoors. You don't mind?"

"No." Marie slipped her arm through Sophia's as soon as they were settled on the bench in the shade of a tree. "I came to see you and to find out how you enjoyed last evening."

Sophia's hair was still slightly stiff from the powder, although her maid had removed most of it when she brushed out the curls the night before. The rest would come out that evening when she had a bath. She did not know where to begin and chose the safest remark.

"Camilla and I were thankful to have such pretty habits to wear. We will have them washed and returned to you." She smiled at Marie. "Your parents must have all of their characters carefully organized in readiness for masquerades, particularly if they are able to lend them to other guests as they did with us."

"Yes, they do keep them fairly well sorted. And yours

weren't the only ones that were lent." Marie's face wore a peculiar expression. "We also lent a habit to Mr. Harwood and another to Mr. Edwards. My father wanted me to wear Diana's, and I suspect it was because Mr. Harwood had been given the one of Endymion." She let that sink in before adding, "But as you recall, I encouraged you to be Diana."

Her regard had enough significance that Sophia was prompted to ask faintly, "Why should you do that?"

Marie lifted a brow curiously, pausing before she spoke. "Should I not have? Is there anything you wish to tell me?"

Sophia knew what she meant and grew warm from embarrassment. It was fortunate they were outdoors and would not be disturbed by other members of her family, for it was time to tell Marie the truth. Or, she would have, if her courage had not fled before she could begin. "I...do not know what you mean."

Marie sighed. "I know you don't disclose your heart readily, and I do not wish to force a confidence you're not ready to give. But from what I could observe, you spent a long time talking and dancing with Mr. Harwood last night and"—she lifted her hands with a shrug—"well, I don't know what else to say about that."

Little tremors went through Sophia at the thought of speaking aloud a subject upon which she had kept still for so long, but Marie had given her an opening. She must take it.

"We did dance, but we spoke in riddles, and I am not entirely sure he knew who I was."

Marie laughed and shook Sophia's arm in affectionate exasperation. "Certainly he knew who you were, for I pointed you out to him when you crossed in front of our booth."

Sophia looked at her in shock. "He knew?"

"I made sure he did because I had my own suspicions."

Sophia went quiet, absorbing this revelation, and Marie continued. "I don't know what he said to you, but Mr. Harwood does not seem like the type of man to seek out the company of a woman he has no interest in." She glanced at Sophia. "And you? Do you have interest in him?"

Sophia drew in a shaky breath. "Did you not have a liking for him? You had expressed as much."

Marie faced forward, studying the neat garden, whose parcels of land where grass and trees grew were dissected by gravel paths.

"I did like him. But when we were at Primrose Hill, I was given the distinct impression that his heart was engaged elsewhere. I received no encouragements in my attempts to interest him in conversation. It stung," she admitted, "but I am not one to set my cap after a lost cause."

Sophia tangled her fingers together, attempting to respond with the perfect words. "I am sorry you were hurt, and that he did not return your regard." At this, her friend turned in her seat, a skeptical look in her eyes.

"Are you?" Marie asked sardonically. "Truly? For it seems to me that you have a very *decided* regard for Mr. Harwood, and that you would be very blue if he did not return it. Fortunately for you both, it seems that he does."

As surprising as it was to hear it, her friend's speech was the opening to the floodgate that sent hope pouring into her, and she swallowed hard. It was time for the truth to come out.

"I have had a very decided regard for him for any number of years. Four, to be precise." She dared to lift her eyes and meet Marie's. "He rescued me four years ago in the drawing room of Chawleigh Manor. Robert said something to me…" She pressed her lips together and shook her head. "Something not worth repeating, and I was sunk with embarrassment. Mr. Harwood came and turned everyone's attention away from me. I don't know how he did it, but he managed to defend me, call Robert a boor, and not set up his hackles when he did so." She puzzled her brow and said again, "I don't know how he did it."

Marie's mouth opened in indignation. "Lady Sophia Rowlandson. All this time you have liked him and have not said a word to me! Even when I said that he was handsome and hoped he would turn his eyes my way." She set her hand on Sophia's arm, forcing her to look at her directly.

"You have to *tell* me these things. I believe I am your closest friend. I dare hope so after all these years, and I know you are mine. I don't expect to know everything that is on your heart, for you have never been one to speak before you are ready. But something as big as this? I should have been made aware. I would have stepped aside right from the beginning." She frowned. "It is what friends do."

Sophia knew Marie was right, and suddenly her refusal to disclose something so important seemed shameful. She covered her face with her hands and leaned forward. "I know I should have told you, yet I could not bring myself to do it. I was certain he would like you better than me."

"That is outrageous," Marie protested. "How can you think such a thing?"

Sophia lifted her head to look at her. "The only qualities I have in my favor are my face and my rank. Some might think those the highest qualifications, but a man who is worthy enough to attract my regard would not. He would hope for something much deeper."

Marie did not look convinced. "But you have something much deeper. You are not simply the sum of your face plus your rank. Your heart is worthy and noble; it is time you started valuing yourself with justice."

The words touched Sophia but did not convince her. "He is a member of Parliament and will need a woman who is capable of organizing social gatherings—of speaking to people. That is not me."

"Not every member of Parliament needs such a wife," Marie retorted. "And I am not entirely certain you are as hopeless at organizing events or speaking to people as you seem to think. Give yourself a chance for these skills to be nurtured. Then, you will see what you are capable of."

A silence fell between them, and Sophia looked at her sheepishly. "I'm sorry I didn't tell you."

Marie let out a huff. After a moment, she put her arm around Sophia and squeezed her in an embrace. "It is all right."

She laughed suddenly. "And it might not all be for naught, for having been spurned by Mr. Harwood, I have been forced into the company of Mr. Edwards." Her eyes twinkled when Sophia turned to look at her. "And I am not finding him as uninteresting as I once did."

Marie did not remain at Grosvenor Square for much longer, and Sophia bid her farewell, then took refuge in her room. She stared from her window at the houses opposite on Brook Street, deep in thought about all her friend had revealed. Marie had suspected Sophia's secret, and she had told Mr. Harwood who she was. The implications were astounding. It meant that when he had spoken those words in the magic of the evening, he had known—had known it was her.

The woman I love is strong and able to raise her voice to defend the weak.

...is pure of heart.

She is the one I am destined to love.

And then...

The woman I love has pierced my heart and made me unfit for anyone else.

Until now, she had not permitted herself to dwell on these words because she had convinced herself that they had been spoken about someone else. But now, she knew he had meant them for her. What did that mean? Would he drift back to how things were before? He had never spoken to her directly of courtship. What would he do now? She longed for direct words. *Oh, if only he would put me out of misery and remove all doubt!*

She went over to her desk and pulled out her memento book. Sitting, she turned to a new page and took a pencil. She was about to sketch a row of Chinese lanterns, but instead drew a wherry pulled up against a bank. On the meadow nearby, a picnic sat on a blanket. When she was satisfied with that, she turned the page and sketched the lanterns, then two loo masks. She added a moon and stars and an arrow mid-flight.

A nervous, happy fluttering had taken flight inside. She had never experienced such a thing and couldn't believe it was real. It was almost impossible to sit still. If only he would come to call. Or she could go to Hyde Park in hopes of seeing him there. But then what if he did call, and she missed his visit? Groaning softly, she dropped her head on her arms. The not knowing was as torturous as Diana and Endymion's plight ever was.

CHAPTER 21

After the masquerade, Felix was easily able to dismiss Robert's confrontation from his mind. However, he went over his interlude with Lady Sophia again and again. She had likely fled during the fireworks because she had seen Robert coming, but could he be sure that was the reason? Perhaps she disappeared because he had overstepped the bounds of what was proper, offering words of love cloaked in ambiguity when they were both in disguise. He had thought…he had been sure that she returned his feelings. There had been evidence of it before, and even that night he didn't think his confession was unwelcome. Was her sudden disappearance due only to Robert, or was it her shyness—or him? If it was because she feared Robert, she should have known he would protect her. Unless she believed he had spoken lightly.

His ardent wish was to see Lady Sophia immediately and give relief to his overmastering desire to let her know that *all* of his words had been spoken in great earnest. However, he had the appointment with his solicitor that morning to sign for the house in Russell Square. This project must take precedence, for it directly concerned his future happiness—and hopefully hers. He would need to have a home to welcome a wife.

The signatures did not take long, and when they were finished, Mr. Burbank handed him the key to his new residence. He stared at the heavy iron skeleton key in the palm of his hand, scarcely able to believe that the house belonged to him.

"If you should require a complete furnishing of the house, I have agents who will handle that. You need only let me know your budget and taste."

"I will think on it." He hesitated, for surely his future wife would wish to have a hand in choosing the furnishings. "There are other things I must take care of first."

Mr. Burbank tidied the stack of papers in front of him. "Had we delayed another day in arranging the signatures, this house would have gone to another. There was a gentleman interested who visited the house before you but took his time in deciding to purchase it. He's son to a baron of some means, I am to understand, for he lives on Grosvenor Square. Just yesterday, his solicitor contacted the seller with an offer to buy and had to be told it was too late."

The words "baron's son" and "Grosvenor Square" struck Felix forcibly and trickled through him like dread. The question "Are we speaking of Mr. Robert Cunningworth?" rose to his lips but he clamped them shut. It was unlikely the solicitor would betray the information, and it was better for Felix to remain in ignorance.

Mr. Burbank walked him to the door, and Felix stuck out his hand. "Thank you."

"The pleasure is mine."

Felix set out from Jermyn Street in the direction of Grosvenor Square but, unlike the urgency from that morning, his steps were slow. Where did one begin?

My words at the masquerade were sincere. Oh, and I have bought a house that I hope you will want to live in. Will you marry me?

The more he thought about it, the more awkward it felt to go there with no other aim than to propose without first having been obvious in his intentions. If he had grossly misread her feelings, he would not be able to face himself in the mirror. The pain of her refusal would be heightened by his having bungled his courtship.

A solution of how to approach the matter sprang to his mind, and he seized it. He had promised to assist Lady Sophia in finding Society members for the naval asylum subscription list. In his weeks in the Commons, he had come to learn what the gossips said of who would be amenable to what scheme. If he could secure the name of a hopeful patron, he would have a useful reason for calling on Lady Sophia, and from there he would see where the conversation led. To that end, he flagged a hackney, heading in the opposite direction to Whitehall.

A session had just come to a vote, and members filed into the narrow lobbies to have their "aye" or "nay" counted. Some exited to go into adjoining rooms while others entered the cramped corridor where Felix waited.

Lord Henry, although a traditionalist, was not opposed to reform, and he was the man Felix sought. Second son to a duke, Lord Henry was wealthy, connected, and—more to the point— had a kind and charitably-minded wife. Felix just hoped the MP would be as amicable. The MP pushed past the throng and stepped into view, and Felix went forward to meet him.

"Good afternoon, Lord Henry." He waited until his greeting was returned before asking, "Did you attend the masquerade ball at Vauxhall yesterday?" The MP looked surprised at being approached, and Felix steeled himself to present his agenda despite a rebuff.

"I avoid Vauxhall when I can, even when a duchess reserving a supper box promises a successful event for the *ton*."

Felix smiled feebly. "Understood. It is always something of a gamble in terms of company. Are you headed to the coffee room? Might I walk with you there?" Lord Henry nodded and moved forward. Felix fell into step beside him, twisting his body to avoid bumping into members coming the opposite way.

"I have yet to learn from Admiral Mowbray how the masquerade ball fared, but I am sure you must have heard that the proceeds will be donated to the Royal Naval Asylum."

Lord Henry nodded his greeting to a colleague before answering. "I am aware of it. I am also aware of your interest in the causes of fallen seamen and their families, for Fox has spoken of you. You must be pleased with the notion of a ball being given for charity."

"Indeed I am—and beginning to feel confident that the act for better provisions for seamen will pass. I shall not attempt to convince *you* of your vote, being only a first-year member," he added with a self-deprecating smile. "I am sure there are others more seasoned than I who would have greater success."

Lord Henry laughed. "Wise, for I would only cut you short if you tried. I am looking for a quiet hour to read the newspaper and drink my coffee before heading into another session." They had reached the crowded, smoky coffee shop where gentlemen populated the tables, some engaged in debate and others reading quietly.

"I will not keep you, then. I had only wished to approach you regarding another topic entirely. Would Lady Henry be open to receiving a call from Lady Sophia Rowlandson, sister to the young Earl of Poole? It also regards the asylum, for although the ball proceeds are intended to build a new ward, the asylum still requires subscriptions for beds, as well as coal, food, and textiles."

"I understand your interest in the pension and the ball's proceeds…" Sir Henry scoured him with his keen gaze. "What matter does a visit between the earl's daughter and my wife have to do with you, if I may ask?"

"Why, purely a benevolent one, I assure you." Felix returned a bland smile. He was not going to reveal his true interest. "Miss Edwards, daughter to a board member for the asylum, and Lady Sophia have taken on the task of seeking subscriptions. I am only performing the role of introductions, as I promised to do."

Lord Henry glanced over at a chair that someone was vacating. "Very well. Here is my card. I will let my wife know of Lady Sophia's visit."

Felix nodded. "Thank you."

He went away satisfied with his interview. He had fulfilled his promise, and had a hand in assisting Lady Sophia with the social calls that would be difficult for her. He was confident she would be successful in her ambition, which would remind her of how capable she was. Now, if only he could summon similar courage and present himself to her as a suitor worthy of her acceptance.

He decided first to send off a note to the earl's household, explaining that he had found a lady from the *haute ton* open to receiving Lady Sophia on the subject of the naval asylum, and that if she were not opposed to the idea, he would come calling for her at five o'clock to discuss it. That was—if she was available. If not, she need only leave word with her butler, and he would wait for a more opportune moment. He jotted off another quick note to his father and sister, apologizing for neglecting them and promising to come the next evening for dinner. He wanted to reserve that evening for a visit to his newly purchased house.

Felix brought the notes downstairs and sent them off with a messenger, glancing at the clock as the man left. He had not given her much time to prepare and hoped she would be at home and open to receiving him. Now, he needed to decide how to broach the more delicate subject. Did he propose to her directly? No, that would not do. It would only be right to inform his father first, both about his purchase in Russell Square and his intentions toward Lady Sophia. He supposed he owed Robert a visit regarding Sophia, too. That would not be an easy conversation to have.

Today, I will speak to her of courtship. She must be certain without a doubt of my feelings for her. This would require him laying his prospects at her feet. She would have to know that he could not keep her in the same style to which she was accustomed, but neither would she be reduced to a mean living. If only there was a male relative he could go to and convince of his worth. Lord Poole was a stripling. Did she have a guardian? Surely she must—he would have to ask.

As for how the words of love would come, he did not know. He would have to let his heart lead the way, trusting that he would say all that was necessary.

By the time Felix arrived at Grosvenor Square, he was rigid with nerves and more than relieved when he was admitted into the earl's residence, where he found Lady Sophia ready to receive him. He smiled as soon as he saw her, remembering only belatedly to bow.

"I see you have received my note. The weather is fair. Would you care to take a walk?" She nodded, and as soon as she had put on her bonnet and gloves, he led her outdoors.

Grosvenor Square's flagway was broad and the day beautiful. People strolled along it in different directions, and he offered his arm, enjoying the warmth and intimacy of walking together.

"How have you been? Not too fatigued from the masquerade?" He felt a little tremble go through her and slid his eyes sideways at her heightened color.

"I am not tired," she replied.

"I spoke today to an MP by the name of Lord Henry Ashford, brother to the Duke of Stanley. He is known for having some sympathy for reform, even if he leans conservative. I asked if Lady Henry would be open to receiving a visit from you, for she is famed for her benevolence and is known to be amiable. I thought you might approach her first about a subscription, for she might lead you to others afterward."

"You are too kind. I have hardly dared show my face to Miss Edwards, for I have not even begun seeking donors. The fact that Lady Henry expects my visit will make it much easier."

"I am delighted to be of assistance and am ready to do more, should you wish it. Would you like for me to accompany you to visit Lady Henry?"

She smiled softly but shook her head. "I believe a visit to a lady with whom one is unacquainted is better done by another woman. I will ask either my sister or Marie—or even Miss Edwards, for she knows more about the asylum than I do."

"You are probably right." They were approaching Park Lane, and the sight of its green trees brought him back to the last time he had come to Hyde Park with Lady Sophia, and to the conversation he hoped to have today. His heart began to chug violently in his chest. He waited for a pause in the carriages and horses on the road before leading her to the other side.

The open path under the row of trees would give them the privacy he needed to begin speaking. It would not allow him to take her in his arms as he wished, should his suit prove successful, but he could speak his heart without fear of being overheard. Now...how to begin without oversetting her?

"I asked if you were tired after the masquerade last night, but I did not ask if you enjoyed it."

Lady Sophia was quiet for long enough that he turned to examine her expression. He guessed that his opening had embarrassed her because it demanded she give voice to what he had not yet had the courage to express.

"Perhaps I shall answer my own question first," he said. "I enjoyed it. Very much. In fact, I do not remember ever enjoying any ball as much as that one, for I was paired with the most charming dance partner." Since he hadn't taken his eyes from her, he did not miss her dimpled smile and gaze directed downward. "There was only one thing that cast me into regrettably low spirits."

Her regard swung to his, and he held it. "I was unable to see the face of my masked partner when all was revealed, and I so should have liked to have."

"Why?" she asked quietly.

"Because then she would know the words I had spoken were meant for her." If he kept his voice light, he might not scare her off.

Felix watched emotions flit through her expression, varying like colors in a sunset and sending a delightful hue to her cheeks. He stopped and gently turned her toward him, reaching for her hands to clasp in his. She looked up at him, a tremulous smile on her lips. Lips he meant to kiss as soon as he was given a private opportunity. But first, she must be convinced beyond a doubt of how he felt.

"I must tell you of my esteem—the depth of love I have come to feel for you." Her hands sat lightly in his, but her regard was unwavering, and he knew he had not erred in divining her feelings.

A stray wisp of curled hair flew loose from underneath her bonnet and caught on her lips; he reached up to free it. "Sophia, I—"

"Harwood!"

Sophia's eyes widened in surprise and alarm, and Felix turned to the unwelcome sight of Robert marching toward him, flanked by Tom Perkins. His stomach plunged.

What wretched timing! At last, he was on the point of declaring himself to Sophia, of asking if they could have an understanding, even if it meant a long courtship—as long as she needed. His hope was only half-formed, but he even thought they might go further and commit to a betrothal. If she was as equally lost to the helpless longing he suffered every time they were apart, perhaps she would be ready for it.

Robert's face was mottled with anger. "Sophia, stay away from this man, for he is an imposter!"

She took a step apart from Felix, sending a wave of disappointment through him that she would so easily credit Robert's denunciation.

"Mr. Cunningworth," she began in a tone firmer than he had ever heard from her. "I do not know what you hope to achieve by telling me what I must or must not do. May I remind you that you are not one of my relations, and therefore I do not answer to you. I wish you would abandon the idea that I have any desire to be guided by you."

For Sophia, this was a long speech, and a decisive one. In any other circumstance, Felix would have wished to shout "bravo!" But he was too filled with fury at Robert's innuendo to rejoice in Sophia's courage.

"What do you mean by coming here with these false accusations—"

"Sophia, it matters little whether you wish to hear what I have to say; *my* information is too vital to be withheld. Although Mr. Harwood preaches reform"—Robert now glared at Felix, letting those words ring out a conviction before continuing—"it is only a convenient pretext to achieve a more exalted position and line his pockets. I have proof of his deeds, and what is more, all of London will be in possession of it by tomorrow morning."

Felix was so bewildered by this accusation—the last one he expected, considering that he thought Robert's objection would have to do with Sophia—he had no ready retort. Robert was so sure of this supposed perfidy that he was ready to smear his name? His hands hung helplessly at his side. "Explain yourself."

"Oh, you need have no fear that I won't. Not only am I going to explain myself to you, but I have exposed the facts to the gossip sheets as well. All of Society will know you for the fraud you are."

Felix stared at him, his brain working sluggishly as he tried to understand what could possibly have caused Robert to act in this way. He was vaguely aware that a crowd had gathered to listen, near as they were to Hyde Park's entrance.

"I am still waiting for you to explain exactly what you mean by these ridiculous allegations."

"You preach reform and merit-based appointments," Robert began again, "yet you have been supported by patrons your entire life. My father paid for your schooling and called in favors to get you your first clerical position in Brighton, and you repaid him by casting his aid aside. Not only you, but your *father* owes his living to mine. We shall see if he will still retain it after my father turns the parish against him."

The reference to his father was a blow from the side, and Felix could scarcely comprehend it, but he would not be deterred. "You have said nothing other than what everyone knows. Anyone who wishes to learn that your father owns the advowson to my father's living, or that the baron paid for my schooling, might have the information simply by asking you or me. I have never hidden it, nor have I disguised the fact that my first clerical position was owing to him."

"Astonishing that you will own it, since you are now

preaching merit-based appointments rather than favors in the Admiralty. You refuse to assist my father in the only favor he asked of you in return."

This stung, for there was some truth to it, but Felix had grown in his convictions on this and would not back down.

"You are right that your father connected me with the customs officer who gave me my first position, but you must own that I had the qualifications for that position. He pulled strings so that I might come under the customs officer's notice, but I was perfectly competent to perform the role. And what's more, my career evolution afterward was entirely based on my own performance and not on any other favors."

"You are forgetting the admiral's patronage in purchasing your seat in Parliament."

Felix tightened his fists. This was another half-truth that he was not entirely comfortable with. His only reason for accepting the seat was for the good he could do in Parliament. And he had done nothing illegal; it did not matter that the town of Gatton was so small the admiral easily persuaded the constituents to elect Felix. With the practice so common, not even his father had expressed qualms about it. He glanced from Robert to Perkins, aware all the while of Sophia standing beside him. He shuddered to think of the impression she would have of him.

"Everyone in White's is saying that the admiral simply bought his mouthpiece. He did not wish to enter Parliament himself, so he found someone he could buy off who would spout the same foolish notions he has."

"I am no one's mouthpiece," Felix said firmly. "The words I speak in the Commons are of my own conviction. I sit in Parliament with the aim to serve crown and country, and everything I do or say—every vote I cast—is to that end."

The argument stretched on painfully, but he was forced to

remain for walking away would only make him look guilty. Sophia had remained silent during the exchange. How he wished he could whisk her away and explain that he had done nothing illegal.

"If you are not bought, then how do you explain your sudden influx of money?" Robert demanded with a glance at Perkins, who nodded. "You stole a march on me by buying that house I wanted in Russell Square—and with what funds?"

It had come down to the house. A heaviness settled in Felix's chest, and he wondered if Robert had wanted it for the same reason he did—to take a wife. He had certainly not intended to steal the house directly from Robert and had not even known that a gentleman meeting his description was interested until after he signed. He had simply been the first to put in a formal offer.

"You did not have the funds to purchase that house," Robert went on, "but I know where the money is coming from. The admiral put you in charge of a subscription fund attached to some widows' pension, and you are pocketing a share from each one."

"That is outrageous!"

"Is it? Admiral Mowbray's name appears first on the subscription list. You're collecting subscriptions from unwitting patrons with talk of widows, but it is all for your own ends. And what is worse," he went on ruthlessly, "your father, who appears to be the picture of piety, is now tangled in a will dispute in the Court of Canterbury. You Harwoods are the greatest hypocrites I've ever seen!"

"I've heard enough of this nonsense," Felix said through gritted teeth, his anger only increasing at the sight of Sophia, who had shrunk into herself. Robert's tirade had hit the wrong victim, and her initial signs of courage in standing up to him seemed to have deserted her. "Step aside and allow me to escort Lady Sophia back to her home."

"As Sophia's oldest friend, I will do the honors," Robert retorted.

Sophia took a step back and put up her hands, which to Felix's dismay, were shaking. "I beg you will both excuse me. I see Marie walking with Mr. Edwards, and I will ask her to accompany me."

She did not give either a chance to answer, but hurried over to the park's entrance, where Miss Mowbray saw her approach and paused. Her expression filled with concern, and she put an arm around Sophia as they spoke. Felix had not been able to shield her, and it was the greatest blow. He turned back to Robert.

"Your father might have paid for my schooling, but it does not give you the right to slander my name just because the woman I love does not return your regard. I can only hope you will think better of this day's work." He walked off, valiantly resisting the temptation to punch the man in the nose.

"Slim chance of that," he heard Robert mutter behind him, followed by Perkins's guffaw.

CHAPTER 22

The pain of watching Felix undergo such a battering was almost more than Sophia could bear, but she'd had no intention of leaving his side. However, when both Felix and Robert turned to her and insisted they each be the one to chaperone her home, she feared it would come to a physical fight. The glimpse of Marie approaching the Hyde Park entrance was timely, and it required no reflection to go and seek refuge in her friend's company. Although Mr. Edwards was with Marie, Sophia could not refrain from pouring the story into her ears, aware that Mr. Edwards would learn the whole. But then, she judged, was he not involved in his own way as the admiral's secretary?

She did not believe Robert. Of course, a tiny doubt wanted to make itself heard that she had been mistaken in trusting Felix, but she refused to listen. He had shown himself time and again to be trustworthy and sincere. As soon as Marie was in possession of all the facts, she was indignant on Felix's behalf. Mr. Edwards, too, was concerned and promised to do what he could to clear his name.

Marie and Mr. Edwards put off their pleasure outing to

accompany her home, and there offered to come in and be of support. Sophia shook her head.

"You were about to go walking, and I do not wish to interrupt your plans. Thank you for your company." When it seemed that Marie hesitated, she added, "I believe I need some time alone."

Marie accepted this, promising she would come the next day to see how Sophia did. Meanwhile, Mr. Edwards assured her that he would talk to the admiral, for he would know best how to produce whatever proof was needed to exonerate Mr. Harwood.

As soon as Sophia stepped into the front hall, she heard the door open from the cloak room. Turton approached with quick steps. "Lady Dorothea and Mr. Shaw are in the drawing room with Lord Poole, my lady."

Sophia removed her bonnet slowly, not wishing to face anyone, even family. Perhaps she would simply greet them and explain that she was tired and wished for a short rest in her room until dinner. Before she could take a step, the door opened and Dorothea looked out.

"Sophia, it's you. Come, you are just the person needed."

Mystified, she followed Dorothea into the drawing room, where Evo sat crosswise to Miles, leaning in and explaining something to him with uncharacteristic gravity. As soon as he saw Sophia, he got to his feet. "You'll never guess what mischief Cunningworth has been up to."

To hear Robert's name while still reeling from what had happened was like pressing on a wound. Sophia advanced into the room, her eyes on him. "What is it?"

"He is rounding up accusations against Mr. Harwood because of his jealousy. He wanted to marry you, and apparently you have turned him down. I must say, that is good of you."

"How...how do you know all of this?" Sophia felt like she was wandering through a fog of confusion.

Miles had waited until Sophia was seated before resuming his own, and he now prodded Evo. "Perhaps you had best start with the mischief."

"It has been so dreadfully dull here. I couldn't bear just sitting in the house and kicking my heels, so I've been borrowing the key to Grosvenor Park, or slipping into it when others enter. I found a tree there that I climbed when no one was in sight. I didn't intend to eavesdrop, but the branches hid me perfectly and no one thought to look up. It's how I knew you liked Mr. Harwood, for I heard you tell Marie."

"Everard!" Sophia gasped, horrified, her mind racing back to that conversation as she struggled to remember precisely what she had said. She knew her face was crimson, for she felt it burning in embarrassment.

"I have given him a rare trimming," Dorothea said firmly before gesturing to their brother. "Go on."

"The people who sat on the bench underneath the tree never had any idea I was there." He shook his head. "You should hear some of the things those gudgeons say when trying to woo a lady. It's astonishing they are not repulsed from the outset."

"We were not talking about that," Dorothea said, cutting him short with another reproving look. Then she turned to address Sophia. "As reprehensible as Evo's actions are, he has provided us with some invaluable insight in this instance. He wasted no time in sending off a note for Miles and me to come. Tell her."

"I climbed the tree again this morning and was trying to see if I could drop twigs and hit my target without people looking up to see where it had come from. Cunningworth walked by with that chap Perkins. And there was another fellow with him whose name I don't know. They stopped under the tree to blow a cloud—"

"Mind your speech," Dorothea said gently.

"It was good they stopped, so I could hear what they said," he went on, ignoring the interruption. "Cunningworth began by saying that he had never been more shocked in his life when some fellow at White's declared that Harwood was accepting bribe money. The other fellow under the tree—not Perkins—said he guessed it was nothing more than idle gossip. But Robert said it could not be. That he'd had his eyes set on purchasing a house in Russell Square, and that Harwood, who should not have had the money, purchased it from under his nose."

"Perhaps he has an inheritance we know nothing about," Sophia said. Her defense was automatic, but her heart was torn between pleasure that he should be in the position to purchase a house and fears that what Robert said was true.

"The other fellow said the same—Grantly, I think Perkins called him. He doesn't appear to view Harwood as a villain. But Cunningworth would have nothing to do with it. Said that he had bewitched you"—Evo brought his eyes to Sophia—"so that you would not hear his suit. That even Harwood's father was involved in scandal. Said he was going to ruin the family, but I like Harwood better than I could ever like Robert."

Miles exchanged a glance with Dorothea, and she swiveled in her chair to face Sophia. "This is the first we are hearing of your confession to Marie," she began with delicacy. "But after sending us a note to come, Evo did seem to think there might be some understanding between you and Mr. Harwood. I do not wish to pry, but is there anything you wish to tell us on the matter?"

Sophia went still as she thought carefully. Did she tell everyone assembled that she loved Felix? No, she could not do so, nor did they have an understanding. Or, at least, even if they were about to have one, he had not been able to finish his sentence.

"I esteem Mr. Harwood. I don't believe he would do any of the things he was accused of. If there is any way we might clear his name, I am in support of it."

Miles nodded with a look that declared him satisfied. "I will speak to Rock. He has more sway than I ever will, particularly in the Lords, where Lord Chawleigh has a seat. Perhaps he can find out more on the matter, but he can definitely spread seeds of truth until they take root."

"Thank you." Sophia clasped her hands, then glanced at Evo, who was examining the toes of his boots. "And thank you," she added, causing him to look up at her in surprise. "Despite your reprehensible behavior, which I *do* hope you will grow out of...I'm glad that you wish to defend Mr. Harwood. I believe him to be an honorable man."

"At least he does not prose on at a fellow," the earl replied.

After his confrontation with Robert, Felix abandoned the idea of visiting his newly purchased house and retired to his rented rooms. Rather than celebrating his hoped-for victory of having laid claim to Sophia's heart, he was in his rooms licking his wounds. He was far from easy about Robert's threat of having sent his so-called proof to the gossip sheets. Felix would face backlash in Society over these rumors, even if they were not true. His only consolation was that his own behavior was above reproach.

However, knowing he was free from blame did not heal the letdown of having been obliged to watch Sophia leave without first being able to convince her of his innocence. The episode had affected her, so he did not impose his continued presence upon her. Nor could he go to her now, as much as he longed to; he had to clear his name first. That night, he was in no position to do so. He would need to evaluate the fallout from the gossip sheets and the precise nature of what he was facing.

The next day he went to the public dining room, where he picked up a copy of the *Morning Post* and sat down to face the worst. Was he imagining it or were people staring at him? He flipped to the last page and skimmed the paragraphs until he found the one he had hoped not to see.

A certain youthful member of Parliament has lately acquired his seat through the persuasion of a certain reform-minded admiral. Lauded a rising star in the Ministry of All the Talents, he delivers affecting speeches on the need for merit-based appointments and support for widows of seamen who have taken part in the recent heroic action in Spain. However, one cannot be convinced that all of his efforts are disinterested, for his recent displays of wealth foil such naivete. Let us hope that the money collected will reach its proper objects...

The blood drained out of Felix's face as he set the newspaper down. It was worse than he could have imagined. Why, even last week, he had spoken about the widows' petitions in a committee, promising to bring them to the House that very week. No one would believe him now. The noise around him became an incomprehensible din, and he recognized the laughter and whispers directed his way.

He had to leave here. The only thing he could think to do was to visit his father, though he had told him and Megs he would come for dinner. Felix stood, just as a servant approached, carrying a letter.

"This has just arrived for you, sir."

"Thank you." Felix glanced down and saw that the seal

belonged to Lord Chawleigh and resigned himself to the inevitable. He slit the seal and spread open the papers.

Harwood—

You will not be surprised to hear from me. Robert has told me all that you are involved in, which he himself heard at White's. I now better understand why you did not wish to help him. You were too busy helping yourself. I must say that I am heartily disappointed after all I have invested in your family that we should be repaid in such a manner. I cannot force your father from his living, but I am no longer complacent about his holding it. I will do everything in my power to dissuade him from remaining. And should he be so stubborn as to ignore my wishes, I shall make it so uncomfortable for him that he will spend his years there in misery. You may be assured of it, for those who try to make a fool of me will not succeed.

Chawleigh

The letter did not surprise Felix, but it succeeded in making him feel worse. There was nothing for it but to go to Searle Street and hope his father and sister were home. He regretted that he would not be good company to Megs, but there was nothing he could do about it. For once, he was in need of their presence and the deep family ties, a balm against the wound he had just suffered.

CHAPTER 23

Margaret opened the door to Felix's knock, smiling broadly, and pulled him by the arm into their house, not seeming to notice that anything was amiss.

"We received your note and expected you for dinner. I am glad you have come early, for I must tell you that I'm feeling quite abandoned! I had not thought you so important as to neglect your own sister who is visiting London, without any other acquaintances or means to amuse herself."

She brought him into the parlor and turned to him, but her smile fell when she saw his face. "What is it, Felix?"

"Is Father here?"

"I expect him at any moment."

The sound of the key in the lock gave Felix his answer. Mr. Harwood walked in, looking weary, but he smiled when he saw Felix. "You have come early. Margaret, will you see to some tea?"

"Yes, Father," she said, but Felix stopped her.

"Don't go for tea yet, I have something to say, and Megs, you should hear it, too."

Their father went still, eyeing Felix, then gestured to the sofa. "Let us sit, then."

They sat facing each other in the comfortable chairs of their rented parlor, and Felix scarcely knew how to begin. He was generally of a cheerful disposition, and this hopelessness—this heaviness—was a first.

"I have not had a chance to tell you, or rather I have not dared to tell you." He smiled feebly. "But I have used half of my inheritance to purchase a house in Russell Square."

Their father absorbed this in silence for a long moment before returning a cautious answer. "It was quickly done, son, but the money was *yours*, and I suppose you must have a house of your own. I had thought that maybe in Sussex..." He let the reflection dangle, but what was done was done.

Felix continued, prey to the feeling that he was climbing a steep hill, each confession harder to make than the last. "I had hopes for Lady Sophia Rowlandson, sister to the Earl of Poole and Lord Chawleigh's neighbor. I do not believe her indifferent to me and had planned to ask for her hand in marriage."

"Oh, Felix," Margaret said, her eyes shining. "I do like her."

Their father studied Felix's expression and appeared to read what was there. "I fear you mean to tell us your efforts were not successful. It is not the moment to remind you of the warning I gave you, so I shall not do that."

Although his father's expression had softened, Felix still felt the reproach in his words—and the injustice in them.

"I would not refrain from speaking to her of my feelings, not for any filial respect I might feel toward you, Father. My feelings could not be suppressed, and I was—am—certain that she returns them. Besides, as owner of a respectable house, and with both annual salary and honorable position to my name, I did not wish to deprive either her or myself of a life of happiness simply out of consideration of a difference in station."

"But she said no?" Meg guessed softly, looking at him.

Felix sighed. "I believe she would have said yes, but we were interrupted. Robert Cunningworth somehow tracked me down and spouted off all sorts of false claims about me in front of her. He called me a hypocrite for preaching reform while living off of two patrons—Lord Chawleigh in my early years and then more recently, the admiral."

"There is nothing in it that he didn't know before." Mr. Harwood furrowed his brows, likely wishing to understand Robert's aim in hurting Felix—especially since he had treated Robert as a son while he boarded with them.

"He created conclusions built on the faulty knowledge he had. He accused the admiral of having bought my compliance, saying that my ideas for reform were not my own. The admiral's secretary has been collecting petitions on the behalf of widows for me to bring before Parliament, and a subscription fund has been started to relieve their greatest needs. He has confounded the two, claiming I am pocketing money for favors given."

Bitterness rose up in Felix as he thought of it. "And he has accused me of using that money to purchase the house in Bloomsbury. Except for a direct mention of Russell Square, it's all in the gossip sheets.

"On—" Felix reached into his waistcoat pocket and pulled out the letter from the baron. "Father, forgive me, but this came from Lord Chawleigh today. It appears the false accusations are to extend to you."

He handed the letter over and waited while his father skimmed its brief contents. Margaret was pale-faced, watching their father. He was sorry to bring her into this as well, but she was old enough not to be shielded from what was to be a family trial. They would need to face it together.

Their father folded the letter and leaned back in his chair. He steepled his hands and lifted his eyes to the ceiling as he often did when he was thinking. "It appears he means to subjugate me by removing his favor."

"Robert also mentioned something about this when he confronted me. But I don't see what the baron could do."

Mr. Harwood brought his eyes to Felix, then to Margaret. "He could be slow in paying my tithes and refuse repairs on the house that were promised. And he could suggest to the more influential members of the parish that I am not to be trusted."

"How could he do something so cruel?" Margaret demanded. "And there is no truth to these claims!"

A faint smile appeared on their father's face. "Although I know I need not defend myself to either of you, allow me to reassure you that Mr. Thurlow engaged me to be the executor of his will with the full consent of his heirs. My coming to London for probate had nothing to do with any question of my meddling in his inheritance for my own gains. I was required to come because he has property in more than one diocese. For these matters, it is necessary for the executor to come and present the will in person."

"I believe you, Father," Margaret said hotly.

"Indeed, I did not need your reasons for coming to London," Felix assured him. "It was just to inform you of what can only affect us all."

After another short silence, it occurred to Felix that he ought to clear his own name as well.

"I hope I need not say that all of these accusations against me are false, as well. You knew of the baron's support in those early years and his leading me to a clerical position in Brighton. As you requested, I continued to show Lord Chawleigh every sign of respect and do what I could for him, short of going against my own conscience. The admiral has not given me any money, other than what is expected to gain a seat. He and I think alike on reform, and that is why I am representing Gatton. It is not for financial gain."

"We know that, Felix." Margaret's eyes still flashed in indignation that her father and brother could be accused of such falsehoods, and Felix felt an outpouring of affection for her.

"Nor did I need your justification in order to believe you," Mr. Harwood stated.

"Robert has created his accusation out of partial truths. Regarding the subscription fund for widows, Admiral Mowbray was the first to put his name on the list, a fact I suppose was easy to distort. It seems Cunningworth has mixed the two up, ignoring certain facts and condemning me for both."

"That is very, very wrong of him," Margaret said indignantly. "I hope he will repent of this slander." She turned to their father. "What can we do now?"

Mr. Harwood was not a man to rush his words, and he took his time before answering.

"I had not thought we would ever move. I am loath to leave your mother's final resting place and start over elsewhere, but perhaps it is time. I met an old Oxford peer at Doctors' Commons, and he offered to recommend me for a very comfortable living in Kent."

"Oh!" Margaret's eyes went wide.

"I told him I would think on it, but I had not seriously intended to take it. I am attached to my parish and to Sussex, and have never had any desire to uproot my family." He laughed softly. "But perhaps this is a sign from Providence. I only hope Caro, Anne, and Mary will not be too overset by the change."

"I think my sisters will look upon it as an adventure," Margaret said with a firmness that showed her growing confidence. "As for myself, I can only think that moving closer to Felix would turn into a happy advantage for us all." She smiled at him.

"Then I will think about it some more and seek out Mr. Blackwood tomorrow." There was warmth in Mr. Harwood's regard when he turned it to Felix. "And what is your plan to be?"

Felix was too weary to think. "Tonight, I shall dine with you. And then tomorrow, I believe I should pay a visit to the admiral and bring the petitions and attached subscriptions to the Commons as proof. I will have to defend my honor."

THE NEXT DAY, Marie came as promised and informed Sophia that her father and Mr. Edwards believed that the gossips were up to mischief and that there was no basis to their claims. They were either purposefully misreading—or accidentally confounding—the subscription fund attached to the widows' petitions, turning it into one where Mr. Harwood funneled the money into his own coffers. But such an offense was not easily done, not without risking exposure and banishment, besides the fact that neither of them thought Mr. Harwood to be such a man. As to the house he had purchased in Russell Square, her father knew nothing of it but vowed not to have given Mr. Harwood a farthing more than what was needed for his seat.

"Certainly he did not," Sophia said. "Even if I do not know Mr. Harwood as well as I do your father, I cannot be convinced that either of them could participate in something so self-seeking."

"And Bartholomew"—Marie looked self-conscious—"Mr. Edwards, rather, has promised to put together all the documentation needed to exonerate Mr. Harwood, so he might present it in the Commons."

"It is good of him. I am very glad to hear it." Sophia was beginning to feel hopeful again. "Thank you, Marie."

Her friend hugged her and did not stay long after that. She had an appointment to meet Miss Edwards to apprise her of the news.

When she was alone, Sophia attempted to calm her mind, but the silence did not sit with her. She wanted to do something to help. The recollection of Felix's mentioning Lady Henry came back to her, this small piece of information having been forgotten among all the rest of what had happened the day before. Even if she had no certain idea of how Lady Henry could assist her on Mr. Harwood's behalf, she would at least be doing something good for the asylum. And she had to do something —anything—that was within her power. It was intolerable to sit and do nothing.

She sought out Turton. "Have a footman discover where Lord Henry Ashford lives, and then have the carriage readied. I must pay a call on his wife, Lady Henry."

"Very well, Lady Sophia." The butler went to do her bidding while she went upstairs and called for Margery to come and help her change into her best morning gown.

The groom was ready to set out within the hour, and Sophia mounted the carriage with her maid. What had seemed impossible before—the idea of paying a call on a woman with whom she was unacquainted to request an annual subscription for charity—suddenly seemed insignificant compared to what Mr. Harwood was going through.

She scarcely spoke on the way there, and when they reached Cavendish Square, George One helped her to alight. She stared up at the front door, her throat suddenly dry. There was nothing for it but to carry out her mission. Trailed by her maid, Sophia moved forward with purpose and presented her card to the footman there, who returned with the pleasing news that Lady Henry would receive her.

The footman indicated for Margery to follow one of their

maids to the servants' quarters, then turned to Sophia. "If you will follow me, my lady?"

Heart beating erratically in her chest, Sophia followed him up the stairs, and when she was led into Lady Henry's drawing room, discovered that there were other visitors. At the sight of two older unknown women of status, her courage failed her. She had not envisioned that she might need to make her request in front of an audience.

"Lady Sophia, please do come in." Lady Henry advanced to greet her, smiling warmly as she ushered her to a seat. "You have fabulous timing, for we have just had the tea set out and my cook is an expert at making scones. Allow me to introduce you to Mrs. Wright and Lady Lockwood."

"A pleasure," Sophia murmured, dipping into a curtsy.

"And this," Lady Henry continued, addressing her other visitors, "is Lady Sophia Rowlandson, sister to the fifth Earl of Poole. I have been expecting her visit on the subject of the Royal Naval Asylum."

Sophia was heartened by these words and was further reassured when Mrs. Wright said, "I am acquainted with Lady Dorothea. As you must know, she is a particular friend of Anne Kensington, who has recently become betrothed to my youngest brother."

"I had not heard, but I am very happy for her," Sophia managed.

"Oh, it is of a recent date. I believe it was only announced in this morning's paper." Mrs. Wright accepted a cup of tea from a servant.

"How do you take your tea, Lady Sophia?"

"With milk and sugar, if you please."

Lady Henry lifted her finger and had the maid prepare the tea, waiting until everyone had been served a cup and her cook's famous scones.

After a proper pause to allow everyone to enjoy their refreshments, the mistress of the house turned to Sophia. "Although I believe I know the purpose of your visit, perhaps you might enlighten the other ladies."

Sophia's hands trembled, and she set her cup down before she spilled her tea.

"I have come to ask for support for the Royal Naval Asylum. I am friends with Miss Mowbray, whose father is the Admiral Mowbray, and he has a keen interest in the widows and children of seamen who have perished in the line of duty."

Her heart hammered in her chest. "I was wondering—that is, I was hoping you might be prevailed upon to make a donation to the cause? It can be in one sum, or perhaps an annual subscription to provide for the needs of one orphan being trained in the asylum? In that case, his bed would be known as 'Lady Henry's bed' as a thanks for your generosity."

"Have you agreed to an annual subscription?" Lady Lockwood asked curiously.

Sophia had not even thought of offering a subscription herself. She scarcely viewed her money as her own and never requested it as she had few needs. But naturally she must and would do that, and answered honestly.

"I had not thought of it, but I would like to. I must speak to my uncle, who is our guardian, for I can think of no worthier cause."

Lady Henry set her teacup down and clasped her hands decisively. "I will honor your request and give an annual subscription." Her twinkling eyes made her look younger. "Mr. Harwood was right to approach my husband, for I find it difficult to say no."

Sophia smiled. "I believe Mr. Harwood approached your husband because you were known to be both benevolent and kind, not because you are easy prey."

"Mr. Harwood!" Lady Lockwood raised an eyebrow. "I was at Mrs. Simpkin's house earlier today, and it appears your Mr. Harwood is guilty of pocketing the proceeds from other subscriptions for widows' relief. As he manages the funds himself, it is not difficult to dip into the coffers for his own use. I am not sure it serves your cause to align yourself with such a man."

"Mr. Harwood was wrongly accused," Sophia said with surety, before she could even measure her words. She felt their combined regard and the embarrassment from having spoken out.

"How do you know this?" Lady Henry asked gently.

"I have had time to come to know him," she replied, stopping short as she realized even this confession gave away more than she could wish. "My friend's father, the Admiral Mowbray, has assisted Mr. Harwood in gaining his seat in the Commons. The admiral is an honorable gentleman and will not be corrupted. The same is true of Mr. Harwood."

"Such rumors are rarely founded on complete innocence," Lady Lockwood maintained, clearly unconvinced.

Sophia was quiet for a moment, wondering whether she could truly convince these women of Felix's innocence. Although it was difficult to speak of, there was one argument that would clear his name.

"I...it is just that the person spreading the rumors is not unknown to me," she said. "I believe he is motivated by jealousy."

"Jealousy over what?" Lady Lockwood said, but Sophia would not answer that.

"I only know that in this case Mr. Harwood's name has been wrongly dragged through the mud, and I believe the truth will come out."

Lady Henry nodded. "We shall see."

CHAPTER 24

The next day, Felix left the admiral's house, strengthened in his resolve to confront the gossip head-on. Mr. Edwards had drawn up a list of all the expenses the admiral had incurred on his behalf and handed this to Felix, along with the widows' petitions, and the subscription list with the corresponding amounts.

A junior member did not generally seek to call attention to himself, but once rumor reached the gossip sheets, it became too important to ignore. Not only did it risk Felix's personal reputation and all he hoped to share with Lady Sophia, but it discredited the actual reform they were trying to bring about.

When he reached Westminster, his heart was pounding. He entered St. Stephen's Chapel and was unsurprised by the mix of reactions he received there. Many ignored him in the smoky, crowded bustle. One or two openly snubbed him, which he did not take to heart because he was still building his connections in the Commons and scarcely knew them. But the occasional whispers and snide remarks that caught his ears stung. Foreign Secretary Charles James Fox entered the fray from the corridor leading to the rooms where the clerks sat. He stopped short when he saw him, and Felix braced himself as he strode forward to meet him.

"Harwood, I take it you mean to address the House today about what I am guessing is a piece of nonsense?"

"Yes, sir," Felix said. "You will have seen the gossip sheets, and I mean to expose them for fraud. It is a distraction from what we are trying to achieve. You may be assured that I have the widows' petitions here as proof, along with the complete list of patrons for the subscription fund and their pledged amounts, which line up with the expenditures."

Fox clasped him on the arm. "Then let your voice be heard so we might put this matter behind us. Using your voice for the widows is the only shield you need for your name."

Heartened by this support from so senior a member, Felix took his place on the benches and waited until the Speaker brought up the order of the day. He listened to the matters put forth, waiting for the widows' pensions to be announced. When it came time, he caught the Speaker's eye and was acknowledged.

Felix stood and bowed to the Speaker, then looked around at the august members of Parliament, pausing until the ripple of murmured comments ceased.

"Gentlemen, I beg a moment of your time in which to present three petitions from the widows of seamen who request adequate pensions after their husbands perished in the line of duty for the crown." There was a swell of murmured remarks, and he raised his voice. "Before I speak on the matter at hand, I feel compelled to address a recent scandal attached to my name. You will not be unaware of the similarities of the paragraph inserted into the *Morning Post* and my own situation."

He held up the offending newspaper. "This speaks of a

young member preaching reform while pocketing proceeds from the subscription fund set up for the widows, also on a petition list—a subscription list which contained the prominent name of Admiral Mowbray, who purchased my seat. I need not go on," he added wryly.

In his other hand, he held the petitions and lifted those for everyone to see. "I have for you petitions signed by widows in Exeter, Plymouth, and Dover, which I will hand to the Speaker presently. Attached to these lists are subscription funds managed by clergymen in each of those towns, whose names are also noted. I have no access to these funds, nor have I received anything in exchange for presenting these petitions.

"The attention given to these false claims should be brought instead to bear on a worthier cause. That is, why should only the families of officers be well compensated for their service? Is the loss of ordinary seamen less valuable?"

He allowed that remark to sink in before lifting his voice again above the murmur of speech that spread throughout the House. "It is true that the Admiral Mowbray assisted in my winning a seat to Parliament. Those who know him personally will know he is not a man to be corrupted. You may not know me as well, but you soon will.

"My interest in reform is pure. Yes, the admiral ensured my election to Gatton, but I am not his mouthpiece. The reform I push for comes from my own desires and experiences."

Suddenly, the memory of all he had seen flashed before his eyes, lending strength to his speech. "When I served in the yeomanry in Brighton, I saw the sailors who came back maimed reduced to begging on the street. I witnessed widows and children seeking alms because they no longer had support sent from their husbands or fathers, who had died at sea.

"*These* issues motivate me, not money. So I beg you will receive the widows' petitions and consider them with the respect due to any living soul. These widows ask only that their request for adequate pensions be heard. Attached to the petitions are the subscription lists of private individuals who contribute to their needs until such a time that Parliament will vote on this worthy legislation. The names will speak for themselves of Society's support for the act."

"You may bring them down and we will read it," the Speaker said in a bored voice with a wave of his hand. Felix wove through the benches and brought it to him, then retook his seat, relieved that he had been given the chance to set the record straight.

It had not been a rousing speech, and was met with only polite applause, but he was not a performer. He simply cared that what he was trying to bring about would succeed. The proceedings passed on to other petitions, and Felix was thankful to have the attention off him once again.

When the Speaker declared the House adjourned, Felix wove his way to the floor, prepared to leave. He was intercepted by Lord Henry.

"Fine speech, Harwood. You almost persuade me to cast my own vote for an increase in pensions."

"I will certainly not dissuade you from doing so," Felix replied with a smile. If Lord Henry was still willing to speak to him, things could not be as bad as he feared. Perhaps he might even retain his seat, something he had hardly dared to hope for.

"My wife received a visit from Lady Sophia yesterday." At her name, Felix went still, straining above the noise in the hall to hear the rest. "Lady Henry has offered to give an annual subscription to the asylum, along with Mrs. Wright and Lady Lockwood, who both happened to be visiting at the time. I thought you might wish to know."

Sophia had summoned the courage to visit Lady Henry? And had applied not just to Lady Henry but to two other women? What was more, she had trusted a recommendation from Felix. He smiled more broadly than was warranted, saying, "I thank your wife for her generous contribution."

Lord Henry studied him for a moment, a wry smile on his lips. "Apparently, she defended your honor while there, assuring the women you could not be corrupted and that the gossip sheets were wrong. My wife assured me that if such a gentle spirit as Lady Sophia could speak so determinedly on your behalf, the claims must be false. And I trust my wife," Lord Henry added.

Touched, Felix could only bow. "Thank you."

As he left Westminster, Felix was conscious of the change that had come over him. He had gone from feeling that all was without hope, impossible to surmount—that he could not approach Lady Sophia, much less offer her his heart and hand—to feeling as though this impossible heaviness had been swept away like dust on a cloud. Suddenly, there were possibilities again. He had not perfectly cleared his record. He supposed such a thing must come with time, as people saw there was no substance to the rumors and the malicious talk died down for lack of fuel. And perhaps, he was in no position to propose marriage to Lady Sophia *now* when all of this was still so uncertain.

But the winds had brought hope, and his feet moved of their own accord, seeking the first hackney he could flag down to bring him to Grosvenor Square. When he arrived at the earl's house and knocked on a front door that was becoming familiar to him, he received the gratifying news that Lady Sophia was home and would receive him.

He was shown into the drawing room, and as he was too nervous to sit, went over to the window that faced the park. He stood there with his hands behind his back, wondering how a man such as he might dare approach a woman such as Sophia, then decided that it did not matter. What mattered was that he loved her. He loved her—and at long last he would discover if she loved him in return.

TREMBLING with happiness and nerves at the thought of seeing Felix again, Sophia slipped through the door into the drawing room. He turned, and their eyes held across the room. She offered him a shy smile, which he returned, as she went to him. He stepped away from the window and reached for her hands, lifting them to his lips.

Sophia spoke first. "How are you?"

He retained her hands in his clasp. "I am well. I am better now that I am with you."

A look of tenderness came into his eyes as he added, "I learned from Lord Henry that you successfully applied to three Society women for a subscription in one visit—and that you also gave me the courtesy of believing me without having proof of my innocence."

"Well, I know Robert—Mr. Cunningworth. And I feel I have come to know you." She plunged ahead, despite the boldness of her words. "Your character does not lend itself to duplicity, Felix." The name had slipped out involuntarily, and she felt the accompanying flush of embarrassment as soon as it reached her own ears.

He smiled broadly. "I cannot tell you how much I enjoy hearing my name on your lips, Sophia."

She bit her lip and glanced down at their joined hands until she had recovered her composure. Allowing her hands to rest in Felix's felt both intensely personal and just right. She brought her gaze up to his.

"You are all that is honorable. I have thought so from the

first time you defended me all those years ago, and I think so today." He rubbed his thumb over hers, causing her breath to dissipate like a puff.

"Had I known that day that you would remember such a small service... There are a great many services I hope to perform for you if I am allowed."

Sophia inhaled, swept along by an overpowering wave of excitement and nerves. *My dream is coming true!* She wanted to tell him that she had loved him since that day in the Chawleigh's drawing room, but she was too nervous. Her beleaguered mind leapt in an entirely different direction.

"My brother, Evo, overheard Robert threatening to bring about your downfall. It seems Mr. Grantly attempted to defend you, but Mr. Perkins encouraged him in it. And our butler was the one who informed Mr. Cunningworth where I had gone. He is not unknown to Turton, you see." She was speaking nonsense. He needed to know this, but not at this precise moment.

"Ah. I had wondered how he knew where to find me—or you, I suppose." Felix straightened his lips. "Robert is jealous. And that trait, combined with being used to getting what he wants, has led him to this unfortunate act of spite. I only hope he will think better of it and turn his life in a different direction."

"I hope so, too," she said softly. A silence fell between them, and the air grew thick with all she wanted to say, all that was bottled up inside. She took a breath.

"I have always loved you."

"Sophia, will you marry me?"

They had spoken at the same time, and it took a moment for his words to penetrate. They had been breathless and rushed, and she wondered if he had planned on asking her. Her eyes grew wide, and she watched his smile grow as her words reached him.

"You have always loved me?" he asked, his voice infused with doubt, but hope and delight, too.

"Since the day I first met you, yes." She nodded, as though to add strength to her statement. And then because he had not repeated himself, and because she wanted to be entirely sure she had heard him, "You want to marry me?"

"Desperately." He briefly tightened his hold as if to punctuate the word. "I know it is not quite the thing to propose to a woman without having disclosed the state of my own affairs, but if you will inform me of your guardian's name and direction, I will contact him."

"I..." She did not know how to respond. Should she say yes to his proposal or give him her uncle's name and direction?

He let out a soft groan. "This isn't going at all as it should. I'm nervous," he confessed. "But I love you, Sophia. And if you will allow me the privilege of doing so, I will cherish you for the rest of my life."

"You love *me*?"

"Yes," he said as though it were evident. He released her hands to caress her cheek and whispered with a lopsided smile, "Goose."

This made her laugh in happiness—and release of all she was feeling. Her eyes were fixed at some point around his mouth, and she lifted them to his, hoping he would ask her again in a way she could answer.

"Sophia, before you give me your answer, allow me to tell you of the bargain you'll be getting in me." His voice was self-effacing and humorous, sincere.

"I promise to see that you have every comfort I can possibly give you. As you now know, I do have a house. To own the truth, I bought it with you in mind, for I could not offer for you without having a home to bring you to. I am hoping you will like it."

He paused and she nodded for him to go on. "Although I think you will have a comfortable life with me, I cannot offer you *all* of the elegancies to which you are accustomed. But I can offer you every elegance of heart. Faithfulness, protection, esteem…passion." His whispered last word sent a shiver through her, and he paused, allowing the stretch of time to carry the significance of his next words. "Will you make me the happiest man alive and agree to become my wife?"

Those elegancies he spoke of were what Sophia treasured most, and she needed no reflection to give her answer.

"Yes, Felix. I will marry you."

His face split into a smile so encompassing it reached his eyes. "I will make you happy. I promise it."

How in the world could one fit so much happiness inside one body, Sophia wondered? She could not say another word but nodded and smiled as broadly as he did.

The clock struck the hour with a loud chime, and he bent down and kissed her. It was a simple kiss, but its effect was just as sweeping as the happiness had been. In kissing him back, she was engulfed with a different kind of sensation.

Love. She was in love. The way his hands cradled her cheeks as he continued to kiss her told her of his love, and the gentleness of his lips on hers showed how much he treasured her. And despite the tenderness, she was beginning to understand just what he meant by *passion*.

Sophia's hands were on his chest, and she had the sudden urge to rise up on her tiptoes and kiss him back just as passionately. She did so, and he dropped his hands from her face and seized her around the waist—

The door to the drawing room slammed open behind them, causing them both to leap apart. Before Sophia could decide if she should feel guilty or indignant at the interruption, Evo's voice rang out.

"Ugh. Now I have to witness kissing in the drawing room. Harwood, I will listen to your petition for my sister's hand, but this I won't have. All kissing will have to be done in your own house."

EPILOGUE

Sophia encouraged Felix to speak to Dorry's husband before approaching her uncle regarding the marriage settlements. Miles was accustomed to the matter, having had to discuss terms when he wished to marry Dorothea. For a guardian, Lady Poole's brother was absent much of the time, but when he wished to, he could be particular. Sophia did not want Felix to be bullied for not having a living her uncle might think indispensable. Miles would understand, for although his own situation had vastly improved by the time he offered Dorothea his hand in marriage, he was sensible of what it was to negotiate from an inferior position.

The terms were agreed upon, and the wedding was set for July. Both Sophia and Felix were eager to tie the knot as soon as possible, but there were many things that needed to be handled first. For one thing, Felix wished to see that his name was fully cleared before Sophia tied hers to it. She had no doubt that it would be, but he insisted on being above reproach. His father had accepted another living that would put him under a friendlier patronage in Kent and would need to move. To everyone's surprise, the patron of the living was none other than Lord

Pembroke, Miles's cousin, though he had not known of the connection when he had accepted Mr. Blackwood's recommendation.

Sophia had a delightful time coming to know Margaret—Megs, Megabits, whichever name Felix happened to bestow upon her in the moment—before she returned to her younger sisters. Sophia promised to come and meet all of them as soon as she and Felix had returned from their honeymoon, a plan to which Margaret gave her wholehearted approval.

After all they had shared in their years growing up, Sophia almost thought Robert might offer Felix an apology, but Felix informed her that he had received none. Instead, Robert appeared to have dug down in his belief, for he avoided him in Society. Fortunately, they frequented different clubs and did not often cross paths. Robert, therefore, would be responsible for his own misery, but he did not affect their happiness in the least.

Felix had not considered Tom Perkins a close friend and was unsurprised when he followed Robert's direction. However, Grantly surprised him by offering an olive branch in the way of sitting down with him at a coffee shop and speaking to him as easily as if there had never been any disagreement. He was assisting Miss Edwards with some of her work in the naval asylum and thought he might try his hand at obtaining a clerical position at the Admiralty. He rushed on to assure Felix that he was not asking for a favor and would find his own way. If, as Felix suspected, Miss Edwards had managed to wiggle through Grantly's usual antipathy toward women, they would all be seeing more of each other.

Marie and Mr. Edwards announced their own engagement shortly after Felix and Sophia, and the two couples were often in company. Felix asked Bartholomew if he would stand up for him at his wedding, having no close male relations, and was gratified to hear that he would. So all that was left for Sophia and Felix to arrange was the matter of decorating their house, a subject they did not easily tire of and which required many visits to the house they were to occupy in Russell Square.

On this particular day, Camilla and Lady Poole were discussing the proper way the new furniture should be arranged in the drawing room, while Tilly and Joanna were running through the empty rooms in a manner that was wholly unladylike but which no one corrected. Evo had gone back to school but would return in time for their wedding, which was to be held in Surrey. And Dorothea and Miles had just arrived in time to listen to Camilla's complaint that it was most annoying to have the seats so far from one another that one had to shout to be heard. This caused their debates about furniture placement to break out once again.

Felix came to stand next to Sophia and discreetly slid his hand into hers. She stayed there for a moment, enjoying the feeling of having him so close. They listened to the discussion with half-an-ear but did not participate.

He released her hand and folded his arms as he leaned. "We might display your memento book right above the fireplace." He had been delighted to learn about its existence and bemoaned that Robert had never returned her silhouette so he might add to it.

She pursed her lips and lifted her chin. "The memento book will remain firmly stashed in my wardrobe."

"Mm-hm." He listened for another beat, then said, "We can always move the furniture after everyone has established it to their liking."

She covered her silent laughter.

"After all, the only one whose opinion matters is yours. You see how wholly I am under your power," he continued, his words coming softly to her ear.

"Are you?" She turned and raised an eyebrow playfully. "I have fully snared you, then, have I?"

"Yes, you've caught me in your net," he replied with playful mockery. A wide grin spread across his face. "I will call you "Sophia-net.'"

Her lips twitched, but she repressed a smile. "I am not sure I approve of you calling me a net."

"Sophia-web?"

"Even worse!" she said, finding it hard to keep a straight face.

Felix sighed as he linked his fingers through hers. "I suppose I shall just have to call you—wife!"

About the Author

Jennie Goutet is the best-selling author of eighteen historical romances, including the **Clavering Chronicles**, **Memorable Proposals**, and **The Bridwells' Grand Tour** series. Her books have received first place in historical romance for the New England Reader's Choice Awards and have hit the number one spot in Regency Romance on Amazon. They have been featured on BookBub and Hoopla, and are translated into six languages. Jennie is an American-born Anglophile who lives with her French husband and their three children in a small town outside of Paris, but her imagination resides in Georgian England, where her proper historical romances are set. You can learn more about Jennie's books and sign up for her newsletter on her author website, jenniegoutet.com.

Printed in Dunstable, United Kingdom